NARCOS™

THE JAGUAR'S CLAW

NARCOS™

THE JAGUAR'S CLAW

JEFF MARIOTTE

TITAN BOOKS

NARCOS: The Jaguar's Claw
Print edition ISBN: 9781789090123
E-book edition ISBN: 9781789090130

Published by Titan Books
A division of Titan Publishing Group Ltd
144 Southwark St, London SE1 0UP

First edition: November 2018
2 4 6 8 10 9 7 5 3

Gaumont Books

Gaumont
BOOKS

Did you enjoy this book?

We love to hear from our readers.
Please e-mail us at: readerfeedback@titanemail.com
or write to Reader Feedback at the above address.

To receive advance information, news, competitions,
and exclusive offers online, please sign up for the
Titan newsletter on our website:
www.titanbooks.com

This book is for Marcy Spring,
with all my love.

1

THE MAN CALLED Luis Roberts—known to his friends and post office coworkers as Lou, even though his real name was Jose Aguilar Gonzales—pushed through the glass doors of the Robinsons-May department store in Arizona's Scottsdale Fashion Square. His hands were laden with shopping bags. He had gone to the mall to do his Christmas shopping, taking advantage of the sales on the day after Thanksgiving.

Lou's habit of generosity had been developed during an earlier phase of his life, when his income had far exceeded what he made now, sorting mail in the back of the post office. He liked giving presents. His colleagues and the neighborhood kids had come to expect them, thinking of Lou as a kind of Santa Claus figure. But with his diminished income, shopping during sales had become a necessity.

His red Ford Escort—another step down from the old days—was parked in the lot that faced onto Camelback Road, outside Robinsons-May. He'd been lucky to get a spot close by; the parking lot was jammed, and vehicles circled like vultures, trying to nab any space that opened up. As he waited on the curb for a chance to cross into the lot, a black Mitsubishi Montero with tinted windows rolled slowly past. Inside, the driver and passenger—both Hispanic men—eyed him. He didn't recognize either one, but that meant nothing. From their expressions, as far as he could tell through the darkened glass, he believed they recognized him.

He dropped the bags where he stood, spun, and hurtled toward the department store. A woman was coming out as he reached the doors; he shoved past her, causing her to drop something that landed with the crash of breaking glass. He kept going. Weaving through the crowded aisles at something less than a full-on sprint but more than a jog, he made it through the store and out into the main area of the mall in a couple of minutes. All the way, his right hand was tucked inside the zipper of his leather jacket, close to his gun.

The wide corridors were jammed with holiday shoppers. Lou's gaze darted this way and that, seeking an escape route and scanning for enemies. Most of the shoppers were white, many with families, children. Of course, anyone could be an assassin, but he had always believed that when they came, they would be Latinos. Colombians, most likely. Possibly even people he knew.

Not seeing anyone who seemed to pose an immediate threat, he started toward another exit, walking quickly but no longer running. He didn't want to attract undue attention to himself. He kept his gun hand inside his jacket, close to his holster, just in case.

The shoppers he passed were largely cheerful; he

heard laughter and uplifted voices. Gloria Estefan's "Christmas Through Your Eyes" was playing over the P.A. system. Lou was glad for her success in the U.S.; he hated Miami, but as long as he could think of her as Cuban, he could ignore her Miami connections. A few minutes earlier, he might have been humming along, smiling like so many of the people around him. Instead, he was sweating, fighting back panic—the price of years of paranoia, of living on the run, always watching over his shoulder.

A Hispanic-looking man shifted course, as if to block his path. Lou cut across to the far side of the walkway. A woman reached suddenly into her purse. For a gun? Lou tightened his grip on his, and moved so that a family was between him and the woman.

Ahead, he spotted a hallway leading to restrooms. They would offer some degree of privacy; he could fight back, if necessary. He started toward them, but before he'd made it halfway down, the hall started to look like a dead end. In there, he would be trapped, with no escape possible. He whirled around and sprinted out, made for the nearest escalator. On the way, he saw a man by himself, carrying a small bag, looking his way. When Lou hit the escalator, he took the steps two at a time, pushing past people standing still and letting it carry them up.

On the upper floor, he no longer worried about discretion. He raced full tilt for the bridge that passed over Camelback Road. Inside Nordstrom, he slowed once again, eyeing everyone around him as he rode the escalator back to ground level. His fingers rested against the butt of his pistol, ready to yank it from its holster.

Sweat beaded on his forehead, ran down his cheeks, stung his eyes. The escalator seemed to crawl.

Finally on the ground floor, he quickly walked toward the exit and outside, across a small parking lot facing Goldwater Boulevard. If the attack came, it would be here. His head swiveled this way and that, seeking out potential threats. Across Goldwater was a bus stop, and a bus huffed its way toward it, less than a block away. At a break in traffic, he raced across the street, arriving just in time to board the bus. He found a seat in the back and rode, no particular destination in mind, watching every passenger who boarded while keeping an eye on the street.

Luis Roberts had to die, so that Jose Aguilar Gonzales could live for another day. Cheerful Lou, beloved by customers and coworkers alike, generous Lou who gave Christmas presents to the neighborhood children and handed out the best candy at Halloween, could exist no more. He would have to leave Arizona; too close to Mexico, which he had always known but tried to ignore.

Where to go, though? Someplace north. Chicago? Minneapolis? Maybe Detroit? Somewhere far from the southern border.

But did distance really matter? According to the news from Colombia, Pablo Escobar was a fugitive in his own land. But *El Patrón*'s reach was long, his memory longer still. Forgiveness was not in his vocabulary.

Lou—Aguilar—rode the bus, and watched, and pondered his next steps.

2

WHEN JOSE AGUILAR Gonzales looked at his wife Luisa, he saw beauty personified, joy made flesh. She didn't resemble the Colombian beauty queens he saw on TV and in the newspapers. Her skin was much darker than theirs, her features less refined, sculpted more broadly. She was sturdy, thick through the middle, with breasts small for her frame and calves that barely tapered into shapeless ankles.

Her brown eyes were flecked with gold, and to gaze into them was the closest thing to heaven Jose had found on this earth. She had a shy, sly smile that alternately charmed him or thrilled him to his toes. He loved to hold her, and when he couldn't do that, he loved to watch her move, or breathe, or simply be. He loved her laugh, her fierce intelligence, the way she sank her entire being into any given task.

She was his, and he was hers, and the day they wed was the happiest day of his life.

The second happiest was the day he graduated from the Carlos Holguín police academy in Medellín, the city where he had always lived.

Most of his fellow graduates were local boys, raised in poverty or the middle classes, like him. They were overwhelmingly dark-skinned—the children of Colombia's white-skinned oligarchy stayed away from such common occupations as officer of the Metropolitan Police. To Aguilar, whose father was a cobbler and whose mother mended clothing when she could and sold lottery tickets on street corners, it was a big step up in the world.

To make things even harder for Aguilar, when he'd been seven years old, a cousin had accidentally spilled a pot of boiling water on him. He'd been badly burned. For a while, no one expected him to survive. He did, but his flesh was mottled, with white and dark patches that he thought made him look like a mangy dog. In some places, hair grew, in others it didn't. As a boy, he'd thought that his disfigurement would doom him to the life of a street beggar or worse. When Luisa fell in love with him, he wondered about her eyesight; his freakish skin didn't seem to disturb her. And when he was accepted into the academy, he had at first thought it was a mistake. But he vowed to become the best police officer he could, to pay back his city for taking a chance on him.

He loved his country, but he knew its history. He had studied the Thousand Days' War in school. *La Violencia* had just ended when he was born; although he had never seen the men cut into pieces, or the "neckties" made by slicing open their throats and pulling their tongues through the slits, he had seen the photographs and heard the stories his whole life. He had been married for a year, he and Luisa were ready to start a family, and he wanted to raise his children in a Colombia free of its violent past. He couldn't tame the whole country, but he could start at home, in Medellín.

At the same time, he wasn't naïve. Everyone in the academy had heard the rumors that some of their fellow students were already on cartel payrolls. Some barely tried to hide it—while most walked or bicycled to classes, they drove convertibles or sports cars or powerful imported motorcycles. When they went out at night, their clothing was flashier than most cadets could afford, and their dates more beautiful.

Aguilar knew that circumstances might one day pit him against brother cadets who had chosen the wrong side. He didn't mind; he almost looked forward to the opportunity to teach them that Colombia could, despite history, despite everything, be a nation of laws. On that graduation day, in his dress uniform, with Luisa by his side, he fairly swelled with pride. He was proud to be an officer, proud to be a husband, proud to be Antioquian, proud to be part of Colombia's future rather than its past. After the ceremony and the drinking that followed, he took Luisa home and made love with her and fell asleep wearing a smile and nothing else.

Then came the morning.

His assigned partner was Alberto Montoya. Barely thirty, Montoya was already a veteran officer, a first sergeant whose arrest record was legendary among the cadets. Aguilar could barely believe his luck when they were introduced.

Montoya was tall and broad-shouldered, with curly dark hair and a jutting chin. His olive drab uniform was wrinkled, as if he had slept in it. He had an easy smile and sleepy eyes, leading Aguilar to wonder at first if he was stoned. But the sergeant's speech was crisp, his intellect sharp. "Welcome to the Colombian National Police, Jose," he said. "You'll find this a rewarding career, I'm sure."

"It's an honor to meet you, sir. I'm so lucky to be partnered with you. In the academy, everyone talks about you."

Montoya chuckled. "You can't believe everything you hear," he said.

"Only good things, I mean," Aguilar said, flustered. "That time you stopped the holdup at the Banco Nationale. Or when you foiled the kidnapping of Señora Guerrero. And—"

Montoya held up a hand to stop him. "I did none of those by myself. You'll see. Police work is teamwork. We cover each other's backs. Nobody's a hero."

"Or you all are."

"Not 'you,' Jose. 'We.' You're one of us now."

Pride filled Aguilar near to bursting, as it had earlier that morning when he'd donned his brand-new uniform. He had a Beretta 92FS holstered against his hip and his usual pocketknife in his right front pocket, and he was ready for anything. "Where do we start?" he asked, to bring himself back to earth.

Montoya ticked his head toward a Nissan Patrol four-wheel drive SUV. It was boxy, a rectangle on wheels, it needed washing, and it looked as if it had been run into once a month for a year or more. But it had a light bar on the roof and POLICIA across the top of its windshield and a green stripe down its side, and to Aguilar it was the most beautiful vehicle he had ever seen. When he looked back at Montoya, the sergeant was holding keys out toward him.

"You want me to—" Aguilar began.

Snapping his fist closed around the keys, Montoya said, "I'm driving." He headed for the four-wheeler, and Aguilar followed, reminding himself to pay attention to everything, to learn, and most of all, to remember to breathe.

It didn't take long for his expectations to be dashed.

Montoya drove all over Medellín, from the Bello, through the *comunas* of 12 de Octubre, Castilla, across the river into Aranjuez, La Candelaria, El Poblado, and up the mountain into Envigado, then back down through Guayabal, Belén, Laureles Estadio, and Robledo. Along the way, he kept up a running patter, pointing out where notable crimes had occurred, or once in a while, where they'd been prevented. He showed Aguilar how to spot likely criminals, *sicarios* he recognized as in the employ of Medellín strongman Pablo Escobar, walls pockmarked with bullet holes. Montoya usually had a Pielroja cigarette burning. Luisa said that spending all of her working hours in a smoke-filled restaurant had made her hate the smell, so Aguilar had quit, but he recognized the Indian on the packaging and the smaller one on the cigarette itself. He wondered how long it would take to get the stink out of his uniform and his hair.

The older officer punctuated his tour with complaints. His pay was too low, especially for someone as decorated as he was. The ranking officers were corrupt or idiotic or both, mentally incapable of working the streets and therefore confined to the safety of their desks in police headquarters. Some of his greatest achievements—and there were many, he insisted—went unrecognized by superiors.

Occasionally, he stopped outside a business and told Aguilar to wait while he went inside. He was never in for long. When he came out of the third place, he had a white envelope sticking out of a pants pocket.

"What are you doing in those places?" Aguilar asked. He thought he knew the answer, but wanted to hear it from Montoya.

"Just dropping in on various business owners," Montoya said. "Public relations. They like to know the police are keeping them safe."

"What's in the envelope, then?"

"Nothing that concerns you."

Aguilar had started the shift expecting to be inspired by riding with his hero, but by the fifth or sixth hour of nonstop bitching, he was discouraged. If even Alberto Montoya was bitter about his career, what chance did *he* have for happiness? Maybe he'd made a mistake. He should have joined the army, or become a teacher. Or let his father teach him how to repair shoes.

The next time he mentioned his paltry salary, Aguilar—already pushed close to the edge by the envelope—could no longer contain his suspicions. "Why do you stay if you hate it so much?"

Montoya shot him a cynical grin. "Not for the pay," he said. "But for the benefits."

"What do you mean?"

Montoya didn't answer for a while. He seemed to be considering how to answer. Then he shrugged and confirmed Aguilar's hunch. "You'll find out soon enough, anyway. Certain people will pay nicely for the favors that a policeman can do for them. Especially a sergeant. But even a rookie patrol officer can do okay."

"What people? That's what the envelopes are, right?"

Even before the question was out of his mouth, Aguilar realized he shouldn't have asked it. "Never mind, I don't want to know."

"Which means you already do," Montoya said.

"Who? Escobar?"

"Among others. But Pablo pays the best."

"You call him Pablo? Like you're friends?"

"Not friends. Business partners, in a way."

"But you're police! You're supposed to *prevent* crime."

"Look, Jose. I'm telling you this because I like you. I think you can go far in this job, but you have to understand how things are here. You think the captain doesn't take money from Don Pablo? That bastard owns three houses, and one of them has seven bedrooms. Who needs that many bedrooms? If you take his money, you take his orders. It's how this city works."

"But—"

Montoya talked over his objection. "You have to be realistic. Don Pablo has more money to throw around than the city does. If he didn't share some of it with the police, he would have to hire more criminals to get his business done. Who would you rather have running errands for him, cops or killers?"

"Is there a difference?"

"Of course there is. I feed him information sometimes. I perform minor tasks—nothing that would threaten the safety of civilians, of course, or harm the working people of Medellín. In return, I get information that helps me keep the peace. And I make a little money to supplement my salary. Everybody wins."

Everybody except those who believe in justice, Aguilar thought. *And the rule of law*.

He didn't say it out loud, though. Montoya had demonstrated who he was, and Aguilar didn't see the point of arguing with him further.

Still they drove. A police radio chattered incessantly, but Montoya seemed to pay it no mind. If he was doing any police work at all, Aguilar didn't see it. He seemed instead to be playing tour guide, showing Aguilar the sights of the city of his birth.

Some aspects of it, like the Point Zero Bridge and Berrío Park, he never tired of seeing, and he had to admit that Montoya's capsule history of the city's criminal past was interesting. Soon, another sight that Aguilar loved—the Iglesia de San Ignacio—loomed ahead of them. Aguilar was Catholic, like most Colombians, and had attended Mass there on several occasions. It was, he believed, the loveliest building in Medellín.

They had almost passed it when the rapid-fire reports of automatic weapons reached their ears. "Guns!" Aguilar cried.

Montoya braked the Nissan, then cranked the wheel and turned into the Plazuela San Ignacio, hitting lights and siren as he did. Now they saw the gunfight under way. Two men were taking cover behind the big statue of Francisco de Paula Santander, and three others were trying to escape, using trees as shelter. One body lay in the street, a pool of blood spreading beneath him. Merchants under broad umbrellas cowered behind their carts.

Montoya brought the vehicle to a shuddering stop, then bolted out his door, whipping his gun from its holster. Aguilar hesitated momentarily. He had practiced this at the academy. He knew what to do. But those were just training sessions, with no actual danger attached. Here, the bullets were real and the people involved were desperate. One man was already bleeding out on the pavement.

His heart pounding, he threw open his door and rolled out of the Nissan. His legs almost gave out beneath him when he hit the street, but he caught himself and drew his Beretta.

Crouching behind a low concrete planter, Montoya fired a couple of shots at the men trying to flee the scene. The two men sheltering behind the Santander statue stepped out and fired bursts from their weapons—an Uzi and a MAC-10, Aguilar thought. Their rounds found a target; the running man jerked spasmodically and fell, knocking over one of the tables at a sidewalk café on the corner. His leg twitched a few times, and then he stopped moving altogether.

The third man had made it around the corner and was gone. Aguilar heard approaching sirens, and was glad that backup was on the way. They still had the two by the statue to arrest, and those men were better armed than he and Montoya.

Instead of turning his weapon toward the gunmen, Montoya holstered it and approached the men with his hand outstretched. One of the men, young and slender, with a mop of dark curls and a wispy mustache and goatee, held the Uzi loosely in his left hand and clasped Montoya's offered hand with his right. The other guy, blond-haired and green-eyed, heavier, really just a kid, held back and kept the MAC-10 at the ready.

Montoya beckoned Aguilar with a jerk of his head. As Aguilar approached, trembling a little from fear—and maybe a little from excitement at witnessing a real gunfight, up close, and surviving it—Montoya waved at his weapon. "Put that away," he said. "You don't need it. The danger's passed."

"Are we arresting these men?" Aguilar asked, confused. His ears were still ringing from the noise. The acrid stink of the gunfire sat heavily in the air.

Montoya just laughed. "This is La Quica," he said, as if that explained everything. "I don't know the other guy."

"That's Snake-eyes," La Quica said. "He's new."

"So is this one," Montoya said. "First day. He'll figure out what's what, sooner or later."

"Sooner would be safer." La Quica extended a hand toward Aguilar. "Welcome to the team."

"I'm Jose," Aguilar said. Maybe the guy was an undercover officer. "Jose Aguilar Gonzales. Are you... one of us?"

La Quica broke into laughter, and Montoya joined in. Snake-eyes stood back, eyeing the whole scene with suspicion. Aguilar felt the same way. "Depends on which 'us' you mean," La Quica said.

"You guys better get out of here," Montoya said, cocking an ear toward the oncoming sirens. "Backup's almost here."

"I'll see you get a little something for your trouble," La Quica said. "Both of you."

Aguilar almost replied, but a stern glance from Montoya hushed him. The two gunmen walked away quickly, fading into the growing crowd. In a few moments, Aguilar could no longer see them. By the time more police vehicles reached the scene, they were gone, and Montoya was clearing spectators away from the bodies of those they'd shot.

Aguilar watched, crestfallen. Was this what he'd signed up for? Covering for killers and letting them walk away? Taking bribes?

He had wanted to make a difference. To arrest criminals, and make the streets of Medellín safe for honest people.

He still could, he supposed. But he would have to start by turning in his hero, Alberto Montoya. As he watched more cops spill out of their cars, flooding the scene, he wondered if he had the courage.

3

THE NEWLY ARRIVED cops cleared the onlookers away from the scene, and kept them out until a crew came to pick up the corpses. Montoya talked to detectives, but kept them away from Aguilar. That was fine; Aguilar was still wrestling with what he had observed and how to report it. If Montoya was right, who could be trusted?

When he was finished, Montoya came back to him and waved him into the Nissan. Inside, with the doors closed, he said, "Not a word to anyone, understand?"

"What was all that?" Aguilar said, struggling to keep his voice under control. "Those guys just killed two people, and you let them walk away! You shook a killer's hand!"

"So did you," Montoya reminded him. "And introduced yourself. You sounded like a nervous schoolboy."

"I'm an honest man. I've never met a murderer before."

"That you knew about."

That was true. After all, he had shaken Montoya's

hand just this morning, upon meeting him. For all he knew, Montoya had killed more people than La Quica.

"I guess," he said.

"Look, kid, I know this is all new to you. But they told me to train you and keep you out of trouble, and that's what I'm doing. You're part of this now. You saw what I saw and what I did. You didn't say anything to the detectives, and that was smart, because you don't know who's on which side. Me, I'm on every side. I'm just trying to stay alive and make a little money. You said you're married, right?"

Aguilar had mentioned Luisa several times during the day. "That's right."

"You want her to be safe, right?"

"Of course."

"Then you've already made your decision. You heard what La Quica said. We'll both get a bonus for letting them go. If you say anything now, your bonus will come in the form of bullets. Maybe you, maybe your wife. Maybe your wife in front of you, after she's been raped by a few guys. Also in front of you. That's not what you want, is it?"

Aguilar's stomach churned. His guts had turned to ice water. "I can't believe you're even asking me that."

"Then you take the money and you keep your mouth shut. You're a witness now, so you're either an ally or a liability. Don Pablo's generous with his friends and deadly to his enemies. *Plata o plomo*, that's his motto."

"But... that was cold-blooded murder."

"You don't know that," Montoya countered. "For all you know, it was self-defense. That doesn't really matter, though. If we had arrested La Quica and that other guy—Snake-eyes, I don't know him—if we had arrested them, they'd be free before we finished writing our reports. If somehow they went to trial, they'd be freed by the judge. But in the meantime, innocent people—witnesses, jurors, and so on—could die.

"Those guys who got killed were bad guys," he went on. "Drug dealers or worse. They had guns and were in the middle of a shootout in a public plaza. The world's better off without them. By protecting La Quica, we're ensuring the safety of citizens who don't even know the danger we could be in. And we're ensuring our own safety, and that of your wife. If we made any other choice, we'd have targets on our own backs, and so would everybody we care about. You don't want your wife to be a widow on your first day."

"Of course not," Aguilar said. "But—"

Montoya silenced him with an outstretched palm. "But nothing. I'm telling you how it is, Jose. You can't deal with the world you wish you lived in. You have to deal with the one you do live in. You can make a difference in people's lives. You can keep people safe. You can arrest bad guys. But you have to do it within the system as it exists, or the system will chew you up and spit you out, like gum on the sidewalk. Understand?"

"Yeah." Aguilar crossed his arms over his chest and dropped his chin. He had expected his first day to be exciting, eye-opening, but not like this. In glum silence, he rode out the rest of his shift.

He hadn't intended to tell Luisa about the things he'd learned. A woman should be protected from such ugliness, he believed. But she had expected him to come home from his first day on the job inspired, excited by all the things he had done and seen. When instead he was quiet, somewhere between gloomy and numb, she pushed and prodded until he gave up and spilled the whole story. He told her about the envelopes, the gunfight, even what Montoya had told him about the possible danger to her.

"If you want to leave me, I understand," he said when he was finished. "If you're not with me, if you're back with your parents, you might be safe. We could make it look like we had a big fight, that I was furious with you. Then they wouldn't think that hurting you would bother me."

The look in her eyes was almost unbearably sad. They'd been sitting at their kitchen table in their cramped hillside apartment, but now she went to the floor, kneeling beside him, and rested her hands on his legs. "Nonsense," she said. "I'm never leaving you. Not for Pablo Escobar or anyone else. You're my husband, and I love you. I'm devoted to you."

"But... they could hurt you. Even kill you."

"If they do, I just want to be beside you when I die."

"Baby, please—"

"That's enough. I'm not going anywhere. You should know me better than that." She pulled herself up on his legs, then wrapped her arms around his waist. He smelled her hair, like a bouquet of flowers from the shampoo she used, and felt her warmth. Her solidity in his arms was comforting, reminding him of why he had fallen in love with her in the first place. She made him feel like he was where he belonged, no matter where they were. Nothing else in his life had ever had that effect on him.

"Maybe I can quit the police. It's only—"

She reared back from him. "No! Don't even say that. You've worked so hard."

"Even if I stay, Escobar surely already knows the things I've seen—I don't think I can just walk away from those. I just want you to be safe."

"Don't worry about me. I'll be fine."

"You can't know that."

She leaned close again, and he stroked her hair as she spoke. "I know you're an honest man, and you want to live an honest life. That's part of what I love about you. But I also want you to live a long life. Maybe your friend Montoya is right—"

"He's not my friend."

"All right, your partner. But think about it. He says what he did there, letting that guy go, will keep other people safe. People who might never know they were in danger, but who, just by happenstance, end up in a position to harm Escobar. But in the fight you witnessed, nobody was hurt except criminals. Right?"

"That's right. There were plenty of people there who could have been hurt, but they got lucky."

"Or maybe Escobar's men knew what they were doing. Either way, no civilians were hurt. By keeping quiet about it and not trying to arrest someone who would never go to jail anyway, you're preventing others from being hurt. That's why you're a policeman in the first place, right? To keep the public safe."

"That's part of it, yes."

"A big part, I think. So nobody gets hurt instead of who knows how many people getting hurt. And in exchange, you earn some extra money. We can use it, especially when we have a family."

Aguilar was confused, wasn't sure he'd heard her right. "Are you saying I should go along with Escobar, Luisa?"

"I'm saying, you didn't make this world. This is

Colombia. From what I understand, this is how Colombia has always been. Maybe if we lived someplace else, it would be different. But we live here. In Colombia. In Medellín. You can't take on Escobar all by yourself. But if you can conduct yourself honestly, and still make some extra money for your family, what's the harm?"

"But how can I conduct myself honestly and still take money from a criminal?"

"Just do what you would do normally. Accept that you can't fix the whole world. Do what you can to help people and keep the city safe. And if once in a while you have to close your eyes or look the other way, is that so bad? That's what you did today, and it saved lives, didn't it?"

"According to Montoya."

"Well, he's been a policeman a lot longer than you have. He knows how things work."

"Luisa, are you really asking me to—"

"I'm not asking anything. I'm just saying, you have to put your family first. You have to keep yourself safe. I need you, and the children we'll have together will need you. So you have to do whatever you have to do. For both of us. All of us. Will you do that?"

When she put it that way, he didn't have a choice. It wasn't quite *plata o plomo*—silver or lead—but it was close.

4

AGUILAR HAD THE next day off, because his next shift was to be at night, so he could learn that routine. He spent most of the day with Luisa, until she had to go to work at Café Parilla Fresco, where she waitressed. They had met there, when he was washing dishes and sweeping the floors.

Then he took a long walk through the barrio. Some kids were playing soccer in a field that would be dark soon. People sat on the steps outside their homes, drinking beer or wine. The smell of marijuana wafted from open windows. Old men sat on benches, gossiping and laughing. Three dogs raced down the street, snarling at each other over a scrap of stolen meat.

In this neighborhood, nobody had much money. He didn't mind that; he'd never had much, either. He and Luisa had moved here after they got married, and while he attended the academy, she paid the rent from her waitressing job. It wasn't far from his parents, or from hers—near enough to visit easily, but enough distance to feel like they were on their own. They still belonged to their families, but they were a family themselves, too.

During the day, he had half-expected one of Escobar's men to show up with an envelope full of cash. When none did, he was surprised to find himself relieved—maybe La Quica's promise was empty, after all. That would be fine with him.

Between the thousand pesos a week he made as a police officer and her salary and tips, they would do okay. They would never be rich, but who needed the headaches that came with wealth, anyway? If they could put a little bit away, so that Luisa could quit her job when she became pregnant, that would be good. Beyond rent and groceries, they didn't need much.

As he walked, hands in his pockets, taking in the sights, sounds, and aromas of his neighborhood— somebody was cooking *bandeja paisa*; he could smell the chorizo and the frying egg—the sun sank behind the Cordillera Occidental, the mountains to the west, and the sky turned crimson, then purple. The lights of the city spread out below and around him, and he remembered a story his mother had told him when he was a boy, about a blanket of fairy dust that kept sleeping children snug and warm. The lights of Medellín reminded him of that blanket, and he wished it was a real thing. Because he knew that within those lights, some people were safe and warm, eating good food and making love and relaxing, watching television, reading books, enjoying themselves. But others were fighting, plotting, killing, stealing, dealing drugs, hurting themselves or one another. Within those lights, there were people sleeping on sidewalks because they had no shelter, stomachs growling because they had no food. Mothers were crying because their sons had been slain or their daughters had run away or their husbands beat them. The rich worried about keeping what they had and how to get more, the poor worried about having nothing, and everyone in between worried about both.

Aguilar despaired. He was one man, insignificant in the greater scheme. He was a tiny candle in that vast sea of lights, unnoticed by virtually all the others. He had entered the academy somehow believing in his power to effect change, and it had taken only one day to drive that notion from him.

He would just do his best, he decided. The best he could do was the best he could do. Where he could make a difference, he would, and he would learn to accept the rest. Having reached this conclusion—such as it was—he realized how dark it was getting, and he ran to catch a bus to the police station.

When he walked in, three minutes late, he felt like every eye was on him. Weighing him, judging him, finding him wanting. Some thought he was a rat, others thought he was already corrupted. If anyone thought he was still struggling, he didn't see that in the way their gazes landed on him.

Montoya waited outside, leaning against the Nissan, smoking a cigarette. "You're late."

"I'm sorry," Aguilar said. "Just a couple of minutes. The bus was—"

"Don't blame the bus. You could have taken an earlier one. You have a responsibility to your partner, the Colombian National Police, and the city of Medellín. Don't let it happen again." He threw the cigarette butt to the ground and stepped on it. "Let's go."

"Where are we going tonight?" Aguilar asked. He couldn't believe the man who had let a murderer walk free was lecturing him about being three minutes late for a shift.

"I showed you the city during the day. Now it's time to see it at night. That's when most of the bad guys are out."

"So we'll be doing some real police work?"

"If we're unlucky," Montoya answered. He opened the driver's door and slid in behind the wheel. "Get in."

Aguilar wondered how long it would be until he could drive. Maybe never, as long as he was partnered with Montoya. Someday, though, he would be the senior officer, training some green rookie like himself.

Then he would always drive.

Montoya was quiet, resisting Aguilar's attempts to draw him into conversation. He drove like he had a destination in mind. He took them up Calle 58 through Enciso, then cut through La Ladera, and continued working his way up the mountain. Finally, they reached the end of the paved road and started along a dusty dirt track. There were no lights anywhere except the headlights of the Nissan and the glow of Montoya's constant cigarettes. He had been lighting each one from the butt of the last, and refusing to talk, answering every question with a grunt or a monosyllabic response, if at all.

Finally, he stopped and turned off the engine. A cloud of dust lifted around them, then settled. The motor ticked. After what seemed an eternity, Montoya opened his door and got out. Aguilar did likewise.

"What are we doing here, Alberto? What's going on?"

Montoya just looked at him. A quarter moon provided faint, silvery illumination. "Well?"

"Well, what?"

"Well, what's your decision?"

Aguilar had suspected something like this, from his partner's odd behavior. They were alone on the mountainside. If he gave the wrong answer, he might never leave here. He would be buried in a shallow grave, or left for wild animals. Luisa might never know what had become of him, and would spend the rest of her life wondering.

Until this moment, Aguilar hadn't been sure what his answer would be. Now he swallowed. He couldn't look at the other man when he spoke. "I'm in."

"Good." The word puffed from Montoya like an exhalation; Aguilar hadn't realized until that moment that the veteran officer was also nervous. Maybe that meant he wasn't so bad, after all. He hadn't wanted to bring Aguilar up here to kill him. "Good, that's the right choice."

"I'm not so sure I have a choice."

"If that's the best way for you to look at it, that's fine. It's true enough. None of us do, really."

"I don't like it, though."

"None of us like it, either," Montoya said. "It's as it must be, that's all."

"Does that mean we can go back to the city?" Aguilar asked. "Maybe do some police work?"

"We can try," Montoya said, coming close to him. "But first..." He unbuttoned Aguilar's shirt pocket and tucked something inside. "That's for you. Don't look at it now. You can look when you get home. Now come on... let's catch some bad guys."

The payment that first night was ten thousand pesos. Aguilar bought a new refrigerator for the apartment;

the one they had was a cast-off that barely kept things cool, and was too small to hold more than enough food for a couple of days. When Luisa came home and saw it, she clapped her hands together, then wept, then pushed him down on the kitchen floor and made love to him right there in front of it.

After, holding her in bed, he thought about it. It was such a small thing, really. He had actually made the decision the moment he got back into the Nissan on that first day, instead of going to the detectives to tell them what Montoya had done. From that point, there had been no going back. All the agonizing, the soul-searching, had been theater, nothing more.

The money wasn't much, either. He wouldn't complain, of course—it had bought him a new refrigerator and an incredibly erotic bout of lovemaking with his Luisa.

And all he'd had to do to earn it was close his eyes. So easy. Any Colombian had to do the same a hundred times a day, or be driven mad. What must his parents have had to close their eyes to during *La Violencia*, the decade-long spasm that had seen two hundred thousand Colombians butchered?

If they could do it then, he could do it now.

For the rest of that week, Aguilar rode with Montoya, and stayed in the SUV while Montoya went into businesses and came out with envelopes or folded cash. They made some arrests, investigated traffic accidents, gave directions to people who were lost. They stayed busy, but Aguilar already found himself getting bored. Compared to that first day, with the adrenaline rush of the gunfight, his days seemed quiet, as if Medellín were a provincial backwater, not Colombia's second largest city.

Aguilar had Sunday off. He and Luisa went to Mass, then took a walk through nearby Parque La Milagrosa, enjoying the crackle of autumn leaves under their feet, with cloudy skies overhead promising rain. Back home, as the rain fell, they made love and lay in bed talking about their future. With two paychecks coming in, and the promise of more from Escobar, they were looking forward to better times than they had anticipated even a month earlier. They talked about getting a bigger apartment, or even buying a house one day, with a room for each of the children they would have. Maybe a car, as well. Aguilar didn't know many people who had moved from poverty to the middle class, but he knew it could be done. And it looked like he and Luisa might do it.

On Monday, he went back to work.

Halfway through their shift, Montoya stopped outside a restaurant in Belén. It looked like a thriving place, in a good neighborhood. He got out of the vehicle, then nodded at Aguilar. "Come on."

It took a moment for Aguilar to comprehend his meaning. "What, inside?"

"We don't have all day."

Aguilar got out and went with him.

It was beautiful inside, the nicest restaurant he had ever been in. Against one wall was a shiny wooden bar, and behind it were brightly lit glass shelves stocked with high-end liquor on the wall. The tables and chairs were wood and steel, the tables inlaid with glass. Ferns hung on chains from the beamed ceiling. Soft lighting gave it all a shimmering glow. Colombian pop music played from hidden speakers, and the aromas from the kitchen made Aguilar's mouth water.

They had come between the lunch and dinner hours, so it was quiet inside; a couple of men in expensive suits drank at the bar, but the restaurant was empty. A young woman in a low-cut dress rushed to meet them when they entered, but a short, balding man came out from behind the bar, wearing an apron over his guayabera shirt and creased pants, and waved her away. "I'll deal with them," he said. "It's okay."

She shrugged and headed back to the kitchen. The man gave Montoya a grin and a handshake, and looked curiously at Aguilar.

"New guy," Montoya said.

The man laughed. "Oh, a virgin? But you're breaking him in, right?"

"Of course," Montoya replied, chuckling.

"What's up with his skin? Why is he spotted?"

Montoya twitched his shoulders. "That's just how he looks. It doesn't make him deaf."

"Sorry, I didn't mean anything." The man reached into his pants pocket. "Bad day for Atlético Nacional. I'm distracted," he said with an exaggerated shrug. When he pulled his hand free, there was a wad of cash in it. He handed it to Montoya, disguised as a handshake, but everybody knew what had just transpired.

Back in the four-wheeler, Aguilar asked, "What was that money for?"

Montoya shot him a stern look. "You're lucky you're asking me that, and not *El Patrón*."

"*El Patrón*?" Aguilar echoed.

"You really are a virgin," Montoya said, shaking his head. "Pablo Escobar. *El Patrón*. It's his money."

"I knew that. I mean, why? Why does that guy pay off Escobar? It looks like he runs a successful business of his own."

"He does. And he owns several expensive automobiles. He has a Mercedes, of course, and a Corvette. He also has one of the only Bentleys in Medellín, and he wants to keep it."

"I don't… I don't understand. I thought Escobar's business was drugs."

"Cocaine is his main business," Montoya said. "But he's a man of many interests. Years ago, before the cocaine, he stole cars. A nice car would disappear off the street, and within a few hours, Don Pablo would have it in pieces, and sell the parts for a big profit. Then he figured out that some people—those with the most expensive cars, and therefore the most money—would pay to have their cars *not* stolen. Less work for Don Pablo, less risk, and more money."

"Smart," Aguilar had to admit.

"He's done it all. Smuggled cigarettes and liquor. Marijuana. Sold counterfeit lottery tickets. Kidnapping. Now, cocaine. Next month, next year, who knows? He gets bored easily, I think. Anything that will turn a profit and interest him, he'll try."

"How well do you know him?"

"Not well," Montoya said. "But well enough. Soon, you will, too."

Aguilar wasn't sure how he felt about that.

He'd heard plenty of stories about Escobar. The man was a ruthless criminal with the blood of dozens on his hands. But at the same time, Aguilar had heard that he shared his riches with the poor. A man who did that couldn't be all bad, could he?

Still, Montoya worked for him, and seemed to be bringing Aguilar into the organization. At some point, he would have to meet his other employer, he supposed. The idea was at once terrifying and thrilling.

For a couple of weeks, it continued like that. Mostly, he and Montoya did police work. Occasionally, they did chores for Escobar. A couple of times, they picked up packages from one person and delivered them to another, always collecting a tip of a few hundred pesos at each end. Montoya introduced him to the people he collected money from regularly, but there was no more talk about meeting Escobar himself.

Then came the day that Montoya held out the keys to the Nissan, and didn't snatch them back. Instead, he dropped them in Aguilar's hand.

"Really? I'm driving?"

"I have other things to do today," Montoya said. "You're driving yourself. You know what to do, where to go, right?"

Aguilar knew the routine by now. "Of course."

"One more thing," Montoya said, handing Aguilar a folded slip of paper. "At noon exactly, you're to meet a man at this address. His name is Hernan Garcia. He needs a ride. He'll tell you where to take him. Don't talk to him, just drive him."

"Is he… one of Escobar's?"

Montoya clucked at him. "You should know better than to ask such questions."

"Sorry," Aguilar said. "How will I know him?"

"He'll know you," Montoya replied. "Now go. And don't forget. Noon exactly. Not earlier, not later. Noon."

5

DRIVING THROUGH THE crowded streets was nerve-wracking. Aguilar had only driven cars a few times; his parents had owned one briefly, but they'd had to sell it. A friend had taught him to drive, and let Aguilar borrow his car from time to time, but he'd never handled anything the size of the Nissan Patrol. At the same time, he had to watch for crimes being committed or people in need.

But none of it made him more anxious than his noon appointment. Who was this Hernan Garcia? Why couldn't he take his own car, or a taxi? Why did he need someone to pick him up in a police vehicle? Various scenarios flitted through Aguilar's head, but he knew that whatever the reality was, it was probably something he couldn't even imagine.

Nervous, he got to the address Montoya had given him five minutes early. Montoya had told him not to, so he stopped several doors down. There were no parking places, but nobody was going to complain if a police vehicle blocked the lane for a few minutes. He'd been driving with the window down, trying to force out some of the stink of Montoya's cigarettes, and he waited with his left arm hanging out the window, enjoying the cool fall day. He heard a radio playing in a nearby apartment, the sounds of children playing in a hidden courtyard.

Then, he heard—from a building three doors ahead of his position—the unmistakable pop of gunshots. Three, then two more. Startled, he almost missed the sound of church bells tolling noon.

He put the Nissan into gear and rolled up to the front door of the address he'd been given.

A man stepped out of the door as he approached, carrying a briefcase in one hand and a pistol in the other. On his gray suit and shiny black shoes were damp spots that might have been blood. He looked over at Aguilar and nodded twice, then headed for the back door.

"Mr. Garcia?" Aguilar asked.

"Yes," the man said. He opened the door and got inside. When he was settled in the back, he told Aguilar an address. "Right away, please," he said.

"Yes, sir." Aguilar put the car in gear and drew away from the curb. He tried not to let Garcia see how badly his hands were shaking.

On the drive, Garcia was silent. He sat calmly in the back seat, as if he had just come from a nice lunch with friends.

Aguilar had to look at a map to find the address he'd been given. It was in El Poblado, high up in the hills. He had never been up in that neighborhood— never had a reason to go there. But he wasn't about to argue with Garcia. He followed winding streets that led past El Poblado's cluster of high-rise apartment buildings, up to where the houses were spaced farther and farther apart, interspersed with trees and surrounded by high walls. The air was a few degrees cooler here than it was down in the valley.

Finally, he came to the address and started up the driveway. It wound up through a wooded stretch, and then took a sharp curve. Immediately after the curve, Aguilar had to slam on the brakes; there was a gate across the road, with a wooden guardhouse nestled in the trees beside it. "Now what, sir?" Aguilar asked.

"Just wait," Garcia said.

After a few moments, two young men emerged from the guardhouse carrying guns. One of them, Aguilar saw, was Snake-eyes.

His anxiety turned to real fear. Was this Escobar's house? Why else would Snake-eyes be at the gate? He gripped the wheel hard to calm the tremors in his hands. Sweat trickled down his sides, under his uniform shirt.

The other guy, still in his teens and armed with a shotgun, nodded to Garcia in the back. "I don't know you," he said to Aguilar. His hair was long, scraggly, and he looked like he was trying to grow a beard but couldn't manage it yet.

"He's cool," Snake-eyes put in. "I know him. Hey, brother."

"Hey," Aguilar said, hoping he sounded half as cool as Snake-eyes had said.

The teenager opened the gate. "Head on up, then," he said.

"Thanks." Aguilar gave them both a nod and pressed on the gas. A little too hard—the SUV lurched, pressing him back against his seat and no doubt doing the same for Garcia. "Sorry," he said, slowing down.

"No problem," Garcia said. They were the first

words he'd spoken since giving Aguilar the address. His voice was smooth, cultured. Aguilar wondered what his story was. Escobar's *sicarios* seemed to be young men, but this guy was middle-aged, in his forties at least. And his suit wasn't typical *sicario* dress, either. "Be calm, everything will be fine. You'll just drop me off. You'll get a small tip, and then you'll be on your way."

"Okay," Aguilar said, his voice catching in his throat.

The drive wound through more trees, then came out into an open expanse, in the midst of which stood a large house. It was three stories tall, stucco-walled, with a red-tile roof. Aguilar wasn't sure if he'd call it a mansion, but it was more luxurious than any house he had ever been inside.

At the front were four steps, leading up to a door tall enough to admit giants. "Just there," Garcia said. "The foot of the stairs will be fine."

Aguilar pulled the car to a stop. He waited there a moment, and when Garcia didn't budge, he realized his error. He killed the engine, got out, and walked around to open Garcia's door. Then the older man climbed out and thanked him.

As he started up the stairs, the massive door opened and a portly man with wavy dark hair and a mustache emerged from inside. He wore a blue shirt with white vertical stripes, blue jeans, and white sneakers. Aguilar had seen his picture many times.

Pablo Escobar.

He froze.

Escobar laughed. "You're the new policeman?"

Aguilar's voice caught again. He cleared his throat, then managed, "Yes, sir."

"What's your name?"

"Jose Aguilar Gonzales."

"You're the one partnered with Montoya."

"Yes, sir."

"He's a good man, Montoya."

"Yes, sir."

"Do you know who I am?"

"Yes, sir. You're *El Patrón*. Mr. Escobar."

Escobar came down the stairs, shaking Garcia's hand as he came. "Everything went well?" he asked. His skin was light, his features more European than native, but his accent was heavy—a Paisa accent. He had come from here, as Aguilar had.

"Very well," Garcia said.

"Go on in, have a drink. I'll be right there."

Garcia obeyed. After he was inside, Escobar descended the last two steps and held out his hand. "Thank you for bringing him up," he said. He clasped Aguilar's hand. When he drew his hand away, Aguilar's palm was full of paper. He started to hand it back, then realized what it must be—his tip—and stuffed it into a pocket without looking at it.

"Thank you, *El Patrón*," he said. "Thank you very much."

"I look forward to getting to know you better," Escobar said. "You must come up for a drink sometime. You and Montoya."

"I would like that."

"You may be wondering about Mr. Garcia."

How should he answer that? It might not be good to show curiosity about such things. But the truth was, he had been wondering, ever since he'd seen the gun and the splattered blood. Instead of speaking, he simply shrugged.

"It was a personal matter, not business," Escobar explained. "Between Garcia and his wife and her lover. Mr. Garcia will be on an airplane to Panama in a few hours. Mr. Garcia did me a favor, so I'm doing this favor for him. He'll never set foot in Colombia again. None of this will fall on you, you have my word."

"Thank you, *El Patrón*," Aguilar said again.

"Until the next time, then," Escobar said. Without waiting for a response, he headed back up the stairs.

The dismissal was unmistakable. Still, he'd had a conversation with Pablo Escobar, and had not only survived it, but been paid for his effort.

Aguilar got back behind the steering wheel and cranked the ignition. As soon as he rested his hands on the wheel, the enormity of what had just happened sank in and he started shivering uncontrollably.

He'd picked up a man who had just murdered his wife and her lover, then delivered the man to the crime lord of all Medellín, to be spirited out of the country ahead of the law. All while wearing the uniform of the Colombian National Police. Escobar had thanked him and stuffed cash into his hand.

What had he become? *Who* had he become? He no longer recognized himself.

Just weeks ago, he'd graduated from the academy, ready to fight crime and uphold law and order. So quickly he had barely noticed, he had become an accomplice to murder—someone he would have felt obliged to arrest, if it had been anyone else. Had he succumbed to the corruption that seemed rooted in Colombia's very soil? Or was his a personal moral failing? He could never confess it to his parents or his priest, he knew. He would have to confess to God, but in his own way, without the intercession of clergy.

Perhaps the more vital question was, if he had so easily slipped across this line, where did his real moral line lie? Was there anything he wouldn't do?

And if so, when would he find out what it was?

He didn't have to wait long.

That evening, Luisa was working at the café. Aguilar treated himself to dinner at the most expensive restaurant in the *comuna*. Escobar had given him thirty thousand pesos, so he could afford it without worry. The food smelled delicious, but he could hardly taste it. All he could think about was the blood on Hernan Garcia's clothing and shoes, the sound of the gunshots, and how disappointed Luisa would be if she knew the whole truth.

He would have to bring her here, someday soon. Maybe if they were together, he could enjoy the experience. As it was, he paid his bill with half his dinner uneaten on his plate, then walked the dark streets until it was time for Luisa to come home. He met her at the bus stop, and they walked back to the apartment together.

It was only after they were inside, sitting together on a couch, that she trained her deep brown eyes on him. "What's wrong, Jose? Don't tell me 'nothing,' I know you better than that."

"It's not nothing," he replied. "But it's nothing I can talk about. So the same thing, really."

"Are you sure? You can talk to me about anything, you know that."

"I'm sure."

"Is it work?"

"Yeah," he said. "Work." He reached into his

pocket and pulled out what was left of the money Escobar had given him: more than twenty-five thousand pesos. "I made this, though."

She took it, flipped through the bills, and her eyes went wide. "For what?"

"For work."

"Your salary? This is far too much."

"No, a tip."

"For doing what? Never mind, if you don't want to tell me you don't have to."

"It isn't that I don't want to, baby. I do. So much. But I can't. I... I just can't, that's all. Ever."

Luisa moved against him, pressing herself close. She smelled like grilled meat and rich coffee. Suddenly, he was actually hungry, and regretted leaving that dinner behind.

"You can trust me, darling," she said. "Always. And if part of trusting me means that you keep things from me, well, then that's how it must be. None of it affects how I feel about you."

"That's good," Aguilar said. "Because it affects how I feel about me, and I'm glad there's someone who still likes me when I come home."

"Not just likes. Loves." She pressed her face against his neck, planted small kisses there. "Always, always, always. No matter what."

After a while, they moved into the bedroom. A while after that, they fell asleep, tangled in the sheets and each other's limbs.

They were still there when pounding at the door woke Aguilar. He rolled away from Luisa, struggled into some pants, and went to it. The door was shuddering from the force of the hammering, and he hesitated, wondering if he should go for his gun.

Then he heard Montoya's voice. "Come on, Jose! We don't have all night!"

Aguilar unlocked the door and opened it. Montoya stood there, out of uniform. His hair was in disarray, his cheeks thick with whiskers. "What is it?" Aguilar asked.

"You're not dressed," Montoya said.

"It's two in the morning!"

Montoya glanced at his gold wristwatch. His manner was urgent, almost frantic—much different than the usual casual Montoya that Aguilar knew. "One-forty. Come on, get dressed."

"Our shift doesn't start until eight."

"This is different," Montoya said. "Not police work. Pablo work."

"Now? In the middle of the night?"

"Right now. You have three minutes to dress. In street clothes, not your uniform."

"I'll be right back, then. I have to tell Luisa I'm going."

"Tell her quick," Montoya ordered. "And bring a gun."

6

A RENAULT 12 waited in the street, its motor running. The car had been dark blue once, but it was at least a dozen years old. The paint had oxidized, and rusted in spots, and now it was almost as mottled as Aguilar's skin. It had, Aguilar thought, more dents than a golf ball.

Montoya got in, and Aguilar went around to the passenger side. The seat was torn, tape curling down in places. "All the money you make, you can't buy a new car?" Aguilar asked.

"What makes you think this is my only one? I needed something that wouldn't attract attention." He pulled away from the curb and tore down the quiet street.

"For what? What have you been doing all day?"

"Surveillance."

"On who? Wait—for who? Escobar?"

"What do you think?"

"Tell me what's going on, Alberto."

Montoya made a screeching right turn and hurtled

downhill. Rain had fallen during the evening, and the streets were slick. "We have to pick somebody up. I know where he is right now, but I didn't want to go in by myself."

"Who? Go in where?"

"His name's Leo Castellanos," Montoya said. "He owes Don Pablo some money. We have to collect it."

"Collect it how?" Aguilar demanded.

"He says he doesn't have it, but his family does. We'll pick him up and hold him until they pay."

Aguilar processed that for a few moments. "Wait, we're kidnapping him?"

"Of course we're kidnapping him!" Montoya braked hard and twisted the wheel left, leaning into the turn. Aguilar grasped the door handle, but let go when it felt like it would come off in his hands.

"But... how?"

"Just follow my lead," Montoya said. "Don't say anything. Remember, no names. Don't do anything stupid. We'll be fine."

He slowed the Renault and watched the street numbers, finally pulling into an empty space at the curb. Rows of apartment buildings flanked both sides of the street. He pointed at one with a light burning on one side of the doorway, and a dark one on the far side. "That's the place. He's on the first floor. It'll be easy."

"How do you know he's still there?"

"I've been watching him all day. He went in, had some wine, and finally turned out the lights. I'm sure he's sleeping."

"How much does he owe?"

Montoya handed him a balaclava. Or Aguilar thought it was a balaclava, at first. Closer inspection showed it was the end of a sweatpants leg, sewed shut at one end, with holes crudely cut out for eyes and mouth. "Half a million pesos."

Aguilar looked at the buildings again. This was not a wealthy neighborhood. "And he lives here?"

"He's *hiding* here. His family has plenty of money."

"How do you know they'll pay?"

"I don't," Montoya said. "But I guess we'll find out, won't we? Put that on."

Aguilar pulled the makeshift balaclava over his head. "It stinks."

"Don't breathe, then." Montoya put his on and opened his door. Outside the car, he pulled a pistol from his belt. "Remember, don't shoot unless he forces us to. We need him alive."

His heart pounding, Aguilar drew his own gun. He'd been swept up by Montoya's intensity, not really thinking things through. Now there was no more time to think, no time to argue. Montoya was already on the move. Aguilar followed, and hoped this didn't go wrong.

Montoya reached the door to the apartment building. It was metal, with a glass panel at the top. The single light shone wanly, making the whole scene appear lopsided. When Aguilar caught up, Montoya yanked the door open and went in, gun first. Aguilar caught the door as it started to swing closed.

Inside, Montoya pointed out a door with a brass 3 on it. There were so many questions Aguilar wanted to ask. *Will he know someone's coming for him? Is he waiting inside with a machine gun pointed at the door? How will we get him to come with us? What if we have to kill him—will we owe Escobar the money, then?*

But he couldn't find his voice, and there was no chance to ask, anyway. Montoya went to the door and tried the handle. He shook his head. Locked.

He turned back to Aguilar. "Go outside, in the alley. There's a window. I'll go in this way, and you make sure he doesn't go out. When you hear me go in, break the glass and come in that way."

It didn't sound like Montoya had thought this through, or he would have sent him to the alley in the first place. He was less confident than ever in this plan—if "plan" even described what was going on here.

Not seeing any better option, he nodded and ran to the alley. The rain had somehow intensified, rather than washing away, the smells of urine and garbage. Two windows on the ground floor faced him; he didn't know which was Castellanos's apartment, or if they both were. He hoped he could tell when Montoya went in.

He was still trying to figure out how to get through the window when he heard crashing sounds from inside. Montoya was trying to kick the door in, or break it down with his shoulder. It didn't sound like he was having much luck.

In the window to Aguilar's right, a light clicked on. He saw a man stand up, wearing a strapped undershirt and boxers. The man snatched up a rifle or shotgun and opened his bedroom door.

Aguilar's thoughts raced. If the man killed Montoya, what then? Would Escobar have Aguilar killed, for failing? He couldn't let that happen.

He fired a shot through the window. The glass shattered, shards of it dropping into the apartment, some tinkling to the alley floor.

Inside, the man spun around and started for the window, bringing the rifle up to his chest. Aguilar didn't want to kill him, but—

Then Montoya smashed through the door behind

the man and charged into his apartment. "Drop it!" he cried. "Police!"

The man hesitated. Looking outside, he saw Aguilar pointing a gun at him. He whirled around, and Montoya was bearing down on him. He threw the rifle down. "Don't shoot!" he cried. "I won't fight you!"

Montoya went closer to him, looming over him, his pistol pointing at the man's head. "Good," he said. He met Aguilar's gaze. "Come on through."

Aguilar looked at the window, chest high, still rimmed with glass shards. No way he was climbing through. "Fuck that," he said. "I'm coming around."

Castellanos was around thirty-five years old. He had a full head of dark hair, a slender mustache, a slim build but with a round belly, and the soft hands of someone who went to work in an office every day. There was nothing personal in the apartment at all. It was probably rented, furnished, by the week or the month. This was where he had gone to ground, not his residence. An overflowing ashtray sat next to the bed, and the room stank of stale smoke.

He was—reasonably enough—terrified. Tears ran down his cheeks and snot bubbled from his nostrils. "Stop blubbering," Montoya said. "We're not going to hurt you. We need you in one piece."

"You're not here to kill me?"

"Nobody wants you dead. You owe money to somebody very important. He just wants to be paid."

"I told him I don't have it! I tried to get it. I tried everyone I could think of. Nobody would help me."

"You need better friends, then," Montoya said. "But we'll find out who your real friends are soon enough." He went to the bed, which had two pillows on it, and shook off the pillowcases. "Get his belt."

Aguilar looked around the room. The eyeholes were hard to see through, but he spotted a pair of pants wadded up in a corner, with a belt through the loops. He tugged it free. Montoya was draping both pillowcases over the trembling man's head. "Loop that around his neck," he said. "Not too tight. We don't want to strangle him, just to keep him from seeing."

"Can I get dressed?" Castellanos asked, sniffling.

"You can dress later," Montoya said. "We need to go."

Aguilar pulled the belt tight around his neck and buckled it. "What about his hands?" he asked.

"He won't try anything." Montoya sounded confident. "If he did, we'd have to kill him, and he doesn't want that."

"You're right," Castellanos said. "I won't try anything. Just don't hurt me, please."

"Only if you force us to," Montoya said. "Come on, let's go."

They led him out of the apartment and onto the sidewalk. A woman looked out a window, and Aguilar waved his gun in her direction until she ducked back in and pulled the curtains tight. At the Renault, Montoya made Castellanos lie on the floor in back. "My friend will be watching you," he warned. "You make a move, he'll put a bullet in your head."

"I promise," he said between sobs. "You don't have to worry about me."

This time it was even harder for Aguilar to survive Montoya's breakneck driving, because he was turned around in his seat, pointing his gun more or less in the direction of Castellanos's head. He probably needn't have bothered; the man curled into a fetal position on the floor, knees and head down, back up, and rocked back and forth like a baby trying to sleep. Aguilar had expected that anyone bold enough to find himself in debt to Pablo Escobar—and then to resist paying that debt—would be made of tougher stuff. Castellanos, by contrast, seemed on the verge of complete collapse.

Soon enough, Montoya pulled the Renault up to the door of a garage attached to a single-story house on a fairly spacious lot. The lights of neighboring houses were visible through a screen of trees, and Aguilar figured the idea behind this house was that a prisoner could scream his head off without being heard. "Get the door," Montoya said.

"What about him?"

"He's not going anywhere," Montoya said. He sniffed the air. "I think he pissed himself."

Aguilar shrugged, got out, and opened the garage door. The garage was empty. He waited as Montoya drove in, then closed the door again. Another door led into the house. "Is anyone else here?" he asked.

"Of course not," Montoya said, tugging open the car's back door. "It's a safe house."

"Who will watch him, then?"

Montoya sighed. "We will. We stay with him until his family pays up."

That was the first Aguilar had heard about staying with the hostage. "Us? But I haven't told Lui— my wife."

"You can call her later, if you need to. Now shut up and help me peel him out of the car."

Montoya tried to pull Castellanos free, but the man was holding onto the carpeting, the bottom of the seats, anything to keep himself from being moved. Aguilar tucked his gun into his pants and went in through the opposite door. He pried Castellanos's fingers away from whatever he gripped, but as soon as he did, Castellanos grabbed something else, or clawed at Aguilar's hands. Finally, Aguilar drew the pistol and shoved it against Castellanos's forehead hard enough to leave a mark. The man's eyes grew wide, and he stopped struggling.

"Please, no, don't..."

"If I were you, I wouldn't want to be too much of a pain," Aguilar said. "The more trouble you are, the less likely we are to keep you alive."

"No, I... I won't. I'll do whatever you say."

"Get out of the car."

Aguilar moved the gun away so Castellanos wouldn't grab it. The man released his hold on the car's interior surfaces and backed out stiffly. As he did, Montoya got a grip on his neck. "Now into the house," he said.

"All right. Whatever you say."

Aguilar opened the door to the house. It was dark inside, but he pawed at the wall until he found a switch. An overhead light came on, showing an empty hallway with a couple of doors and an opening at the far end.

"Have you been here?" he asked.

"Once," Montoya said. "We can take him in there, second door."

Aguilar opened that one, and switched on a lamp inside. The room contained a steel bed frame with a thin mattress on it. No bedding, no pillows. A cockroach scuttled across the wood floor when the light came on, squeezing into a crack at the base of the wall. Another door led into a bathroom, with a sink, a toilet, and a bathtub. The only window was covered by a sheet of thick plywood, nailed to the frame.

Montoya shoved Castellanos into the room and closed the door. "Welcome home, Leo," he said. "Make yourself comfortable. You're going to be here a while."

7

CASTELLANOS HAD BEEN married once, but not for long, and his wife had moved to Mexico, so that first morning, Montoya called his parents on a portable phone and then passed him the handset. "Tell them you need them to gather the money. Five hundred thousand pesos. I'll call them back in two days, and if they have it I'll tell them where to deliver it."

"They don't have that kind of money," Castellanos objected. "They're simple people."

"They own a house. You own a house. They can sell both and get it."

"That could take weeks!"

"I'm not in a hurry," Montoya said. "But the quicker they act, the sooner I can let you go."

Castellanos's father had answered the phone while they were talking. Aguilar could hear his voice coming through the speaker, thin and distant. Castellanos almost seemed like he'd forgotten who would answer. "Hello? Father? Is it you? It's me, Leo."

A query came across the phone. Castellanos

listened, then explained his predicament. "They need half a million pesos, or they'll murder me. Yes! Yes, they will, I swear to you. No, I can't explain, just... you have to get the money. You have to."

Montoya snatched the phone away from him. "He's right, Mr. Castellanos. You get the money together. I'll call back in two days to see if you have it. If you don't, I'll start hurting Leo. I won't kill him right away, but I'll hurt him. The sooner you get the money, the better shape he'll be in when you see him. If you call the police, though, you'll never see him again. Not this side of the grave."

He hung up without waiting for an answer.

"Two days, Leo. Then...?" He ended with a shrug. "I wouldn't want to be you."

After they secured Castellanos in his room, Aguilar used the phone to call Luisa. When she answered, she sounded almost hysterical.

"Where are you? What's going on? I've been so worried!"

"I can't tell you where I am, baby," he replied.

"Why? What are you doing?"

"I can't tell you that either."

"Jose, tell me what's happening here! I don't understand!"

"I can't tell you anything, Luisa. I'm fine. I'm not in trouble, and I'm not in any danger." He hoped that part was true. "I won't be home for a while, maybe a couple of days. But I'm all right. You just have to trust me. Do you trust me?"

"Of course I trust you. I just... I don't know. I never thought something like this might happen. He pulled you from the apartment and you just went with him, leaving me... I'm so scared, Jose."

"There's nothing to be scared of, baby. You'll be okay for a couple of days. I'll call when I can, but you can't call me. Don't worry, Alberto and I have everything under control." Montoya was listening, so he didn't want to tell her that there would probably be a nice bonus at the end of the process. But that was true, too.

Once she was marginally more calm, he told her he loved her and would try to call again soon. Then it was just him and Montoya and the drained feeling that came when the adrenaline rush had ended. He collapsed into a chair.

"Two days, right?" he said.

"At least two days. We might be here longer. Depends on his family now."

"Then we let him go?"

"When they pay, we let him go. If they pay."

"But they'll pay, won't they?"

Montoya scoffed. "I don't know them, do you? Some families pay. Some don't. You can't know until it happens."

"Have you... done this before?"

"Once. I was like you, not the guy in charge. This is my first time in charge."

"How was it?"

He made a face and spread his hands. "It was... it was not good. Hopefully this time will be better."

It took five days. Montoya let Aguilar call Luisa twice more during that time. Each time, she was increasingly impatient, angry, and concerned. Each time, he did his best to reassure her, but the truth was, he didn't know how it would all play out. He was worried about their shifts on the police force, but Montoya told him they were "covered," whatever that meant. Aguilar was afraid when they did go back, everyone would know they were on Escobar's payroll. When he raised that with Montoya, the older man just laughed, and wouldn't discuss it further.

The house had a TV, a radio, beds, couches, a dining table and chairs, and a kitchen stocked with food and alcohol. Castellanos never saw those parts of the house. He was either tied to the bed or chained in the bathtub. Sometimes, if he refused to cooperate, he was left in the bathtub with cold water running for an hour or more. Mostly, he cooperated. They prepared him simple food in the kitchen, or went out for food and brought him some back. He complained a lot, but when he got too annoying, they reminded him of the bathtub and he shut up. They kept the hoods on whenever they were near him, so he wouldn't see their faces. When they were in the other room they drank and ate and smoked marijuana, listened to the radio, talked, played cards. When they could, they slept, never knowing if Castellanos was going to start making a fuss and have to be quieted down.

Finally, his parents and family friends scraped up the half-million, and delivered it to an address Montoya gave them. Shortly after the delivery, he got a call on the portable phone. He listened intently, his face grim, then set the phone down on the table. It was dark outside; the phone had awakened Aguilar. "Money's there," Montoya said.

"So now we let him go?"

"Now we kill him."

"But he paid the money!"

"Escobar wants people to know that if they owe

58

him, they have to pay without being pressured to. Think how much this has cost him—this house, our salaries, the other expenses. He'll get back what was owed, but not the other money that went into all this."

"But—"

Montoya cut him off. "He used to kidnap people for ransom. He doesn't do that anymore. Now he only does it to get back what's his, what's owed to him. He doesn't even want to do that, but some people—like Castellanos—force him to. He wants to send a message."

"I don't want to kill anyone," Aguilar said. "That's not why I joined the police."

"He's heard our voices. Memorized them."

"So? He can't prove—"

"It's been decided," Montoya said, interrupting him again. He dug into a pocket, handed Aguilar the car key. "We do what we're told. Move the car out of the garage."

Aguilar took the key. As he went into the garage and opened the big door, he briefly considered simply driving away. He could go pick up Luisa and…

And what? Where could they go? Bogotá? Panama? Mexico? How would they live, with no jobs and little money? What about their families? Surely Escobar would punish them for Aguilar's treason. No, running away was no answer.

Instead, he drove the Renault into the street—it was just after four in the morning, still dark—then went back into the garage and closed the door.

That was the first time he saw the drain in the floor, in the center of the room, and how the concrete sloped gently toward it.

When he was back inside, Montoya donned a

sweatpants balaclava and tossed Aguilar the other. Aguilar followed him into Castellanos's room. "Your lucky day, Leo," Montoya said. "Your family paid up. Let's go."

"Really?" Castellanos asked. "How?"

"Why should I care?" Montoya replied. "They did, that's all I know. Come on."

Castellanos was grinning. Montoya freed him from his bonds, and the man rubbed his wrists where they'd been tied. "Can I get dressed?"

"Of course." His clothing was piled in a corner. Aguilar picked it up and handed it to him. "Quickly," Montoya said.

It wasn't quick. Castellanos hadn't moved much for the past five days, and his joints were stiff. He winced, in obvious pain, as he tried to pull on his clothes. Montoya lit a cigarette and scowled.

When their captive was dressed, they started toward the garage. Aguilar was in the lead, but Montoya shouldered past him and made Castellanos get in front. He paused at the garage door, and Montoya gave him a shove. "Go on," he said. "Don't you want to get out of here?"

"I certainly do," Castellanos said. He opened the door and went out, took a couple of steps, then stopped and turned. "Where's the car?"

His mouth fell open when he saw Montoya standing there, arm extended, gun in his hand. "N-no," Castellanos said.

Montoya squeezed the trigger.

The first round hit Castellanos at the inside corner of his left eye, and sprayed blood, bits of brain, and skull fragments across the empty garage. Fluid from his exploded eye ran down his face.

Castellanos buckled, as if his legs had turned to water beneath him. Montoya stood over him and fired twice more, into his chest. The body twitched as the bullets slammed into it, but only from the impact. Castellanos was already gone.

Aguilar watched it all with a kind of bland disinterest. He expected to be sick, but he wasn't. He was numb. It was as if Castellanos had never been human at all, like he'd been a store mannequin or a character from a cartoon. Aguilar couldn't summon any sense of horror or sorrow, although since moving the car out, he had been dreading this moment. Now it was here and he couldn't even feel it.

He wondered what that meant about him. He didn't much like it.

"What are you standing there for?" Montoya asked. "Get that door open and bring the car as close as you can."

Aguilar obeyed, stepping around the gore as best he could. He threw open the garage door and pulled the Renault partway in. When he started to open the trunk, Montoya said, "No, put him in the front seat. You'll ride in back."

"The front?"

"That's what I said."

Montoya still had that gun in his hand, and a strange half-smile played about his lips. Aguilar was afraid to push him. He opened the front passenger door. Together, they lifted Castellanos off the floor and hoisted him to the car, pushing him in and positioning him so he looked like he was going for a ride. Trying to avoid the blood was useless; by the time they had him in place, Aguilar's shirt and jeans were soaked. Once, Castellanos's head lolled over onto his shoulder, his cheek caressing Aguilar's like a lover's. Finally, he felt his gorge rise and bile stinging his throat.

So he did have limits, after all. He found that strangely encouraging. Still, he helped set the dead man into the Renault, then when Montoya had backed it out of the garage, dutifully climbed into the back.

"What about the garage floor?" Aguilar asked. "All that blood?"

"Somebody will come along and clean it," Montoya said. "Not our problem."

They drove for about thirty minutes, into Medellín's downtown, past parks, museums, churches, and tall office buildings. Montoya rejected all of Aguilar's efforts to learn where they were going. Finally, he pulled onto Carrera 55, where the city's administrative offices were. Aguilar noticed Montoya's eyes tick to the mirror, and he turned to see a police car pulling out behind them.

"It's the police!" he said.

"So?"

"So, we have a dead body in the front seat!"

"And?" Montoya capped that with a shrug, then he pulled to the curb. The mayor's office was less than a block away.

"What are you doing?"

Montoya shut off the engine. "Getting out. You want to stay here with him?" He stepped out into the street, then walked around and opened the passenger door wide.

Aguilar bolted from the car. "But—what about the police?"

"That's our ride," Montoya said. He waved to the police car as it cruised to a halt behind them.

Aguilar felt stunned, shell-shocked by the whole

sequence of events that had played out over the last hour. A moment later, he was ensconced in the rear of a police car that stank, like Montoya's, of bitter Pielroja smoke.

When he passed through the door of their apartment, he was engulfed in shame. He had been part of the kidnapping and murder of another human being. For his trouble, he'd been handed a stack of bills that he hadn't bothered to count yet, but that must have exceeded fifty thousand pesos.

Somehow, being paid for it only made it worse.

He took off his shoes and went into the bedroom. The bed was empty, but the bathroom door was closed. "Luisa, I'm here," he said.

"I'll be out in a minute."

He went to the kitchen sink and washed his hands and face as best he could. She still hadn't emerged, so he returned to the bedroom and peeled off his bloody clothes. Instead of putting them with the dirty laundry, he wadded them up and stuffed them into the trash. Nothing he had on was salvageable. He wished he could strip off his skin as easily.

Finally, Luisa came out. She saw him standing there, naked, and hurried to him. Early morning sunlight was beginning to filter in through the window. "Oh, Jose, are you all right?"

"I'm fine, baby," he said. "How are *you*?"

"I'm... I've been lonely. And worried."

"There's nothing to worry about. It was just some business. It's over."

"Business? You're covered in blood! You smell like smoke and liquor and the slaughterhouse."

"I need a shower."

"What's going on, Jose? You can tell me. I'm your wife."

"I know you are, baby. That's why I can't tell you. The less you know…"

"What? The less I know, what?"

"Nothing. I just don't want you hurt. I don't know what I would do with myself if you were ever hurt."

"Is someone going to hurt me? Am I in danger? Are you?"

He put his hands on her shoulders. She was edging toward hysteria, and he had to calm her down enough to get in the shower.

"There's no danger, baby."

"Are you sure? Do you promise?"

"I promise."

He had sworn never to lie to her, when they were courting and again when they were first married. He had broken that vow, but he didn't think he'd ever done so as fully as he did just then. He'd helped kill a man. That man didn't seem to be a gangster, but Aguilar really didn't know that much about him. Anyone who had wound up indebted to Pablo Escobar must have some criminal connections, and if that were the case, somebody could come looking for those who'd killed him.

Then there were the police—the honest ones, anyway. They had left the body on a street that would be busy with morning traffic, just down from the office of the mayor of Medellín. An investigation would be demanded. How hard would it be for them to connect him to the crime? At least three police officers had participated; if even one of them talked, he was finished.

She didn't look like she believed him, and he didn't know how to convince her of something he knew was a lie.

"Baby, I need a shower. It's been a hard few days. I'm tired."

"Are you drunk?"

"No. I had a little tequila last night, with Alberto. Some beer the night before. That's all."

She looked sad. She chewed on her lower lip and lowered her eyes. "I don't even know you."

"Yes you do, baby. I'm just me. I just had a job to do. It was bad, but it's over now."

"All right," she said after a moment. "You take your shower. When you come out, I have something to tell you."

"Is it something good?"

"I thought so. I hope so. But now, I'm not so sure."

"What is it? Tell me now."

"Later, after you're clean."

If she had news that would help him scrub his mind of the image of Castellanos on the floor, blood puddled beneath him, a gruesome hole beside his ruined eye, he wanted to hear it.

"No, now. Please, Luisa, now. I need to know."

"Well, this isn't exactly the way I pictured telling you, but…" Her face visibly brightened, a smile curving her lips and shining from her eyes. "…I'm pregnant!"

Tears came to Aguilar's eyes, overflowed, spilled down his cheeks. He began to sob, then to weep.

He held her tight against his naked, bloodstained form, and tried to convince her they were tears of joy.

He wasn't sure he succeeded.

8

NONE OF THE things Aguilar had worried about happened. Instead of being ostracized or punished by his fellow officers, he was lauded, congratulated. Some—the honest ones, he guessed—ignored his five-day absence, but even they knew better than to criticize. The bosses seemed to view him as though he'd passed a test of some kind, and now, his loyalty assured, were willing to trust him with greater responsibility. He was assigned his own vehicle, a Nissan Patrol older than the one Montoya drove, but one that hadn't been so saturated with tobacco that just entering it was like swimming in an ashtray. Often, he still rode with Montoya—they were partners, after all, and becoming something like friends—but sometimes he was given tasks to perform by himself. He was allowed to take the vehicle home, too, so his bus-riding days were at an end.

He still performed police duties, but more and more, he was pulled aside to handle tasks for Escobar's organization. Each of those came with a cash bonus, and since he was now saving to prepare for a child, the money was more important than ever.

One afternoon, two weeks after the death of Leo Castellanos, he and Montoya were in Montoya's Nissan. Although afternoon traffic was busy, they sat blocking the right lane of Carrera 34A, a major thoroughfare, watching cars pass. Motorists honked and made obscene gestures, but Aguilar and Montoya only laughed them off. They had a job to do, and they would be here until they had to go.

Then a gray Mercedes rolled past, with a driver in front and a single passenger in the rear, a graying eminence wearing a homburg. That was their quarry. They let the Mercedes get a block ahead, then pulled into traffic—prompting more horns and shouted curses—and followed. Stealth was unnecessary; a police vehicle could travel anywhere in the city, with no explanation or justification required.

After following the Mercedes for a couple of miles, Montoya switched on the lights and siren. The vehicles between them and the Mercedes gradually pulled out of the way, and finally the Mercedes slowed and stopped in an open space beside the road. Montoya and Aguilar got out and approached it, one on either side.

The driver exited the Mercedes before they reached it. He was tall, sturdy, and he led with a prominent, uptilted chin, as if to show that he was afraid of nothing. Montoya was on that side, Aguilar on the other.

"Have a problem, officers?" the driver said. "Do you know who my passenger is?"

"We do," Montoya said. "That's why we're here. Why don't you take a walk?"

"A walk?" the driver repeated, outrage in his tone. "He's in my charge! I—"

Montoya yanked his pistol from its holster and pushed the barrel against that massive chin. "Your choice," Montoya said. "Take a walk, or your loved ones can pick up pieces of your skull from the gutter."

The driver looked like there were many things he wanted to say, but he didn't dare. Instead he turned quickly and started walking.

The passenger in the Mercedes watched his driver go, confusion and fear warring on his face. Aguilar pulled open the back door and slid inside.

"See here!" the old man said. "This is my car! That's my driver! And—"

"We know who you are, Judge Molina. Don't worry, you and your driver won't be hurt, as long as you cooperate."

"Cooperate? You're wearing a police uniform. Driving a police car! Are you working for the Medellín Cartel?"

Aguilar had seen the words bandied about in the newspapers, but it was the first time anyone had spoken them to his face. *Medellín Cartel.* It had a businesslike ring to it, he thought.

He chose to ignore the question. "You're overseeing a case against a man named Alejandro Costa. He's innocent."

"Guilty or innocent is not for me to decide," the judge countered. "It's for the jury."

"Perhaps usually," Aguilar said. "Not this time."

The door on the other side of Judge Molina opened, and Montoya got in. The judge scooted to the center, to avoid touching either of the men. Aguilar could see his driver, almost a block away already and still walking. "We're not asking, Judge Molina," Montoya said. "We're explaining to you how it will be. Must be."

"And if I refuse?"

"You see how easily we can get to you," Aguilar said. "Obviously, we know where you work. We know where you live. We know where your wife Sylvia shops. We know where your daughters go to school. We know where your mistress's apartment is."

"If I were you," Montoya added, "I wouldn't refuse."

"That would be a very bad idea," Aguilar said. "And expensive for you."

"Expensive?"

"Making the right decision here could be financially lucrative. Wrong decision, people get hurt. Right one, people get rich. It's not complicated."

"You criminals think you can order decent, law-abiding people around. Well, I won't stand for it! I..." He let the sentence trail off. Probably, Aguilar thought, he was working through what they'd told him about his private life: his wife and daughters, his mistress. If they knew about those things, then he truly was safe nowhere. He was probably also thinking about the money.

"Innocent," Aguilar said again. "The evidence is lacking, the witnesses flawed."

"To be honest, the prosecution has done a poor job presenting its case," Molina said.

"That's what I thought, too," Aguilar said. He hadn't been present for any of the trial, or heard any reports about it. But he wanted to encourage the judge.

Alejandro Costa was a banker who had conducted several real-estate transactions for Escobar. Officially, the properties were very valuable, having been bought for considerably more than they were worth. Unofficially, much of the purchase price was refunded to Escobar as soon as the deal was completed. Later, the properties would be sold, again for an inflated price, making Escobar's "profits" clean, legal money. Costa had foolishly confided in a junior member of his banking staff, who had gone straight to the authorities. The prosecutor, a politically ambitious young man from an elite Colombian family, wanted to press for the severest possible penalty, in hopes of persuading Costa to turn on Escobar. So far, he hadn't, and Aguilar and Montoya had been charged to see that he didn't.

"I could probably arrange that verdict," Molina said.

"That would be best," Montoya agreed. "For everybody. Especially for you."

"And you should do it quickly," Aguilar added. Costa was growing more worried by the day. "One week. No more."

Molina nodded. They had him. Aguilar and Montoya both got out of the Mercedes at once, almost as if they'd rehearsed it.

"Wait!" Molina cried. "How do I... how do I get home from here? You've sent my driver away!"

"You don't know how to drive?" Aguilar asked.

"No," Molina said. "I've never had to."

"I guess it's time to learn," Montoya said. He and Aguilar walked back to the Nissan, laughing. The judge exited his back seat on unsteady legs, and climbed awkwardly behind the steering wheel. He was still sitting there, looking forlorn, as they drove away.

"You have any money on you?" Montoya asked. The question seemed to have come out of nowhere. They'd been driving aimlessly ever since the confrontation with Judge Molina.

"Some."

"How much?"

"Maybe thirty thousand pesos," Aguilar said. A short time ago, he could only have dreamed of having that much money at any one time. Now it was walking-around money.

"Good," Montoya said. He made a right turn, seemingly with a destination in mind for a change. "Let's go shopping."

"Shopping?"

"Have you ever had enemies, Jose? I mean real enemies, the kind who would kill you or somebody you love, without hesitation."

Aguilar didn't have to think about it for long. "Not really. Fights in school, but nothing serious."

"You do now. You might not know them yet, and they might not know you. But the work we've been doing… some people will resent it. Dangerous people. How do you keep Luisa safe?"

"I've never had to worry about it," Aguilar replied. "I have my sidearm. A knife."

"A knife?"

"Swiss Army. It has a blade for everything."

"It's not very good for killing."

"I just like to carry a knife."

"Why? Do you do a lot of woodcarving? Open wine bottles? What's it for?"

Aguilar pondered for a few moments. Montoya was driving into a neighborhood he wasn't familiar with. The blocks were packed with small houses, their yards thick with flowering trees. "When I was a boy, we couldn't afford a television. But sometimes my father

71

took me to a friend's house to watch *Tarzan*. He grew up in the forest, my father. He always loved Tarzan stories, so when the North American TV show came along, he wanted me to see his hero. I still remember the actor's name, Ron Ely. He always carried a knife; that was his main weapon. So after that, I always carried a knife, too."

"Because of Tarzan," Montoya said.

"That's right. He was my father's hero, and my father was my hero. It made sense to me then."

"Can you use it?"

"I once killed a rat with it. It was in the house, scaring my mother. I cut its throat before it could bite or scratch me." He shivered at the memory. "Blood everywhere."

"All right, I'm sure we can get you a knife, too. But I want to have some serious protection. You don't want anyone to hurt Luisa, do you?"

"Of course not."

"Then it's settled." Montoya made a final left, and came to a stop in front of a house that looked like all the others in the area.

"This doesn't look like a store," Aguilar said.

"Then it's just what we need. Come on."

Montoya led him up to the house's front door. It was wood, painted bright red, with polished brass hardware. Aguilar noticed that the yard was well kept, the adobe walls clean. Montoya knocked twice, then paused, then twice more.

A young woman opened the door, beaming a smile at them. She was attractive, Aguilar thought, long-haired and bright-eyed, with a sturdy, muscular body packed into a tank-top and snug blue jeans. She threw her arms around Montoya's neck. "Alberto!"

she cried. "So lovely to see you!"

"Good to see you, too, Juliana," he said, returning her embrace. After she released him, he said, "This is my friend Jose. Juliana will be able to provide everything we need."

"Can I get you some wine? Or yerba?"

Yerba mate sounded good to Aguilar; the adrenaline from stopping Molina had passed through his system, leaving him feeling tired, his senses dulled. But Montoya said, "Oh no, we can't stay long. We just need to pick up a few items."

Juliana frowned, but let them inside. The front room looked like one that could be found in almost any house: chairs, a couch, a low table, bookcases. But she led them through that into what looked like a bedroom.

From the outside.

Inside, it looked like an armory.

Gun racks had been mounted on every wall, and they displayed rifles and machine guns of every size and variety. Tables held RPG launchers, pistols, submachine guns, knives, swords, axes, and more. Most of one table was given over to hand grenades and other explosive devices. A bazooka leaned against the wall in one corner. The smell of gun oil was almost overpowering.

"Look around," Juliana said. "Let me know if you see anything you like."

"I see something I like," Montoya said, grabbing Juliana's ass.

She gave a laughing squeal and spun away from his grasp. "You could have it," she said. "But I don't think you can afford it."

"Really, Jose's the one looking. For guns, anyway."

"Any special type?" she asked. "I can order others, if there's something special."

"No," Aguilar said. "I didn't even know we were coming. Montoya surprised me."

"He does that," Juliana said. "He's surprised me plenty of times."

He studied the walls. He recognized a Remington shotgun, an Uzi, an HK. Others he recognized by type, even if he didn't know the brands. He wasn't sure what Montoya thought he would need at home. The bazooka would intimidate attackers, but he didn't think Luisa would stand for it.

"Take your time," Montoya said.

Aguilar did. He picked up weapons, feeling their heft, holding them to his shoulder and sighting down them. Some felt too heavy, some too light, others unwieldy or too seemingly flimsy.

Finally, he settled on a MAC-10 machine pistol with a thirty-round magazine. At the last minute, he added a 23.5-centimeter Bowie knife. It was North American-made, a thing of almost indescribable beauty. The top edge of the blade was serrated until the last seven centimeters, when it curved down to a wickedly sharp point. The curved part was honed as sharp as the blade. The upper cross-guard bent forward, toward the point, and the lower bent back to protect the hand. In his fist, it felt like it had been made just for him. It came with a leather sheath that had a snap pocket with a sharpening stone inside. The leather was browned with age, sturdy enough to hold the knife but soft enough to feel like a lover's caress.

"And this," he said, putting it with the MAC-10.

"He likes knives," Montoya said. "Because of Tarzan."

"He has good taste," Juliana said. "Just those two, then?"

"And eight boxes of ammunition for the MAC," Montoya replied.

Aguilar blushed. He'd almost forgotten about that. The gun wouldn't be much good without it. The knife, though—it could hold its own.

He hated to blush in front of strangers, because his peculiar spotted skin didn't blush evenly. The white areas, scar tissue from the burn, never turned pink. The fleshy areas did, so it accentuated his disfigurement.

Juliana gave no sign of noticing. She did math in her head, then named a price. Aguilar looked at Montoya, who nodded. It was well within the thirty thousand he carried, so he counted out the bills and handed them to Juliana.

When she walked them to the door, she hugged Montoya again. Then, to his surprise, she turned to Aguilar and drew him into a tight embrace. She surprised him further by planting a kiss on his cheek. "Come back any time, Jose," she said. "I'm always getting in new merchandise."

Back in the Nissan, Montoya shot Aguilar a wide grin. "You're all set now, brother. That knife is better than Tarzan's."

"Thanks for taking me there," Aguilar said. "She was nice."

"Very nice indeed," Montoya agreed. Then, his face suddenly serious, he added, "Be sure you teach Luisa how to use that."

"The MAC?"

"Yes. You're not always home, you know. She needs to be able to defend herself."

He drove away from Juliana's. Aguilar was lost in thought, wondering how to explain to Luisa that she needed to learn to handle an automatic weapon. He barely heard Montoya say, "Your life has changed, Aguilar. More than you know. It will be better than you ever imagined. But more dangerous, too. Often, the two go hand in hand."

9

ONE WEEK LATER, Alejandro Costa's trial was over, and he was a free man.

That night—really the next morning, after two—Montoya called Aguilar at home. "You have to get dressed and meet me," he said. "There's a problem."

"What kind of problem?"

Montoya named a street corner. "Twenty minutes," he said. "I'll explain when I see you."

Aguilar explained to Luisa, who greeted the news with a pout. "I don't like this part," she said.

"I have to do it. When there's business, I have to take care of it. You like the money, right?"

"Not if it takes you out of our bed." She stood up, put her hands on his shoulders, and tried to pull him back down. Her body was warm and yielding, her hair tousled, her face adorable. "Please, Jose, stay with me."

"I can't, baby. You know that."

"I'll make it worth your while."

"I would if I could. I'll be back soon. You'll be fine. Just go back to sleep."

"I can't sleep when you have to go out at night. What about that time you were gone for five days? I worry about you."

"It won't be that long, I promise." He knew, even as he spoke the words, that it was a promise he couldn't hope to keep. How could he? He had no idea what was going on.

Over her objections, he dressed, strapped the knife to his ankle, put the MAC-10 in a gym bag, and was out of the apartment in a few minutes. He made it to the intersection before Montoya. There were some shops there with a small parking lot on the side, so he sat in his Patrol and waited. Montoya was five minutes late. When he got out of his vehicle, he was smoking, and he looked bleary-eyed. Drunk, maybe. He had been drinking a lot lately. Sometimes Aguilar joined him.

"What's going on?" Aguilar asked. "What's the big crisis?"

"He's been kidnapped," Montoya said.

"Who? Kidnapped? What are you talking about?"

"Costa."

"Costa who?" Aguilar asked. Then it dawned on him. "The banker?"

"His mother called a couple of hours ago. After he got out of court, he went to the apartment his parents are staying in since they sold their house. A little while later, some men came to the door. They shot her husband, knocked her around, and took Costa."

"What are we supposed to do about it? You didn't tell me to put on my uniform."

"It's not a police matter," Montoya snapped. "We're going to get him back."

"How?"

"Don Pablo has eyes everywhere. We know who took him, and where they have him. We just need some men."

"Us?"

"And others. They'll be here soon, and we'll all go together."

"Who kidnapped him?"

"Some guys who work for a man named Carlos Rodrigo Muñoz. He wants to cut into Escobar's business. He wants to know what Costa knows about it. We have to get Costa back before he talks."

"Or kill him?" Aguilar asked.

"What?"

"Get him back, or kill him before he talks. That's what you mean, right?"

"Listen, man, I don't give the orders. I follow them."

"That's always the excuse, isn't it?"

Montoya shrugged. "Look, if you don't want to be a part of this, you don't have to. You can always walk away. I'm not sure how Don Pablo would react, but it's your decision."

Aguilar thought he knew how Escobar would react. He would consider it treason. That, Aguilar had realized, was the real cost of taking Escobar's money. Once you were on the inside, indebted to *El Patrón*, you had to stay inside. To do otherwise was to put your life in danger, as well as the lives of everyone you cared about.

Anyway, he had been raised in poverty. Indebtedness was all he knew. At least this way, he had something to show for it.

"I didn't say I wanted out," he said. "I just want us to be clear about what it is we're doing."

"I think we're clear," Montoya said.

They waited in Montoya's SUV until the others arrived. They came in six vehicles. Aguilar recognized Poison, Blackie, Trigger, Pancho, Shorty, and Snake-eyes, *sicarios* he had already met. The other men were strangers. Most were young, in their teens or barely out of them. They looked like street kids who'd come into some money and spent it on gaudy clothes and stylish haircuts, but didn't know what else to do with it.

Aguilar wasn't much different, except he had a wife, and a baby on the way. Responsibilities. Those weighed on a man, made him more inclined to be careful with his spending.

Poison seemed to be in charge. He was lean, and wore his hair combed up, making him look taller. He had an anchor-type beard that ran straight down from the middle of his lower lip, then spread like the flukes of an anchor under his chin, a bushy mustache, and cool, appraising eyes.

"Place we're going used to be a *mercado*," he said, addressing the entire assembly. "Rodrigo will have a lot of guys there, and Costa will probably be in the back." He bisected the group with an outstretched arm. "You guys will go in the front," he said, addressing those on his left. "And you guys in the back." Aguilar and Montoya were on Poison's right, in the back group, along with tall, skinny Blackie, whose skin was so dark it was no mystery where his nickname had come from. "We'll roll up, pile out, and hit it fast, all at the same time. It's gonna be bloody." He paused for a moment, looking serious, then unleashed a brilliant grin. "That's what makes it fun, right?"

The crowd responded with a lusty roar. Aguilar didn't join in until Montoya nudged him. Then, he opened his mouth along with the others, but stayed silent. Walking back to Montoya's Nissan, he offered a silent prayer for protection, for himself and for Luisa, in case anything happened to him.

The vehicles peeled out one after another, tires squealing, engines loud in the quiet of the pre-dawn morning.

"Who's Rodrigo?" Aguilar asked when they were en route.

"Some *pendejo* from Cartagena who saw Don Pablo, the Ochoas, and Gacha making a lot of money. Decided he wants to get in the business, too. I guess he figured Costa knows all the secrets, so he would grab Costa while he was at his most vulnerable."

"Does Costa know all the secrets?"

"Nobody knows all the secrets, except Don Pablo. Maybe his cousin Gustavo knows most of them, but not all. I'm sure Costa knows plenty, though."

"How do they know he's the one who took Costa?"

"Nothing happens in Medellín that Don Pablo doesn't know about."

"How does he know where Costa's being held?"

"I told you, he has eyes *everywhere*."

"Even inside Rodrigo's organization?"

"Look at it this way. Rodrigo wants to move up, but he's small-time. If you worked for a small-timer who couldn't pay you much, and someone like Don Pablo wanted to pay you ten times as much to spy for him, would you do it?"

"It'd be dangerous, though."

"So would saying no."

"How long have you been part of all this, Alberto?"

"A few years. Since before he even started moving cocaine. Don Pablo knew it would be good to have some people inside the police. I could have joined him full-time, but this way I still get my police pay, and I can provide intelligence from time to time."

"Is this what you thought you'd be doing, when you first went to the academy?"

"I grew up with nothing, brother. Poor as dirt. I didn't want to stay that way. Whatever I can get my hands on, I'm going to take. Anybody gets in my way, fuck them."

Aguilar didn't ask any more questions. He was growing increasingly anxious as they neared their destination. The men he would be fighting alongside seemed more than ready for battle. But he had never been the target of gunfire, never had anyone trying to kill him. Or tried to kill anyone else.

Tonight, in the next few minutes, both of those things would no longer be true.

"Get your gun out," Montoya said, rounding the last corner. Ahead, brake lights from the other vehicles in their convoy showed. Some looped around to the front of the building. Montoya joined the chain at the rear. "We're there."

With shaking hands, Aguilar unzipped the gym bag and pulled out the MAC-10. He checked the magazine, slipped two more into his pockets. He felt the reassuring weight of the big knife around his left ankle.

"You ready?" Montoya asked.

No.

"Yeah."

Ahead of and behind them, doors opened and men poured out onto the ground, slamming doors behind them.

Stealth was no longer the watchword, if it ever had been.

* * *

Aguilar estimated twenty men in the alley, at the rear of the former market. There was a loading dock for trucks, a little more than waist-high, with five concrete stairs leading up to it from the street. A big roll-up steel door led inside, for pallets of merchandise, and next to it was a regular door for people. Those would both be locked, of course.

He'd expected to see armed guards outside, but there weren't any. That didn't mean they weren't right behind those doors.

And, as it turned out, on the roof.

Pancho—so called because he wore his mustache like Pancho Villa, and favored crossed bandoliers—happened to look up, or heard the scrape of a shoe, or something, and shouted out a warning just as the gunfire started. It was too late to save any lives. Four men on the roof opened fire with automatic weapons, and lead rained onto the attackers. Immediately, six of them went down.

Others scrambled for what little cover the alley offered. A rolling steel dumpster halfway down the block, some concrete bollards a man could duck behind if he was skinny enough.

Aguilar didn't even try for those. Instead, he lunged forward, sprang up onto the loading dock, and rolled to his feet. Here, the overhang protected him from the men on the roof. A few others saw what he'd done and followed suit, one of them catching a round in the top of his head as he tried. Still more stood their ground, trading fire with those above. A body dropped from the roof, landing on the alley floor with a damp thud.

The gunfire tapered off, then died. Aguilar could hear more, from in front of the store, but for the moment it was quiet at the rear. The survivors, twelve in all, gathered on the loading dock.

Then rounds punched through the roll-up door from inside, and two more men went down.

The rest returned fire, including Aguilar. He couldn't see who he was shooting at, could only see the now-perforated steel door and estimate where people were on the other side. He was fighting for his life, and he was scared, and he squeezed the trigger with everything he had, watching his rounds penetrate the door and disappear. The recoil made his gun barrel float higher and higher, until he realized it and brought it back down. He was still holding the trigger for several seconds after the magazine was empty. In the noise and smoke and fear and heat of the moment, he hadn't realized it was spent.

He ejected it and slammed another one home. A couple of minutes had elapsed, he had yet to see an enemy gunman, and he'd already burned through a third of his ammunition.

What am I doing here? he asked himself. *I could be in bed with Luisa.*

Too late to worry about that now.

One of Escobar's men trained his gunfire on the human-sized door instead of the big one, shooting around the lock. When he'd done sufficient damage, he kicked it open and hurled something inside. It wasn't until he threw himself to the floor, hands over his head, that Aguilar realized it was a grenade. "Down!" Aguilar shouted, dropping and covering his ears.

The explosion came a few seconds later. The steel door absorbed most of the blast, but through the holes in it Aguilar caught a glimpse of a flashing light. The boom was deafening, and he felt the concussive waves even on the far side of the door.

He could only imagine it was much worse for those on that side.

The gunfire from inside had stopped, at least in the rear of the store. From the front, sounds of battle still raged.

"Come on!" someone shouted. He charged through the small door, gun ready. The rest found their feet and followed. Montoya, Aguilar noted, still lived, and he raced inside like he couldn't wait to kill somebody.

Aguilar was the last man in.

10

INSIDE WAS CHAOS.

The store's back room was full of freestanding steel shelving units, empty of everything except for the dust of the years since it had closed. The grenade had collapsed some of them, and those had knocked over others. Bodies were strewn amidst the debris. Smoke hung in the air like a heavy fog. Light fixtures dangled from the ceiling, but they were shut off, so the place was dark except for what little light filtered in through the open door.

Through the ringing in his ears, Aguilar could hear Escobar's men moving, some speaking in low tones, and the thunder of the ongoing gunfight in front of the store.

He didn't believe the rear was so sparsely defended. There must be more men somewhere, lying in wait. An ambush. Poison had expected Costa to be held back here, but who knew how many rooms there were? Surely more than this storeroom. A market had to have a walk-in freezer, cold storage, offices.

If only he could see. And hear. If only his knees would stop threatening to give out beneath him, and his hands weren't sweating so much he was afraid of dropping his gun.

Blackie found a steel door leading toward the front of the store. He hesitated before it, then waved people away from it so they wouldn't be in the line of fire when it opened. Standing well to one side, he pulled the big handle. The door swung wide.

Three men on the other side of it opened fire, raking their gun barrels this way and that. Aguilar dropped to one knee and opened fire. Four more of the attackers went down, dead or wounded, before they were able to put down those three. Then, Blackie still in the lead, they passed through that door and into a nearly pitch-black warren of offices and storerooms.

"Spread out," Blackie said. "You see anybody, kill them. Anybody at all."

That answered the question Aguilar had asked Montoya earlier. The important thing wasn't rescuing Costa, it was making sure Costa couldn't spill what he knew. A dead banker was better than a live one who talked.

Montoya brushed against Aguilar, gave him a "come with me" nod. Aguilar stuck close. They went off to the right, where an open doorway beckoned, black against black. Two of the other guys followed them.

They'd just reached the doorway when a muzzle flash farther down the hall blinded Aguilar. He swore and fell through the doorway, Montoya tripping over him as he ducked in as well. One of the guys following was hit, but the other joined them.

Aguilar reached around the door and unloaded a burst from his MAC-10. He heard a squeal of pain and some muttered swearing, so he kept firing, moving his barrel up and down, side to side, hoping to find the gunman wherever he was. A heavy thump, followed by silence, rewarded him.

Montoya found his feet, then Aguilar did. The other guy was still there, a shadow in the darkness. Aguilar could hear him moving, sense his presence, smell the cologne he had seemingly bathed in, but could see no detail.

They were in another hallway. Doors were barely visible down its length, steel ones with big handles. Coolers, Aguilar thought.

If he'd been hiding a prisoner, this was where he'd be.

Which meant there would be guards.

He was sure of one thing: Costa was still alive. Rodrigo didn't want any ransom, he wanted information. Killing Costa would defeat his whole purpose. He would have him protected, and he'd be keeping the banker quiet.

Imitating what he'd seen Blackie do, he stood to the side of the first doorway and opened the door. It swung wide. Silence.

Montoya did the same at the next one. As the door swung open, men burst through it, guns blazing.

Aguilar felt a tug at his sleeve. For a brief instant, he thought it was Montoya. Then he realized Montoya was on the far side of the doorway, and the tug was a bullet. He wondered if he'd been hit, wondered if he would feel it if he had. Wondered what it would be like to bleed out on the dark floor of an abandoned grocery.

Those thoughts flashed through his mind in a heartbeat. In the same moment, he was stepping back until he ran into the corridor wall, firing his gun as he did. He couldn't see Montoya or the other guy anymore, couldn't see where Rodrigo's men were; his own muzzle flash had blinded him. The rumble of footsteps told him men were still charging through the doorway, maybe others coming down the hall. He realized—too late, again—that he had once more emptied the magazine.

He dropped it, fumbled in his pocket for another. Someone slammed into him and they both went down in a heap. At the impact, the MAC-10 flew from his hands. He felt something hard against his lower back and he knew what it was: the other guy had a gun, but his arm was pinned under Aguilar's hip and he was trying, one-handed, to bring it into a position in which he could shoot Aguilar in the back, and if that happened he'd be crippled for life, or dead, and dear God what he wouldn't give for some light, any light, even the distant glow of a saint candle.

He tried to bend his leg up to where he could reach his ankle, but it was trapped between them. He realized then that if he was able to, it would shift the pressure off the other guy's arm. But he had to try. He could feel the gun against his back, could feel the barrel was almost there.

Desperate, Aguilar clawed at his leg. He caught the edge of his jeans cuff, tugged it up.

The gun moved against his back, its barrel pressing against him. The guy was trying to reach the trigger.

Aguilar touched the big knife's grip, got his hand around it. It slid easily from its sheath.

He lashed out, felt the blade connect. Heard a cry. Warm blood splashed his hand. He struck again and again, until the other man stopped moving. Aguilar disentangled himself and rose to his feet.

Not counting the dead, he was alone. He didn't

know where Montoya had gone, or the other guy. He wasn't even sure which direction he'd come from. He was lost in the dark, surrounded by enemies.

He went to his hands and knees, feeling around the floor until he'd located the MAC-10. From its weight, he knew he hadn't succeeded in getting the third magazine in. He patted his pockets. Not there. It had to be somewhere in the hallway, then, but where? Someone could have kicked it three meters away. In the meantime, sounds of the continuing gunfight reached him.

He tucked the useless weapon into his waistband, kept his right fist wrapped tightly around the knife.

At least he had that.

The dark hallway still needed to be cleared. The other doors hadn't yet been checked, as far as he knew. Stupid to try it, with no gun. But he was convinced that Costa would be down here, somewhere, and it sounded like the other guys—those who yet lived— were busy.

He went to the next door, opened it. Nothing.

Same with the door after that.

The next one was locked. He pounded on it, shouted, "All clear!" in what he hoped was a convincing tone. No response.

Nothing more he could do here, then. He couldn't break through a steel freezer door, if that's what it was. Couldn't shoot through it without a gun.

Then Aguilar remembered the guy he'd stabbed to death. He'd had a gun. It must still be near him. He went back the other way, almost tripped on an outflung leg. When he hit that, he knew he was there. He pawed around, his hands landing in puddled blood and bits of chopped-up flesh.

He was still on the floor, patting the corpse, when he heard movement in the main hallway. He looked up, saw a lanky form that could only be Blackie, wrestling with two guys. Nobody was using guns; either they'd all run out of ammunition, or they were trying to keep quiet. That seemed unlikely, given the racket still reverberating from elsewhere in the building.

Still, it was two against one, and Aguilar knew Blackie was one of Escobar's most trusted *sicarios*. He abandoned his fruitless search for the gun, rose silently, and worked his way behind the struggling shapes. He could tell which one was Blackie, which meant either of the others were fair game.

He held the knife ribs-high and stabbed.

The double-edged blade sank deep and the man it struck screamed. "Fuck!" he cried, trying to reach whatever was cutting him. Aguilar gave the blade a little twist, then yanked it free. Blood spurted out, and stringy tissue clung to it. The man was still shouting, "Fuck! Fuck!" when Aguilar stabbed him again. His cries turned into wordless grunts. Aguilar drew the knife back, slashing out at the second man. It struck home, sliced through something, and that man gave a pained screech.

Blackie took advantage of his distraction. He kicked the man in the groin, and when the guy started to buckle, grabbed his head. Aguilar heard the cracking of bones as Blackie twisted the man's neck, then released him. The man folded to the floor.

"Thanks, brother," Blackie said.

"No problem."

The two men stood there, breathing hard—glad to still *be* breathing. The sounds of battle had quieted. Instead of gunfire, raised voices cried out. Aguilar recognized Poison's. That meant the men who'd gone in the front had worked their way back. Blackie came to the same conclusion, and started to laugh.

"We won!" he said. "Motherfucker, we won!"

In another minute, men came in with flashlights. Trigger was there, carrying a flashlight and a shotgun. Montoya was there, too. "I think we got them all," Montoya said. "We're just clearing all the rooms." He chuckled. "As police do."

"What about Costa?" Blackie asked.

Snake-eyes drew a slash across his throat.

"Excellent," Blackie said. He turned to Aguilar. "Man, you're *something* with that blade. Like some kind of demon."

In the glow from someone's flashlight, Aguilar saw that the knife was slick with blood and viscera. His hand and arm were soaked. He felt like a *Muisca* warrior from ages past.

Or Tarzan.

Except he doubted that Tarzan had ever been sick to his stomach from slaying his foes. Looking at the gore and thinking about what he had done, back there in the dark, he had to swallow hard to keep from puking. It would have been worse, he supposed, if he'd seen what he was doing, the damage his blade was doing to other human bodies.

Still, if it hadn't been them it would have been him.

At least he'd be going home to Luisa.

Probably with a bonus in his pocket.

11

Twenty-eight men had gone into the market.

Eleven came out.

Poison carried Costa's head, holding it with his fingers twined in the banker's thick black hair.

Aguilar felt queasy, unwell, but he seemed to be alone in that. The others—despite the losses they'd suffered, and the wounds some bore—seemed almost jovial. Drunk with bloodlust.

Aguilar had to admit that he felt some of that, too. Sick, but thrilled. And all the sicker because of the thrill. It was wrong, he knew. He would have much to confess, the next time he went into a church. He wanted to throw up, to cleanse himself from the inside out, but didn't dare in front of the other men.

He thought now that they were done he could go home, take a shower, and let Luisa hold him for the rest of the day. He wanted that more than anything.

Instead, Montoya spoke with Blackie, and when they got back in the SUV, he said, "*El Patrón* needs to see you, brother."

"See me?"

"That's what I said. Blackie was really impressed with your knife skills. He wants Escobar to meet you."

"He has met me."

"I mean, really meet you. We're invited over."

"When?"

"This morning."

Aguilar looked at the sky. The sun had come up, and it was rapidly lightening to a pale, cloudless blue. "This morning? Can I go home first? I'm a bloody mess."

"Escobar's version of morning isn't the same as most people's. Anyway, it's a long drive. I'll pick you up about nine and we'll head over, okay?"

It wasn't perfect, but it would give him some time with Luisa. Maybe he could even squeeze in a short nap. "Sure," he said.

"Dress decent," Montoya said. "Don't look like a bum. And be sure you bring that knife. He'll want to see it."

No problem, Aguilar thought. He didn't think he would ever leave home without it. The thing had saved his life, several times over.

Best money he'd ever spent.

They reached Hacienda Nápoles, Escobar's hilltop *finca*, around noon. Aguilar had heard stories about it—who in Colombia hadn't?—but they hadn't prepared him for the reality.

As they drove up the road approaching it, they passed what seemed like kilometer after kilometer of tall wire fence, topped with razor wire. The landscape was mostly rolling grasslands, dotted with trees, green on green on green. In the distance, Aguilar was sure he spotted a Tyrannosaurus Rex. "There's a dinosaur."

"He's got a bunch of them," Montoya said. "Don't worry, they're not real."

"What are they?"

"Sculptures, I guess you'd call them. Fiberglass, I think. But the elephants and rhinos and zebras and giraffes and shit, they're real."

"Elephants and rhinos? I heard he had sort of a zoo here, but I thought maybe some horses, goats, that kind of thing."

"He doesn't do things halfway. And he has so much money pouring in, why not? He lets the public visit his zoo, for free."

"A generous man," Aguilar said. He almost believed it.

At the gateway, they were waved through by guards who expected them, then passed underneath a small airplane. "That's supposed to be the plane that carried his first load of cocaine to the United States, right?" Aguilar asked.

"Some say that," Montoya replied. "Others say that plane was wrecked, and this is a reproduction of it."

"Which do you believe?"

"Whatever Don Pablo wants me to believe. That's always the best idea."

"How well do you know him?"

"I've met him five or six times. Not well, but a little. He's always been kind to me."

"He seemed nice the time I met him."

"As long as you don't cross him, I think he's always nice. And the people who do cross him don't usually live long enough to complain."

They drove up a long road, from which they could

catch occasional glimpses of other structures, some of the many separate houses Montoya claimed he had on the vast property. The noontime sun glinted off lakes and swimming pools and showered down on kilometer after kilometer of fruit trees. Finally, they pulled up to the main hacienda, a massive house that Montoya said could sleep twenty or thirty people, if necessary.

A mustachioed man in a flat snap-brim cap and sunglasses stepped out of the front door and met them as they exited the Nissan. Other men stood within eyesight, watching with hard eyes. "It's not often we have police cars up here," he said, grinning. "At least, not by invitation. Welcome to Hacienda Nápoles."

"Thank you for inviting us," Montoya said. "Gustavo, this is Jose Aguilar Gonzales. Jose, this is Don Pablo's cousin and closest friend, Gustavo Gaviria."

"It's an honor to meet you, sir," Aguilar said. He'd been raised to be polite. He had put on an off-white silk shirt and Jordache jeans with elaborate white embroidery on the rear pockets, and his best ostrich-skin boots. He wanted to make a good impression on the gangsters, though he couldn't have said precisely why. He did not intend—as Montoya apparently had—to swear allegiance to them. He didn't mind taking their money—indeed, he didn't seem to have a choice—but he was a policeman, first and foremost. And he intended to remain one, to rise through the ranks. One day, he might find himself looking down the barrel of a gun at any of Escobar's people. It wouldn't hurt to know their organization from the inside, if only to someday bring it down.

"It's good to meet you," Gaviria said. "I've heard stories about your knife skills."

Aguilar wanted to tell him that they were

exaggerated, but he reconsidered. Gaviria's tone was admiring, and he didn't want to shatter any illusions. Besides, although he thought he'd just been lucky, the truth was that he'd survived a bad situation. Maybe he was good with a knife, after all.

"I've always liked knives," he said. That much was true, at least.

"Come in," Gaviria said. "Pablo's not up yet, but you can relax by the pool. Do you want something? Beer, wine, Coke?"

A cola would have been fine with Aguilar, but considering where he was, and with whom, he wasn't sure if he'd been offered that, or cocaine. "Pepsi?" he asked.

"Beer would be great," Montoya said, speaking over him. "For both of us."

Gaviria snapped his fingers at a waiting attendant Aguilar hadn't even seen until that moment. There seemed to be an unlimited supply of men around, and they'd all mastered the art of being still and silent. Unless they were needed; Aguilar was certain that if they saw trouble, they would respond with swift ferocity.

"This way," Gaviria said. He led them through a luxurious home that opened on one side onto a swimming pool. The furniture looked comfortable, and works of art that Aguilar thought were expensive were scattered here and there. He thought he saw a famous Picasso on one wall that he recognized from art classes at school. He dismissed it as a mistake, at first, but then thought better of it. Why not? Who could afford Pablo Picasso more than Pablo Escobar? He knew that artwork sometimes was sold at auctions, and there were many reasons he wouldn't have wanted to bid against *El Patrón*, even if he had the money.

Gaviria showed them to some plush chairs beside the pool. The beers were already standing on a table beside the seating area; two sweating bottles, accompanied by elegant glasses. A gentle breeze stirred the water, sending glittering daggers of light into the air.

"I have some business to attend to," Gaviria said. "I'll make sure Pablo knows you're here. In the meantime, if you need anything at all, just ask Ernesto." He nodded toward one of the hard men. Ernesto gave a slight nod in return, but his expression didn't change. He was a big man, broad-shouldered, and he stood with his hands behind his back and his feet spread. Except for that nod, he could have been cast from bronze.

Montoya sat back and took a long pull from his beer, directly from the bottle. "Ahh," he said after he swallowed. "This is the life, eh? All that's missing are some beautiful women in the pool."

"I haven't seen any women at all," Aguilar said. Sitting in a comfortable chair felt good—he was still aching from the fight the night before, and the long ride in the Nissan hadn't helped.

"Victoria, Don Pablo's wife—he calls her Tata—is probably here somewhere. His mother, too. Unless they're out spending some of his money. He's a real family man. I mean, he has his fun, you know. But not when his family's around. He makes sure to keep things separate. It's only respectful."

Aguilar could imagine what Luisa would say if he suggested that kind of "respect." He kept quiet, pouring his beer into the tall glass.

They waited. For a while, they made small talk, and Montoya filled him in on what he knew about

Escobar. Every now and then Gaviria came out to check on them. More often, Montoya summoned Ernesto to ask for refills. Aguilar worried that by the time Escobar came out, they'd be too drunk to carry on a conversation. He tried to sip his, making it last. But the day was warm and the pool was pretty and it was easy to forget. Montoya dozed off once, but only for a few minutes.

Finally, he heard a small commotion inside, and glanced up to see Escobar coming toward them. A couple of men hovered around him, but he dismissed them and came out alone. Aguilar and Montoya both jumped to their feet at his approach. Even Ernesto seemed to stand a little straighter.

"Alberto, Jose," he said. "Thank you for gracing my home with your presence. I hope you haven't been waiting long."

"Not at all, Don Pablo," Montoya said. "Thank you for inviting us. It's beautiful here."

"Yes, it is," Escobar said. "Sit, sit." He took a chair for himself, gazed at the pool for a few moments. Aguilar could smell weed on him; he'd smoked some before coming out. "It's peaceful, that's what I like about it. The mountain breeze, the trees, the water. It's not like the city, anyway. Sometimes I can lose myself up here, forget about all my troubles, all the demands on me." He chuckled. "I've been very fortunate. I'm a successful businessman, and sometimes it sounds like I regret my own success. I assure you, that's not the case. It's just nice to be away from it once in a while."

"I'm sure it is," Montoya said. "It'll be hard to go back to Medellín, after this."

"We need you there, though," Escobar said. "You've been doing good work. Important work. Both of you."

Aguilar felt an unexpected flush of pride. The first time he'd met Escobar, he had just accomplished a very simple task. Now, though, it sounded like Escobar was aware of what they'd been doing, keeping up with their efforts. For such a busy man to take notice was a high compliment.

"We do what we can," Montoya said. "We're happy to serve."

"I trust we're taking good care of you?"

"Very good care, Don Pablo. We're very grateful."

Aguilar had never seen Montoya so deferential, even when he talked to the colonel in charge of the police force. The worst the colonel could do would be to fire them, though. From what he'd heard of Escobar, his version of firing them would be a very different process, possibly involving actual flames.

Escobar turned to Aguilar. "I hear you're handy with a knife."

"I like knives," he said. It had been enough for Gaviria.

Not for Escobar, though. He held out a hand. "Let me see it."

Aguilar hesitated. He'd considered leaving it at home. Now he wondered if he should have, after all. What would the men watching them do if he reached under his pants leg and pulled a knife? They were close enough to see, but not necessarily to have heard Escobar's request. He regretted having so much beer— what if he accidentally dropped it and cut *El Patrón*?

He caught Ernesto's eye as he reached for the cuff of his jeans. Once again, Ernesto gave that briefest of nods. Aguilar took it as permission, and with broad motions, obviously not disguising his intentions, drew the leg up to reveal the knife. He tugged it from its sheath and gave it, handle first, to Escobar. "Here it is."

Escobar gave a low whistle. "Nice. It looks deadly."

"It is."

"I wouldn't want to mess with you, if you had this," Escobar said with a laugh. He handed it back, and Aguilar gingerly replaced it in the sheath, then pulled his jeans back down to cover it.

"I'm glad I had it last night," he said.

"I heard all about it. Blackie was most impressed. And lucky you were there."

"It was an honor to be asked to help."

"I'll see that you're taken care of," Escobar said. "But you could make more money. Much more. Serious money. Would you be interested in that?"

Montoya perked up at that. "Absolutely," he said.

Escobar shot him a withering glance that made it clear he'd been addressing Aguilar. "Both of you, of course," he said when Montoya shrank back into his seat.

"We'd be glad to do whatever we can," Aguilar said.

"It's helpful to have police officers in Medellín," Escobar said. "But there are additional tasks you could handle for me. If I could rely on you two, I wouldn't have to have so many people in the city. I don't know if you can be spared from your official tasks, but—"

"That's not a problem," Montoya cut in. "Whenever you need us, we're allowed as much time as necessary."

"Yes, well, your colonel gets his cut, too. And the captain."

"We can do whatever you ask us to, Don Pablo," Aguilar said. It was the beer talking—beer and adrenaline, from knowing he was sitting here at the Don's *finca*, negotiating a business deal with Escobar himself. He wasn't even sure what he was volunteering for, but he had an idea it was more of the same sort of thing. "You have only to tell us what's required."

"Very well," Escobar said. He held out a hand, and Aguilar shook it. Then, almost as an afterthought, Escobar reached out to Montoya. Montoya pumped his hand like he was trying to draw water from a well. "We have a deal, then."

"We have a deal," Aguilar repeated.

"Here's the thing," Escobar said. "This bastard Carlos Rodrigo is a pain in my ass. He's from Cartagena. It's an easy trip to Jamaica or Panama from there, even Cuba, so he's using boats to carry his product. I don't have a problem with that; there's so much demand in the U.S. that we can all make some money. But he's moving so much that he's having a hard time with supply, and he's trying to cut into my supply chains. I can't allow that."

"Of course not," Montoya said.

"You guys helped take Costa off the board, and eliminated some of Rodrigo's men. I appreciate that. But Rodrigo is still out there. I'm not even sure now if he's still in Medellín or in Cartagena. I need him found, and I need his head on a post somewhere, as an example to anyone else."

He was soliciting murder. If he'd been almost anyone else in Colombia, he could have been arrested for that alone. But Aguilar knew that not only would Escobar never make it to trial, but if he tried to arrest him, he would never leave this hillside retreat. He'd be buried up here somewhere—or else his head would decorate a post in Medellín, maybe alongside Rodrigo's.

Anyway, he'd already killed for Escobar. No sense in pretending he was innocent. He would carry the guilt of what he had done for the rest of his days, and pray for forgiveness at the end of them.

12

AGUILAR AND MONTOYA had left Hacienda Nápoles with a hundred thousand pesos each. Aguilar felt rich, but soon learned that he would have to share the wealth to get the information he wanted. A contact working for the telephone company could provide phone numbers for Carlos Rodrigo Muñoz. Another could tap Rodrigo's lines. But both cost money. With those arrangements made, he and Montoya visited every luxury hotel in and around Medellín, asking if Rodrigo had been or was currently a guest there. Through a friend of a friend, Montoya acquired Rodrigo's addresses in Cartagena. There were six of them, but nobody knew for sure if that was all—those were just the homes that he owned legally.

He wasn't as rich as Pablo Escobar—few people were, in Colombia or anywhere else. But he had the resources necessary to disguise his whereabouts.

As he spread money around in return for information, Aguilar realized that he was replicating, in miniature, the economy of so much of his country.

The drug lords sucked vast fortunes from markets elsewhere, mostly the United States. They spent some of their profits on their employees—servants, *sicarios*, sources, government officeholders and judges and police officers and lawyers—and more buying goods— aircraft and boats and cars, guns and bullets, homes, furniture, artwork, LaserDiscs, clothing. Still more went to entertain themselves, to the nightclubs and restaurants they frequented, the musicians and florists and decorators and caterers for the lavish parties he'd heard about. All those people made money indirectly from the cocaine trade, and they spent it on their own goods, on their groceries and cars and electricity and schooling. Drug money permeated society, from top to bottom. He wondered if there was a single peso in Colombia that didn't have cocaine residue on it, at least metaphorically.

They took a few days off and drove to Cartagena in a rented Corvette convertible. Aguilar had never been there, and what intelligence they'd been able to gather indicated that Rodrigo was in one of his houses in town. Montoya drove fast, where the roads allowed, and they reached the city late in the afternoon.

Hot and hungry, they grabbed some *paletas* and walked the weathered stone walls around the Old City, on fortifications put in place to defend against pirates, among other dangers. The sun set while they were looking out toward the Caribbean, so after they descended from the walls, they found an outdoor café and ordered dinner and drinks. Their fellow diners were mostly tourists and young couples making eyes at each other. At one point, Montoya reached over and gently stroked Aguilar's hand, then started giggling uncontrollably.

"What?" Aguilar asked.

"There are so many lovers here, I figured we should let them think we're gay," Montoya managed. Then he lost it again, laughing so hard tears squeezed from his eyes.

"You're crazy," Aguilar said. But Montoya's hysteria was infectious, and soon they were both laughing too hard to finish their *camarones al ajillo*.

After dinner, they retired to their separate rooms on the tenth floor of the new beachfront Hilton for siestas, then met again at midnight to hit some clubs. The women were beautiful and willing, and Montoya took one back to his room. He offered to share, but Aguilar declined. Dancing wasn't cheating, he decided, as long as there wasn't much touching. Anything else was out of bounds. He wished Luisa were here with him, rather than Montoya. One day he'd bring her back.

In the morning, over a breakfast of strong coffee and fried *arepas de huevo*, Aguilar asked, "So, do we try for Rodrigo today?"

Montoya said, "There's one more place I want to show you before we get down to business."

"I need to get home," Aguilar said. "Luisa needs my help around the house. She's getting big."

"She won't get too much bigger over the next twenty-four hours or so. She'll be fine."

"I'm a little concerned about taking him out anyway," Aguilar said. "He'll be protected, right?"

"Most likely, sure. But nobody will be expecting an attack from just two guys. They'll be looking out for an attack, like on the market back home."

"If they're any good, they'll be ready for anything."

"Cartagena's a backwater," Montoya countered. "And he's strictly small-time."

"Big enough to be a problem for Don Pablo."

"Not a problem. A nuisance."

"Okay," Aguilar said. "What's this place you want to show me?"

"Finish your coffee," Montoya said. "It's not going anywhere."

The Palacio de la Inquisición, facing the Plaza de Bolívar, was an eighteenth-century building that had housed the Holy Office of the Inquisition. Its ornate Spanish colonial architecture was striking, to Aguilar's eyes, but what interested Montoya was what was inside: a display of instruments of torture, including an inquisitor's rack and an elaborate construction of wood, iron, and rope. "What's that?" Aguilar asked.

"It's a witch scale."

"Scale? How does that work?"

"If a witch can fly on a broom," Montoya explained, "she doesn't weigh as much as she should, for her size. They weighed suspected women on these, and if they were too light, they were executed. Exorcisms were popular here, too. Satan was active in those days."

"We have our own devils now," Aguilar said. He was thinking of Escobar and his kind, but he found the whole place a little spooky. A lifetime of Catholicism had taught him that devils were real, and not to be toyed with.

They spent another half-hour examining the other implements of torture on display: thumbscrews and boots, a Judas Cradle and a crude wooden "donkey," and an elaborate bronze device that Aguilar couldn't figure out until Montoya told him it was called the "head crusher." At that point, its mechanism and purpose were obvious.

"We can update these for our own purposes," Montoya said. "Who would refuse to talk once they were placed in a head crusher? You wouldn't even have to tighten it; just the idea would loosen tongues."

"Threats and bribes seem to work," Aguilar said. "*Plato o plomo.*"

"For most people, sure. I'm talking about the extreme cases."

"Hopefully we won't have many of those."

They drifted away from the torture implements and browsed through other historical artifacts. At one point, Montoya started laughing out loud, and Aguilar joined him in front of a glass display. "What's so funny?"

"Apparently, Don Pablo's ideas aren't all original." He pointed at a slip of paper with faded, purplish ink on it. "This is a receipt from the pirate Francis Drake. For ten million pesos, he agreed not to burn Cartagena to the ground. And when they paid, he gave them a receipt."

"Just like Escobar and the stolen cars," Aguilar said. "Except he wasn't stupid enough to put it on paper."

"Exactly. Maybe he's thinking too small. He should ask Medellín for a hundred million dollars to not destroy it. They'd probably pay."

"What would he do with another hundred million?" Aguilar asked. "He'll never be able to spend what he already has."

"No wealthy man ever has enough money," Montoya said. "Just like no powerful man ever has enough power. They all want more, and the more they have, the more they want. Speaking of which, let's go take care of Rodrigo. Killing him won't make us powerful, but it'll help make us rich."

According to their telephone company contact, Rodrigo's most recent phone call had been made from his penthouse condominium in the Bocagrande district, a strip of land that lay between the Caribbean and Cartagena Bay. The Hilton was there, too, on a spit that jutted out, so the Caribbean surrounded it on three sides, with the bay a few blocks behind it. Rodrigo's building was four blocks north, visible from their rooms. After visiting the museum, they had lunch at the hotel, and Aguilar made a quick call to Luisa. Then they walked over and strolled back and forth in front of Rodrigo's local headquarters, then through the alley in back, where they found an entrance to an underground parking garage.

The ground floor housed a bank and a fashionable dress shop. Between those, double glass doors led into the building's lobby. A security guard sat behind a high counter, flanked by video screens that showed him the sidewalk just outside the doors, an alley behind the building, and the interiors of the two elevators that faced him. Aguilar looked over the counter and saw a Glock at his waist. Another guard, similarly armed, stepped off an elevator and came to the desk to chat.

"We're not going to be able to get to him inside," Montoya said when they'd finished their reconnaissance there. "But he can't stay inside forever."

"We can't stay in Cartagena forever."

"Why not? Don't you like it here? Nice hotel, good restaurants, pretty girls."

"We have jobs. And Luisa needs me at home."

"I know, you're a devoted husband. Maybe a little stupid, to marry when you were young and poor, but it's too late now."

"I don't think it was stupid. I love Luisa."

"And you'll still love her when your house is full of little no-neck monsters and you're changing dirty diapers all night long, right?"

"Of course."

"That's no life for me, brother, but you're welcome to it."

"Thanks for nothing," Aguilar said. "What now?"

"Now we try to figure out his routine," Montoya replied. "When he comes and goes. How many guys with him. What does he ride in?"

"That could take days. Weeks."

"Look, man, if you want I'll ask Don Pablo to replace you. You can go home to Luisa and think about all the money I'm making here. Or you can go home with your pockets loaded, and take good care of her financially. Up to you."

"I'm not saying I want to go, Alberto. I'm just saying, let's try to get it over with in a hurry."

"It'll take as long as it takes." Montoya nodded toward a café across the street. "Let's get a window seat," he said. "We can watch the door from there."

Before leaving Hacienda Nápoles, they'd been given an intelligence folder detailing what was known about Rodrigo. He had attended the University of Cartagena, and after graduating, had gone into business with two partners, buying houses in disrepair, restoring them, and selling them. They'd plowed their early profits into ever more real estate, and soon became some of the largest landowners in the city.

Somewhere along the way, Rodrigo had realized

how much more could be made smuggling drugs, especially with Cartagena's convenient location on Colombia's northern coast. He'd continued to invest in real estate, building several large ranches—cattle ranches were ideal for laundering money, Montoya explained, because on paper, a man could buy ten thousand cows at 100,000 pesos each, and who would ever count them?—and acquiring office and apartment buildings throughout the region. The partners had disappeared along the way, and were presumably buried where some of those cattle grazed.

Photographs included in the folder showed a slender blond man with a receding hairline and a heavy mustache. He favored shirts open to halfway down his chest, usually worn with a white suit, and a gold chain or two around his neck. He wore expensive wristwatches, a different one for each day of the month. Aguilar was sure he'd recognize the man if he saw him. "What if he uses the garage, and never comes out this door?"

"Then we'll figure that out after a little while. Harder to watch the garage, though, without being seen by the guard. Maybe we'll get lucky."

When they were seated in the café with drinks in front of them, looking over at Rodrigo's building, Aguilar asked a question that had been nagging at him all day. "Why us?"

"What do you mean?"

"Escobar has dozens of *sicarios* to call on, right? And he could buy any information he wants about Rodrigo—price is no object for him. So why send us after him?"

Montoya raised two fingers. "Two things. One, just because he can buy anything doesn't mean he wants to pay top dollar. This way, we're buying the information out of what he's already given us, in hopes that success will lead to more. And two, he's testing us. I don't believe Rodrigo is a huge problem for him. Kidnapping Costa was an affront that had to be answered, but I'm sure Don Pablo's not losing any sleep over it. So he points us toward a minor concern, in order to see how we handle it. If we do well, there'll be more work. If Rodrigo kills us, then it's no loss for him."

Aguilar raised his glass and clinked it against the rim of Montoya's. "That's you, always looking on the bright side of things."

"Life's too short to sit around moping," Montoya said. "I want to get everything I can out of every day. And hey, at least you got to see the torture museum."

13

It took four more days.

Whenever Rodrigo left his building, it was in a limousine. The chauffeur wore a uniform with a cap, and two thugs sat in the rear with Rodrigo, one facing front, like him, the other watching out the back window. The first time they spotted him, they had walked over and couldn't follow. The next day, they parked the rented car near the alley and killed time wandering through shops or sitting in the café until the limo appeared. Then they raced for the Corvette. The traffic in Bocagrande was such that for the first few blocks the limo crawled, so they were able to keep it in sight.

At mid-afternoon that day, he went to a hotel near the Old City. His men accompanied him inside, then came back by themselves and waited at the limousine for ninety minutes, until he returned. When he showed up again, he was tucking his shirttails into his pants, carrying his suit jacket over one shoulder, and his hair—usually neatly combed—was mussed.

"A mistress, then," Aguilar said.

"So it appears."

Montoya was just sitting there, and hadn't keyed the ignition. "He's getting back in the car," Aguilar said. "Do you want to follow?"

"No," Montoya said. "He's probably going home. Let's go see where she is."

"How will we know?"

Montoya just flashed him a grin. "We'll know."

They left the Corvette parked and went into the hotel. The lobby was quiet. A desk clerk was busily tapping at a keyboard, and a bellman lounged in a chair at his station. The only guest in sight was an old man with bad eyesight, reading a newspaper that he'd folded to the size of a book and held up almost against his birdlike nose.

The bellman glanced up when Montoya and Aguilar entered, but saw that they weren't guests and had no luggage, and went back to picking at his fingernails. Montoya walked over to him.

"The man who just left here. Blond hair, white suit."

"I didn't see him."

Montoya tucked some folded bills into the bellman's shirt pocket. "Okay, thanks." He started to walk away, then stopped, turned back. "But if you had seen him, what room would he have gone into?"

The bellman frowned, wrinkled his forehead. Montoya showed him more bills.

"Two-ten," the bellman said. "Second floor, third on the left."

Montoya put the additional bills in with the first ones. "You didn't see us, either," he said.

Aguilar watched the desk clerk while Montoya negotiated with the bellman. If he was aware of the conversation, he didn't show it. The old man on the settee couldn't have seen or heard anything. Montoya ticked his head toward the lobby's back door.

It opened onto a courtyard with trees, a fountain, and several stone planters full of flowering plants. Birds chirped and flitted from tree to bush to balcony. A staircase to the right of the door led to the four upper floors. To Aguilar, the place held the elegance of a world gone by, a Colombia that might never have existed except in the romantic imagination.

At room 210, Montoya tried the knob, then rapped twice on the door. When he heard a rustling behind it, he mumbled, "*Cara mía*."

The lock clicked back and the door started to open. "What did you forg—"

Montoya shoved the door open and clapped a palm over the woman's mouth. She was barefoot, wearing only a skirt and a bra. She was in her twenties, pretty, her pale skin still flushed from her recent encounter. Montoya pushed her into the room, and Aguilar stepped in and closed the door, locking it behind him.

"We're not here to harm you," Montoya said. His tone implied the unspoken threat. "As long as you don't make a fuss. If I take my hand off your mouth, will you be quiet?"

She nodded, eyes wide with fright.

Montoya removed his hand. The woman touched her mouth, as if to make sure he'd left it in place.

"What's your name?" Montoya asked.

"Amparo."

Montoya took her in, and let his gaze wander around the room. "This isn't a bad place, Amparo," he said. "But Rodrigo could afford far better. Why hasn't he bought you an apartment, or a house?"

"I don't know who you mean," she said.

"Don't be stupid. I'm not interested in you, only in Rodrigo. You help us and you'll be fine. Maybe Rodrigo's too cheap to buy you a place, but my employer isn't. And you won't even have to put up with his unwanted attention." He sniffed the air. Aguilar smelled it, too. It was overpowering and reminded him of fermented fruit. "Or his cologne. It can't be fun to breathe in that stuff while he's on top of you."

"You don't know anything about it," she said.

"I know everything about it," Montoya said. He picked her blouse up off the floor. "Rayon, not silk. That skirt is cheap, too. Your sandals are leather, but not good leather. You think being mistress to a mid-level gangster is going to elevate you financially? I understand that. But Rodrigo's never going to be more than that. He'll never leave his wife for you. He'll put you up in decent hotel rooms until he's bored with you, and then one day he'll stop calling.

"Or you can cooperate with us. I can make one phone call and have two hundred thousand pesos transferred into your bank account in a day."

"I don't have a bank account."

"You should. Every working woman needs a bank account."

"How about cash?" Amparo asked.

"We can do that."

Aguilar didn't know why Montoya was willing to make such promises without even checking with Escobar, but he didn't want to interrupt. The older cop's patter was calm and confident, and she seemed to be buying into it.

"And let's make it two-fifty," she said.

"Why not three?" Montoya asked.

"Why not? Three. What do you need from me?"

"How often do you see him?"

"The same time, every other day."

"Always here?"

"Different hotels, but most often this one."

"How do you know where to go?"

"He makes a suggestion when he calls in the morning. I come to the hotel he suggests and arrange the room. When he comes, he covers the cost. I can stay in the room overnight, or go home, whichever I choose."

"Where's home? Getsemani?"

She turned up her nose. Getsemani was an impoverished neighborhood, blighted and crime-ridden. "Of course not. Pie de la Popa."

"Handy. You can walk here. Save the bus fare. You have your own house?"

"I live with my mother. She's not well."

"So you have medical bills, too?"

"Some."

"And he's not helping with that either?"

"He helps," she said, her tone defensive. "He takes care of us. And I work, too."

"He treats you like a prostitute. You deserve better."

"How do you know what I deserve?"

"I cherish women," Montoya said. "And I honor them. You all deserve better than that."

"Speaking of work, I need to get back there," she said. She snatched away the flowered blouse that Montoya still held. "What is it you want from me?"

"The next time he makes a date, we'll be here, too."

"And then what?"

"Then you get the three hundred thousand."

"It's that easy?"

"For you. We'll do the hard part."

"How do you know I won't call him as soon as you leave, and tell him what you offered? Maybe he'll do better."

"You already know he won't. You're getting what you can, a little at a time. Like I said, I have no problem with that. We all do what we have to do. But he's never going to give you a big payday, because then you'd stop seeing him. He wants to stop when he's ready, not when you are. And until then, he wants you to be available to him, which you wouldn't be if you got what you're looking for."

Amparo considered his request as she pulled on her blouse and tucked it into her skirt. She shuffled her feet into the sandals, lifting each foot one at a time to buckle them. When she was fully dressed, she said, "All right. To tell you the truth, he's not much of a lover."

"Guys like him don't need to be," Montoya said. "You should try a man like me sometime."

She gave him a flirtatious smile. "Maybe I will." She started for the door, then stopped beside Aguilar. Putting a hand on his chest, she said, "Or maybe this one. I like the quiet type. And I've never had a spotted one."

Aguilar felt himself blushing—at least, in the places where he could blush. Self-consciousness about that just made it worse. She tried to make eye contact, but he looked away. "You're shy," Amparo said. "That's sweet. A shy killer."

"He's married," Montoya said.

"So is Carlos Rodrigo."

"But for my friend here, promises matter. For me, too."

He gave her their phone number at the Hilton. "As soon as he calls you, call us. We'll have the money with us when we come, and you'll be considerably wealthier than you were before."

"Is that a promise?" she asked.

"You'd better open that bank account," Montoya said. "So you have someplace safe to put it all."

Back at the Hilton, Aguilar called Luisa and tried to pretend he wasn't taking part in a murder plot. Montoya called Gustavo Gaviria and explained the need for the cash, and Gaviria promised to have it delivered.

The next day, they kept an eye on Rodrigo's building in case a better opportunity presented itself. He only came out once, for what appeared to be a business lunch in the back room of an expensive restaurant. His *sicarios* were present, as were those of the men he met with. Montoya and Aguilar agreed that their chances of success were slim, so they didn't try an attack.

That evening, Poison and Shorty brought a suitcase full of cash to the hotel. "Nice place," Poison said, looking out the window at the beach below. "Does *El Patrón* know where you're staying?"

"We're paying for it ourselves," Montoya said. "We're covering all the expenses."

"Except one." Poison kicked the suitcase.

"That's a special one. Unavoidable."

"I'm sure it's worth it to him. He didn't complain about the money."

"We're just doing what he told us he wanted," Montoya said. "The cheapest way we can."

"When's it going down?"

"Tomorrow," Montoya said. "We'll head back to Medellín right after." As if suddenly realizing why Poison was asking, he added, "We don't need any help."

"I wasn't offering. Unless you wanted some. But I thought maybe we'd get a room for the night, sample some of Cartagena's flavor. As long as we're here, I mean."

"Help yourselves," Aguilar said. "Like Alberto said, we're cool." He needed to back up his partner, and he still wasn't over Amparo calling him the quiet type. Maybe he was, but around Montoya, who talked constantly, it was hard to be anything else. He wondered if he would be like Montoya someday, unafraid to say anything to anyone.

"If you're sure," Shorty said. He weighed almost as much as any three of Escobar's other *sicarios*. He didn't seem like an athletic type, but he must have had some special skills or Escobar wouldn't have kept him on the payroll.

"We're sure."

"Have a good night, then," Poison said. He opened the door and waited for Shorty to exit, then added, "Spend that money wisely. *El Patrón* doesn't like waste."

After the door was closed and the *sicarios*' footsteps had receded, Montoya caught Aguilar's eye. "Unless *he's* the one wasting it. Giant dinosaurs? Sometimes I wonder if Don Pablo is truly sane."

14

AMPARO CALLED AT twelve-thirty and told Montoya the date was at three that afternoon. Same hotel, same room; she'd just checked in. Montoya told her that if Rodrigo called back, she should act like she always did. They had the money, he said, and would be there soon.

They checked out of the Hilton and threw the suitcase of cash into the Corvette's trunk, along with their own suitcases and the duffel bag of weapons they'd brought with them from Medellín. By two o'clock, they were carrying the cash and guns up the stairs to the second floor and knocking on 210.

Amparo opened the door right away and beckoned them inside. "Did anybody see you?" she asked.

"Just the desk clerk, I think," Aguilar said. "No problems."

"I just don't know who's on Carlos's payroll," she said.

"Not the bellman," Montoya replied. "He sold Rodrigo out for next to nothing."

"I've found that it's usually cheaper to buy men than women," Amparo said.

Montoya chuckled. "I've often thought that."

"Did he really?" Aguilar asked. Something about this plan had been bothering him, but he hadn't been able to figure out what it was until just now.

"What do you mean? Did who really what?"

"When we asked the bellman what room Rodrigo had been in, he knew right away. He didn't mind telling us—but Rodrigo was already gone. If we'd meant to harm him, we'd have done it before he drove away. He wasn't putting Rodrigo in any danger by telling us then, only Amparo. He might have thought she was a prostitute, and we were her next clients."

"We meet here all the time!" Amparo objected. "At least once a month. He knows I'm not..."

She let the sentence trail off. Montoya—his tone cruel, Aguilar thought—said, "Call yourself what you will, but we all know why you're here. Why you see him."

"My point is, Rodrigo might be warned before he comes up," Aguilar continued. "Do we even know who owns this hotel? What if it's him?"

"Well, we're not going to find out in the next hour," Montoya said. "Anyway, I didn't even see that bellman down there. Just the desk clerk, and he didn't see us the first time."

"That we know of. He might have seen us on our way out. Also, Rodrigo came out by himself—he must feel safe here."

"Do his men come to the room with him when he arrives?" Montoya asked Amparo.

"They don't come inside. They stop at the door. When I open it, then they go. They know I wouldn't hurt him."

"I guess they don't know you that well."

"How could they? I've never spoken three words to them. I act like Carlos is all I can see."

"I'm sure he likes that," Aguilar said.

"Who wouldn't?" Montoya added. "Anyway, the plan is set. We'll wait in the bathroom when he arrives. Once his men are gone and you two are alone, we'll come out. It would be good for you to be well away from him at that point."

"Should I leave the room?"

"I wouldn't, if I were you." Montoya unzipped the suitcase and showed her the cash. "When you leave, you won't want to come back. And you'll want to take this with you."

Aguilar briefly scanned the room. A big brass bed stood against one wall, perpendicular to the door. Across from it were a table holding a vase of fresh flowers, and a cabinet that doubled as closet and TV enclosure. To the left of the bed, a wall separated the room from the bathroom.

He pointed to the corner at the head of the bed, nearest the bathroom. "This is the best place for you to be," he said. "You'll be safe there." He didn't add "out of the line of fire," but he was sure she understood.

"Can you get there?" Montoya asked. "Make up some excuse."

"He likes me to be nude when he arrives," she said. "And ready for him. Once he's inside, he wants to get right to it."

"Break away from him. Say you need to pee, and head for the bathroom. Then turn, as if you've forgotten something, and duck down in that corner. We'll take care of the rest."

She took in their instructions. Aguilar saw her hands trembling, and a quiver in her lower lip. Now that it was getting real, she was afraid.

He didn't blame her. He was, too. Only Montoya seemed to be looking forward to it. When Amparo nodded her agreement, he unzipped the other bag and started checking to see that the guns were loaded and spare magazines were ready to go.

At ten minutes to three, he handed Aguilar a shotgun and an automatic pistol. He took out a pistol and an AK-47 for himself, zipped the bag, and shoved it under the bed. "You have your knife, right?" he asked.

Aguilar tapped his left leg. "Of course."

"Good."

"Time?" Aguilar asked.

"Yeah." To Amparo, he asked, "You okay?"

"No," she said. "I'm a wreck."

"Hold it together. Security for you and your mother is only a few minutes away."

"I know. I'll be fine."

As she began to undress, Montoya and Aguilar went into the bathroom. Lights off, door slightly ajar, they waited. Aguilar could smell Montoya's sweat, and his own, could hear the ticking of the clock on a little table beside the bed, traffic sounds outside, and the birds in the courtyard.

Then he heard footsteps on the stairs. Several men, it sounded like. Heavy, unconcerned that anyone might hear.

He breathed out, as quietly as he could. This would be over soon.

Knuckles rapped on the door.

Barefoot, Amparo crossed to it. It swung open, hinges squeaking.

"Mmm, baby," Rodrigo said. "You look good."

"You look delicious," Amparo replied. There was a moment of rustling, probably her pressing against him, kissing him. Then: "I just have to pee, love. I'll be right back."

Aguilar tensed. It was time. Montoya stood at the door, waiting to hear Amparo move away. Then she said, "Oh, there it is," and touched the wall nearest the bathroom.

Montoya yanked the door open and rounded the corner, AK in his hands, already squeezing the trigger.

Three men fired back.

Montoya took a round in his left arm and fell back against the wall, still firing. Aguilar unleashed a blast from the shotgun and one of the men exploded into a gruesome red rain. The other two turned their weapons toward him, but Montoya's AK-47 raked across them and their shots went wild. Aguilar pumped another shell into the chamber, fired again, then again.

The third man hadn't made it all the way into the room when rounds from Montoya's gun stopped him; when Aguilar's shot slammed into him, he staggered back against the railing, then went over, landing with a splash in the fountain below.

The room door stood open. When Aguilar went to close it, a bullet crashed through the big window beside him. He looked out and saw the bellman standing in the courtyard, firing up at them with what looked, from here, like a .22. Aguilar yanked the automatic from his pants and fired five times. At least two of his rounds hit the bellman—center mass; Aguilar's range instructor would have been proud—and he sat heavily against a tree.

"We have to get out of here," Aguilar said. "Now!"

"Give me your knife!" Montoya demanded.

"What?"

"The knife! Hurry!"

He was holding up the head of one of the dead men, and Aguilar could see by the white suit and blond hair that it was Rodrigo. Then he understood: Montoya wanted the head.

Reluctantly, Aguilar handed over the knife. "Be quick, though."

Montoya started sawing with it, blood and stringy flesh splashing around his hand. His own blood ran down his arm, mixing with Rodrigo's. Aguilar turned to Amparo so he wouldn't have to watch. She was already getting dressed. "You said his men wouldn't come inside."

"Someone must have tipped them off. The bellman, maybe."

"Then Rodrigo wouldn't have come in."

Montoya stopped what he was doing, rose to his feet, drew his pistol and shot Amparo twice in the face, spraying the wall behind her with gore. She sank to the floor, leaving a trail behind her.

"What the fuck, man? She didn't rat us out! If she did, you think Rodrigo would've come up? He would have sent an army!"

Montoya returned to his task. "She lied to us. She wanted Rodrigo *and* the money. She knew his *sicarios* would come in with him."

"She probably thought you were going to kill her."

"Well, she was right about one thing, then."

"What happens to it, now? The money?"

"Do you have her mother's address?"

"Of course not."

"Then I guess it's ours."

"We can't just keep—"

"Worry about it later!" Montoya interrupted. "I'm really hurting here. Can you finish this?"

Aguilar risked a quick glimpse of the grisly sight. Everything he'd eaten for breakfast and lunch threatened to return. "No way."

"Fuck," Montoya said. He pressed harder with the knife and finally the last bit of tendon snapped. He held the head up. Drops of blood pattered to the floor like light rain. "Where can I put this?"

Aguilar scanned the room, saw Amparo's purse. It was big, leather or fake leather, with fringe hanging from the bottom seam. He grabbed it, dumped its contents, and held it open as wide as he could. He still got blood on his hands when Montoya shoved it in.

"Let's get out of here, man," Montoya said. "Grab the money and the guns."

Aguilar zipped the money case closed and tugged the duffel bag out from under the bed. It still had a couple of guns in it. He started to put the shotgun back in, but Montoya said, "Better hang onto that until we're out of here."

Hearing distant sirens, Aguilar agreed.

The money case was heavy, but it had wheels and a handle, so he slung the duffel over his shoulder and rolled the suitcase. It made carrying the shotgun awkward. Montoya only had Amparo's purse, which was already discoloring at the bottom.

Montoya in the lead, they descended the stairs. Onlookers had gathered on the walkways, looking down at the bodies in the courtyard and the armed men, but nobody tried to stop them.

In the lobby, the desk clerk studiously avoided

so much as glancing at them. "Doctor!" Montoya shouted. "Where?"

The clerk waved an arm. "Three blocks, on the left," he said. "Please go."

They went.

15

AFTER SOME SPIRITED discussion on the way back to Medellín, Aguilar and Montoya agreed that returning Escobar's money would be safer than letting him think they'd stolen from him. Escobar had strict rules against internal theft, and nobody ever made that mistake twice.

They delivered the suitcase of cash to him late that night at Hacienda Nápoles, along with some Polaroid pictures of Rodrigo's head impaled on the spike of an iron fence outside the Casa de Justicia Robledo. Escobar flipped through the photographs, his expression serious, even stern.

"You did this? You two?"

"Yes, *Patrón*," Montoya said.

"By yourselves?"

"We thought that's what you wanted," Aguilar said nervously. "You said—"

Escobar burst out laughing. When he was able to compose himself, he added, "Excellent work! I was right to trust you."

"You like it?" Montoya asked.

"I love it."

"We thought about putting up a sign. 'Don't mess with Medellín,' or something like that," Aguilar said. "But we decided that anyone who knows who Rodrigo is will understand the message without that."

"True, true," Escobar said. "There's no sign needed. By tomorrow this will be in every newspaper in Colombia. The shootout in Cartagena, and then this. Everyone will know what it means." His smile faded as he handed back the pictures. "Do you know why I wanted you men to do this thing?"

"We thought it was a test," Montoya said. "To see how well we'd do."

"A test, yes, of course it was that. Also, to see if you would steal from me."

"Never!" Aguilar said.

"Yes, the money has already been counted. You clearly passed those tests. But more than that, I wanted you to see how hard it is to operate on your own. You did well." He touched Montoya's left arm, below the bandage. "But you were hurt. Just a flesh wound, yes?"

"Grazed me," Montoya said. "I needed a few stitches, that's all. And something for the pain. Jose had to drive home."

"Two men can kill someone, no problem," Escobar said. "But sometimes more is better. You were able to catch him with just a few of his men around, because he was careless. If he'd been smarter, you might have needed more. Five, ten, or more, like the night you went after Costa."

"I think he felt safe in Cartagena," Aguilar said.

"And I feel safe at Hacienda Nápoles. But that's

130

because I have thirty or forty men here most of the time. If we need to, we can hold off an army." He nodded at his own sagacity, looking around as if to see his defenses. Aguilar could see three or four guys, playing cards by the pool, but nobody looked like they were on high alert.

"Strength in numbers," Escobar went on. "I wanted you two to understand how important it is to be part of an organization. Not like your police force, but a real organization that's dedicated to a cause." He chuckled. "In this case, the cause is Colombia itself. Everything I do—everything we do—is for Colombia. I will be president of Colombia one day—no more of these politicians who are only out for themselves and their wealthy friends. It's time for the people to take back the power that's rightfully ours. So that, my friends, is what we're doing here. What you're a part of. There has been no greater cause, no worthier crusade, in history."

Aguilar felt a flush of pride at being involved in Escobar's undertaking. He had seen the man only as a gangster, a drug trafficker, but he was obviously so much more than that. And his ambitions were greater than Aguilar had known. So far, Escobar seemed to have succeeded at everything he had ever tried to do. He'd risen from a simple upbringing to be one of Colombia's richest men—one of the richest in all of South America. He'd built a huge organization from nothing. If he thought he could be president, Aguilar saw no reason to doubt him.

"And also," Escobar added, "Rodrigo had to pay. I hope he suffered."

"I think he was still alive, Don Pablo," Montoya said, "when I started to cut."

Escobar grinned. "Too bad you didn't get pictures of that."

After receiving their reward—each got a third of the three hundred thousand pesos, and Escobar kept his own third—Aguilar and Montoya were invited out to party with some of Escobar's men. They drove in a convoy back to Medellín and hit the clubs, drinking and smoking pot and dancing with the local girls for most of the night. Finally, with the sun just breaking the horizon, Aguilar dragged himself home. He was almost afraid to walk in the door, and did so sheepishly, half-hoping Luisa would be sound asleep.

She wasn't.

She sat at the kitchen table, with a mug steaming in front of her. She wore a bathrobe over fuzzy cotton pajamas with rabbits on them. Her hair was down and her jaw was set, thrust slightly forward, and her expression bordered on ferocious. "Good morning," she said without a trace of warmth.

"Hi, baby."

"How long have you been back in Medellín?"

He hesitated, trying to figure out how to answer the question while causing the least amount of damage, and also because the floor seemed to be moving underneath him. He held onto the arched opening between the kitchen and dining room and waited for it to pass. "We got back from Cartagena yesterday, but had to drop something off at Hacienda Nápoles. Then some of the guys wanted us to go out with them."

"I was at the window for a while, when you drove up. I was so excited to see you, but you drove like a crazy person, and when you parked I was afraid you were going to hit the building. Then you sat there for so long I got bored and made some tea."

"I kind of fell asleep for a few minutes, I guess."

"More like twenty or thirty. You smell like a liquor store after an earthquake. There's lipstick on your shirt collar and glitter in your hair."

"I'm sorry, baby. The guys wanted to go to these clubs. I drank and I danced with some girls, but that's all, I swear."

"You danced."

"Yes."

"And the lipstick?"

"I guess somebody must have put her head on my shoulder. When we were dancing."

"I guess. Jose, I need to be able to trust you. Our baby needs a good father. But this..." She blinked back tears, and Aguilar felt like something people would scrape off their shoes.

"Baby, I'm so sorry," he said. "I didn't want to go out, but Alberto did, and everybody insisted. I didn't really know what they meant when they said they wanted to party. Some of the guys got with girls, but I didn't, except for a few dances. I swear. I would never be unfaithful to you. I love you too much."

"You have a funny way of showing it," she said. "You've been away for days. I thought you would want to hurry home."

"I *did* want to. But the guys—they're not the kind of people you can say no to, you know?"

"Then maybe you shouldn't be hanging around them."

That reminded him of the bag of cash he had in the car. At least, he hoped it was in the car. He was pretty sure it was. "Luisa, I know it's awful, but I'm just doing what I have to for our futures. For you and our baby. We need to start looking for a house to buy this week—I don't want our son to grow up in this apartment."

"Or our daughter, you mean. Anyway, we can't buy a house yet," she said.

"We can! Baby, I have money—it's in the car; I forgot to bring it in, but I'll go get it. We have more than enough to start paying for a house. I've made so much in the last couple of weeks. You can quit your job, like we've been talking about, and just rest up and get ready for when the baby comes. After, you'll be able to stay home and just be a mother. No more waiting tables."

"What did you have to do for that money?" she asked.

Again, Aguilar paused, trying to think through the fog of liquor and dope. "You don't want to know."

"I do, though. I really do."

"No, baby. You don't. Not only that, but you *can't*. The less you know, the better for all of us. You just have to trust me, that's all. I'm looking out for us. I'm going to make sure our child grows up with all the things we never had. Whatever I do—everything I do—it's for you. For our family. Everything I do is because I love you."

At that, finally, her face softened. She pushed back from the table, her tea forgotten, and took him in her arms, drawing him close. He could feel the bump at her belly, where their child was growing. "Just remember that the thing our family needs the most is you," she said. "The money's nice, but we need you. I need you. I need you to be here, with me."

"There's nowhere I'd rather be," Aguilar said. He

buried his face against the spot where her neck and shoulders met, inhaled her scent, kissed her. Working his way up to her lips, he kissed them and said, "Make love to me."

She put her fingers against his chin, pushed him away. "First, take a shower. Then brush your teeth. If you're still conscious after that, then we'll see."

He was.

16

THE DEATH OF Carlos Rodrigo Muñoz didn't mean the end of the Cartagena smuggling operation. It merely delayed shipments for a few weeks, while three of Rodrigo's lieutenants went to war over who would succeed him. Most of Rodrigo's men remained loyal to one of them, but another controlled the docks, and therefore the shipping process. The third, Mateo Quiroga, had been in Medellín since the botched Costa kidnapping. He was quietly trying to amass an army so that when the first two killed each other, or sufficiently weakened each other through combat and attrition, he could swoop in and take over.

To that end, he approached some of Pablo Escobar's *sicarios*, offering half again what Escobar paid them.

Don Pablo didn't appreciate that. To make things worse, when he approached Quiroga with an offer to work for him, to run Cartagena on behalf of Medellín, giving Escobar easy access to the port for shipping as well as for receiving shipments of the precursor chemicals necessary to make cocaine in large quantities, Quiroga turned him down.

Aguilar learned of all this from Montoya. They were working a swing shift, each in his own vehicle, and had met for a quick drink about eight o'clock. Sitting at the bar, Montoya explained what had been happening, and what Escobar's response would be.

"We're going to hit that bastard," he said. "Don Pablo's had a couple of guys watching him. As soon as they know where he'll be, someplace vulnerable, they'll put out the word, and we'll move in. He won't live through the night."

"You'll let me know, right?" Aguilar asked. There would undoubtedly be some cash in it for all participants, with a bonus for whoever actually killed Quiroga.

"As soon as I find out," Montoya said. "Keep your radio on."

After, Aguilar buzzed with tension. He wanted the money—needed it, because in the last few days he and Luisa had been looking at houses, and the ones she liked were invariably the larger and more expensive ones. To be honest, those were the ones he liked, too, but he told himself that the most important thing was to satisfy her.

But he also knew that if Quiroga had indeed raised a force of men, it could turn into a firefight. He'd survived the one at the market and the smaller one at the hotel in Cartagena. How long could his luck hold out? As Luisa never tired of telling him, what she needed even more than money was her husband, her baby's father.

That was easy for her to say. Aguilar thought if she had enough money, she could live without him. But without money, Aguilar would just be a nuisance, another mouth to feed.

So, he'd made Montoya promise to radio him the moment he found out where it would go down. Two hours later, he got the call.

"He's having dinner at Café Parilla Fresco," Montoya said. "Isn't that where your wife worked?"

"She still does," Aguilar said. "She's working tonight! Tomorrow's her last day."

"I thought she was already at home."

"No, tomorrow! You have to stop it!"

"I can't stop it, Jose. The guys are already on their way."

"But she's in there!" He felt panic rising in his gorge. He was forty minutes away. Thirty, if he used lights and siren and broke every law. He didn't know how much time he had, but probably not that much.

"Get her out."

"I can't! I'm all the way in Pedregal!"

"Call her, then. I wish I could do something, Jose. I just found out myself."

"Where are you?"

"Calle 67, at the hospital."

He meant the Hospital Universitario San Vicente de Paul, Aguilar knew. "That's in Prado. You're closer than I am!"

"I'm leaving now, Jose. I'll try, okay? Just do what you can to get her out of there."

"I'll try, man. But hurry."

To minimize Luisa's danger, Aguilar had never let her meet Montoya. She'd heard stories—those he felt comfortable telling her—and she'd seen a picture of him once. He'd seen the three pictures of Luisa that Aguilar kept in his wallet, too, but had never seen her in person. Who knew if he would even recognize her, at work with her hair up and the restaurant's required dress?

He'd been on his way to answer a call when Montoya had radioed him. It was a vagrancy call; a store owner complaining about a man sleeping on the sidewalk in front of his shop and urinating in the doorway. It wasn't something he felt bad about ignoring.

The guy probably just had too much to drink, or maybe he had a mental problem. Either way, he was down on his luck, maybe homeless like so many others throughout the city. The best Aguilar could do would be to put him in jail for the night, and someone else would take his place. And it wouldn't do anything to solve the man's problems. Or the shopkeeper's, for that matter.

He turned around and flipped on his lights and siren, watching for a phone booth from which he could call the restaurant. He didn't know this area that well yet. Finally, he spotted one and pulled in at an angle, blocking part of the nearest lane. He left his lights on but killed the siren, and fed some coins into the slot.

The phone rang and rang. Finally, someone answered, but over the din from the restaurant he couldn't hear what they said, couldn't even tell if the voice was male or female. "I need to speak to Luisa!" he shouted.

"What?"

"Luisa! Please, it's important! This is her husband!"

"I'm sorry, I can't—"

"This is the police! Put Luisa on!"

"I can't hear you," the voice said. "Try again later."

The line went dead. He dropped the receiver, letting it dangle on its cord, and raced back to the car.

He'd wasted precious minutes on that. He flipped the siren on, backed away from the curb, and started out again. He could look for another phone, but with no guarantee that the results would be any better. And each time he stopped would slow down his arrival there.

Instead he weaved through traffic, driving one-handed and using his other to key the radio and call dispatch. "Call the Café Parilla Fresco," he said when he got through. "Tell my wife Luisa that she needs to go home at once. It's an emergency!"

He'd debated how much to tell dispatch. Even with cooperation from the police commanders, he could hardly warn the department about an attack at a restaurant. They would swarm the place, and Escobar would be furious if his intended target escaped with his life. He just had to hope the message got through.

Then he focused on driving, tearing down the city streets faster than he ever had. People screeched their brakes trying to avoid him; pedestrians lunged for safety. After about fifteen minutes, he tried Montoya on the radio again, but got no answer. He passed another pay phone and considered stopping, but didn't.

When he reached the restaurant, the shooting had not yet begun.

Café Parilla Fresco stood in the middle of a block. A meter-tall brick wall was topped by a large window that let passersby watch the diners inside, and let them watch the people on the street. A green awning with the restaurant's name printed on it in gold letters provided shade for the lunch crowd. Inside, Aguilar knew, wide-bladed ceiling fans joined by rubber belts cooled the air.

As Aguilar rounded the corner, La Quica and Big Badmouth were just going in the front door, guns in hand. Other guys stood outside, including Montoya, Jairo, and some Aguilar didn't know. Montoya wore his police uniform, with a bandanna covering his nose and mouth. Someone in the restaurant had spotted them; he could see people screaming, ducking behind tables and one another.

Aguilar abandoned his SUV in the middle of the street and sprinted for the sidewalk, shouting, "No, wait!"

He couldn't know for sure who fired first. He saw the distinctive glow of a muzzle flash through the window, just before all hell broke loose. Then Montoya and the others started shooting in through the window, and someone inside was shooting back at them. The glass shattered, raining onto the sidewalk and into the restaurant. People were screaming.

Getting closer, Aguilar saw individual faces inside, frozen in terror.

One of them belonged to Luisa.

She stood between tables, holding a tray full of dishes. As Aguilar watched, seeing it as if in slow motion, she lost her grip on the tray. It tilted and the plates slid off, landing on the diners, who in their panic were barely aware of it. *No tip for her*, he thought, and for an instant he looked forward to being able to laugh about it with her, after the horror had worn off.

Then he saw the man behind her, shooting over her shoulder toward the street.

Saw Montoya shooting at him, the recoil of his submachine gun twitching it to the left with every round it fired.

Saw two of those rounds hit Luisa, pulverizing her head in a pinkish mist.

He screamed her name, slammed into Montoya from behind, hurtled past him and through the open window, ignoring the shards of glass jutting from the edges. Inside, he knocked over tables and chairs. Bullets whistled past him.

He found her on the floor, lying in spilled food and drink and so much blood.

She was alive, but barely. Her fingers twitched and her heels tapped against the floor and her lips moved. Aguilar thought she was trying to say something, and he gathered her close to him and tried to hear over the gunfire and the wails of the hurt and dying.

Then she was still. He felt the life leave her body, like a released breath, and he knew she was gone.

He stayed there, holding her. The gunfight ended, and Montoya showed up, that bandanna still across his face. "Come on, man," he said. "We've got to get out of here." Then he seemed to realize what Aguilar was doing. His eyes softened. "Oh no, is that her?"

"Yes, damn it," Aguilar said through his tears. "It's her. What's left of her."

"Oh, shit, what happened?"

"You know what happened."

"Man, that sucks," Montoya said. He didn't seem to know—or wasn't showing it, if he did—that he'd killed her. Nor did he seem to care.

Aguilar wanted to tell him. He wanted to pull a gun and blow Montoya's brains out, like his partner had done to Luisa. He almost did it, but that would mean releasing her, and he wasn't ready to do that.

Sitting on the restaurant floor, with wine and coffee and never-to-be-eaten meals soaking through his pants, drenched in Luisa's blood, he decided that Montoya would have to pay for what he'd done. Whether he had been aware of it in the moment or not, Montoya had killed Aguilar's wife, his love, and his unborn child—had killed the only part of him that really mattered.

But not right now. Not while Luisa was still warm.

As Aguilar held her, he could feel that warmth fading and with it, the last link to whatever was good in him being severed. He could feel his heart hardening in his chest.

And he liked it.

17

PABLO ESCOBAR PAID all the funeral expenses for Luisa, and he even spoke at her graveside, though he had never met her. He bought new clothes for the entire funeral party, and arranged for the city to shut down the streets between the church and the cemetery. He bought a marble monument a meter tall, shaped like an obelisk. He put her parents and sisters up in Medellín's nicest hotel and covered their meals for a week. Finally, he bought the block where the restaurant had stood, razed the buildings, and built a grassy park called Parque Luisa. Aguilar received a bonus of half a million pesos.

It didn't come close to making up for his loss.

He made it through the closed-casket wake, the vigil service, and the funeral Mass, alternately weeping or numb. The hugs, handshakes, and back-pats of friends and family members went almost unnoticed. People brought food by the truckload; he picked at it, with no appetite. Others brought liquor or pot; those he consumed greedily. Christmas came and went. He didn't attend Christmas Mass, for the first time in his life.

Two weeks later, he went to Hacienda Nápoles by

himself, and met with Don Pablo. They sat alone in Escobar's formal dining room. Escobar's expression was somber, his forehead furrowed, and he picked at his mustache. Aguilar folded his hands on the table, ignoring the glass of wine placed there for him. Escobar hadn't touched his, either.

"Don Pablo," he said. "I want to thank you for your generosity and your understanding, these past couple of weeks. It's been hard for me, as I'm sure you understand, but you made it easier through your many kindnesses."

"The least I could do," Escobar said. "I gave the order to hit Quiroga. I feel partly responsible."

Aguilar silently agreed, having thought that from the beginning, but at least Escobar had made an effort to atone.

"Of course, I didn't order them to hit him there, in a crowded public place. I would have done it when he was on his way, or after, when he was leaving, with a full stomach and maybe a little drunk on wine."

That, Aguilar would soon learn, was a habit of Escobar's—just when it seemed he would accept the blame for some outrage, he would subtly shift it into someone else's hands.

He wasn't the only one who dodged responsibility, though. When they were drinking together late one night, Montoya had said, "She shouldn't have been working in a place where criminals eat." The fact that he was a criminal himself—or that every time Luisa went into her own home, she was someplace where criminals were—didn't seem to occur to him. Aguilar didn't think Montoya was even aware that he was at fault.

But he was—Aguilar had watched it happen. There was no doubt in his mind.

"You're not responsible, Don Pablo," he said. "But Alberto Montoya is."

Escobar arched an eyebrow. "You're sure?"

"I saw it. I had just arrived—I was trying to get past him, to stop the shooting. He was trying to shoot someone behind her, but his aim wandered and he hit her twice in the head. I was too late." He dropped his chin to his chest. "I guess it's as much my fault as anyone else's."

"You didn't pull the trigger."

"No. But I was too late to stop it from being pulled. Same thing."

"It's not," Escobar said. "We know the risks. We understand the dangers. But family? Family is everything. If anything like that happened to Tata, I would want to burn down the world."

"That's how I feel," Aguilar said.

"How can I help?"

"You've done so much already."

"But there's something else you want. Otherwise you wouldn't be here."

"Your blessing," Aguilar answered.

"My blessing? For what?"

"I want to kill Montoya."

Escobar considered for several long moments. "Are you sure?"

"Yes. He killed Luisa. He needs to die."

"Believe me, I understand the impulse. But he's your friend. Your partner. I'm sure he didn't intend to do it."

"He didn't, I know that. It doesn't matter. He still did it. I can't live knowing she's under the ground, and he's still walking around above it."

Escobar nodded. "I understand that. I do. But I

have a problem. He's one of mine. He's worked for me longer than you have, in fact. Done me many favors. And he was doing what I'd ordered him to. Do you also want to kill me?"

"It's crossed my mind," Aguilar said. The words almost caught in his throat, but he got them out. "But no. You didn't know she was there. He did, because I told him. You couldn't have known that he might shoot her. He knew, and fired anyway. He didn't control his weapon. He's a danger—not just to her, but to you. A man who can't control his fire…"

He knew he was reaching, trying to make Escobar think it was a sound idea.

Escobar narrowed his eyes, and Aguilar thought he'd made a mistake. *He could kill me right here*, he thought. *Bury me on the grounds somewhere, or feed me to the zoo animals.*

Instead, Escobar said, "I would. I would want to kill me and everyone else involved in the operation. You're a kinder man than I am, Jose Aguilar Gonzales. Tell me this… how do you intend to do it? Fast and painless?"

Aguilar eased the knife from its sheath. "With this," he said. "Not fast. Or painless. I want him to know why. I want him to apologize, and to beg for mercy."

Escobar nodded again. "At first, I wondered if you were too gentle for this life, Jose. You're educated. Most of my *sicarios* are just boys from the streets, with no money and no opportunities in life. I give them a sense of purpose, and they can make a good living. You could have remained a police officer, done your duty, arrested criminals, and made a decent living. But you chose to throw in with me. I'm glad you did, but I've sometimes wondered whether you made the right choice.

"I see now that you did. What I took at first for

softness was a disguise—maybe one you didn't even know about. But now I see the fire in your eyes, the steel in your spine." He smiled, and added, "Yes, Jose, you have my blessing. You've always been more interesting to me than Montoya. Now I see why."

"Thank you, Don Pablo," Aguilar said.

"No need to thank me. Once again, you have my deepest sympathies. Go, Jose." He rose, but before he left, Escobar added, "And make it hurt."

Montoya lived in a small, stucco-sided house in the Francisco Antonio Zea neighborhood. It sat back from the road, with a small yard and a few trees screening it from view. He could afford something better, but he liked what he had. It was comfortable, he said, and he didn't need a lot of space.

Aguilar went in the early hours of morning, parked three houses down, and watched the street for a while. Nothing moved except a gray cat and some leaves blown by a passing breeze.

Finally, he got out and pounded on Montoya's door. It took several minutes for Montoya to unlock and open it. He was unshaven, wearing only boxer shorts. Rubbing his eyes, he scowled at Aguilar.

"What the fuck, brother? What time is it?"

"You don't want to know."

"What's going on?"

"Can I come in?"

"I'm not alone," Montoya said.

"That's okay." Aguilar pushed past him. Montoya was heavily muscled, his chest and arms covered with a mat of fur. But Aguilar was propelled by adrenaline and rage, rage that had been building for weeks. It would have taken three of Montoya to bar his way, and the man was still half-asleep.

"Get dressed and get out!" Aguilar called as he entered. "Alberto's finished with you for tonight!"

"Hey!" Montoya said.

A high-pitched squeal came from the bedroom. A minute later, a young woman—a girl, really, no more than sixteen—came out, clutching a shirt around her to hold it closed, carrying a purse and her shoes.

"Don't come back," Aguilar said. "Don't you know he's a police officer? He'll get in trouble if he's caught with someone your age."

She shot him a look that was, in his experience, universal among teenagers, implying, "Of course I know that. Do you think I'm stupid?" In fact, he thought most teenagers were stupid, but he tried not to let it show.

"Don't listen to him," Montoya said, but she had already run out and slammed the door. He whirled on Aguilar. "What was that about? What are you doing here?"

"Do you like her?"

"She's okay. She's fun."

Aguilar walked away from him, and went into the kitchen. It was at the back of the house, with a window and a door that opened onto a yard like a small jungle. He'd seen a wild monkey back there once. "Come in the kitchen," he said.

"Why? What's going on, Jose?"

"Just do it," he said. He didn't turn the light on, and crouched just inside the door. When Montoya entered, he hesitated at the doorway, pawing at the light switch.

Aguilar lashed out with his knife, slicing through Montoya's right Achilles tendon. Montoya screamed in pain and collapsed on the kitchen tiles, blood spurting from the wound. He tried to clutch his ankle, but the agony was too severe, so he held the leg above it. "What the fuck?" he cried. "What...?"

Aguilar slashed out again, drawing his blade across the back of Montoya's right wrist. It didn't bite as deeply this time, because Montoya snatched it away, but it tore through veins and more blood splashed onto the floor.

"Aren't you glad I brought you in here?" Aguilar asked, finding his feet and moving away from Montoya. "Much easier to clean the floors in here. And nobody can hear your screams."

He wasn't sure that was true—the street was quiet, and Montoya was loud. But much of the noise would be muffled by the backyard jungle. Still, maybe he should quiet the man. He moved closer, and Montoya snatched at him with his left hand. Aguilar easily dodged it. He closed in again. Montoya reached for him, but Aguilar brought up the blade, and Montoya jerked his hand back. When he did, Aguilar reversed the knife and slammed the pommel into Montoya's throat.

The older man gagged and choked. His eyes watered, and he clawed at his neck. He looked a question at Aguilar.

"Okay," Aguilar said. "You want to know why? You shot Luisa, you motherfucker. Shot her right in the face, and you didn't even care. You didn't even notice."

"I... no, you're wrong," Montoya managed to croak. His face was turning purple.

"I was there. I saw it. You were shooting at the man behind her, and you hit her."

"That was... Luisa?"

"Yes, you fucker. That was her. You killed her, and

150

then you told me she shouldn't have been working there anyway."

"It was… an accident…"

Was it? Aguilar was no longer so certain. After all, Montoya had shot Amparo in the face, too. Maybe he liked to do that to pretty women he knew he could never have. "Doesn't matter. You have to pay."

Montoya looked at him with sad eyes. Pathetic. Aguilar lashed out again, drawing the blade across his forehead. Blood beaded at the slash, then started to run down into his eyes, and down his cheeks. Crying tears of blood, along with the saltwater ones springing from him.

He had stopped screaming. Now he was alternately whimpering and begging for his life in a hoarse rasp. Aguilar took no pleasure in his actions. He felt sickened, but powerless to stop. If he let Montoya live, the man would surely recover and kill him. And he would lose face with Escobar. He had to continue. He had chosen this path, now it was time to walk it.

He had wanted it to go slowly, or he'd thought he did. Now, though, he didn't want to watch Montoya's suffering any longer than he had to. Luisa had suffered, but only for a short while. Aguilar was suffering, and would for every day of his life, with every breath he took. Montoya had to pay for that.

No longer able to hold himself up, Montoya had curled into a fetal position. He winced and cried out when Aguilar cut him, but weakly. Aguilar moved quickly, slicing Montoya's other Achilles tendon, his arms, his face. Blood pooled around him. Finally, to finish it, he drew the blade across his partner's throat, feeling flesh tear and cartilage snag. Montoya made a choking noise as blood gushed from the wound.

Minutes later, he was dead.

Aguilar found Montoya's Polaroid camera in the bedroom; he'd been using it to photograph himself with the young woman. Aguilar wished he could stay and burn the photos, but he'd been here longer than he'd intended anyway.

He took a few shots of Montoya, figuring Escobar would want to see the proof that Aguilar wasn't as "gentle" as he'd thought, and left the house.

He had thought killing Montoya would make him feel better.

It didn't.

But it didn't make him feel any worse, either.

18

ESCOBAR HANDED BACK the photos with a grin. "You're like that North American, Ansel Adams," he said. "A master of the photographic arts."

Aguilar had seen the photographer's work in a Medellín bookstore. He took pictures of trees and rocks, all in black and white. These photos were primarily red. Still, Escobar seemed to mean it as a compliment. "Thank you."

"You should study his work," Escobar said. "It's beautiful. I wish he would photograph Colombia, to show the world the raw power of our landscapes. I don't know as much about art as I would like to—Tata chooses most of what we have—but I know some things. Such as, the best art is the most expensive. Also, private buying and selling is good, because nobody knows how much you paid, or what profit you earned. In my business—our business—it's good to be able to disguise such things sometimes."

"I understand," Aguilar said. "Montoya explained some of that to me."

"You're a smart guy, Jose. And observant, like all good policemen." Escobar leaned forward in his chair, and lowered his voice, as if to stress the import of what he said next. "So, I know you noticed when I started to say 'my business,' and changed it to 'our business.'"

"I did."

"Do you know why?"

"Tell me."

Escobar smiled. "Ordering me around? That's good. Within limits, of course."

"Of course," Aguilar said. He had already grown more comfortable with the gangster than he had ever expected to. Escobar had an easy charm about him. Aguilar had heard he was interested in politics, and could imagine him doing well at it.

"I want you to join us," Escobar said. "Keep your police job, for now. It has come in handy in the past, and without Montoya on the job, you'll be one of my main connections in the department. I'll pay you regularly, and far better than that job does. You can buy a house in Medellín, but often you'll stay here at Nápoles, or wherever I am."

"You want me to be a *sicario*?"

"More than that. A *sicario* is just a kid with a gun and a chip on his shoulder. I can afford truckloads of those. Yes, you would fulfill that function when needed, but you'd also be someone I can talk to when I want intelligent conversation. A bodyguard and driver for my family. Perhaps one day a lieutenant or a captain in the organization, if you have the aptitude for it."

Aguilar didn't have to think it over for long. Since Luisa's death, he'd been living in a nice hotel, because he couldn't bear to spend time in the apartment they had shared. He was burning through money fast, and he hadn't been earning.

He didn't know yet what effect Montoya's death would have on his police work, but since he and Montoya had been partners and friends, people would expect him to be in mourning. Thanks to Luisa's death, he knew how to behave, and could probably fake it.

He would have to.

"Thank you for the opportunity, Don Pablo," he said. "I will serve you faithfully, and will put your life and the lives of your family ahead of my own."

"That's all I can ask," Escobar replied. He clasped Aguilar's hand and held it tightly. "Welcome to the organization, Jose Aguilar Gonzales."

When he released the hand and sat back, his brow furrowed. "You need a nickname. I probably have seven or eight Joses working for me already, and one of my partners is José Rodriguez Gacha. But I think I already know what I'll call you. With your spotted skin and your initials—J.A.G.—the obvious name is Jaguar. Even better, your knife will be the Jaguar's Claw. Do you like it?"

Aguilar didn't think it mattered whether he liked it—Escobar had already made up his mind. But in fact, he did like it. It sounded exotic, dangerous. There were jaguars in the Colombian jungles, he knew, but he had never seen one. They were sleek, muscular beasts.

They were born killers.

"It's perfect," he said. "I'll do my best to live up to it."

* * *

At work the next day, Aguilar had to feign sorrow over Montoya's reported murder. The captain called him into his private office, where some of the other brass had gathered.

"I'm sure you've heard about your partner by now," the captain said. "Your partner and friend, I understand. I want to offer my deepest condolences. And so soon after the tragic loss of your wife—nobody could blame you for being completely shattered. If you need some time off, we'll understand."

Aguilar had expected something along those lines. But Escobar wanted him to remain on the force, and taking time off would negate whatever advantage came from that. Better to stay put, and use the sympathy offered him to further whatever *El Patrón* needed done.

"Thank you, sir," he said. "But I think I should keep working. Keep my mind occupied. If that's all right, of course."

"Oh, yes. I understand completely," the captain said. "If there's anything you need, anything at all, just let me know. Of course, you can avail yourself of our department counselor, if you feel the need."

"I'll keep that in mind, sir. Thank you again."

The men sat quietly for a couple more minutes, with occasional attempts at conversation. Nobody knew what to say, though, and soon, Aguilar was dismissed. In the hallways and locker room, others tried to express their sorrow, and Aguilar tried to respond appropriately.

It didn't take long for his usefulness to Escobar to make itself known.

Aguilar was out on patrol when the dispatcher radioed him and directed him toward a downtown intersection, without explaining further. When he arrived, he found Poison leaning against a motorcycle.

Aguilar pulled up beside him and lowered his window. "Waiting for me?"

"Yeah," Poison said. "We have a problem."

"What is it?"

"Police have retrieved a car they say was stolen. There's some product in it, and we can't let them have it."

"How much?" Aguilar asked.

"Twenty kilos," Poison said. "It was a special sale to an ally of Don Pablo's, somebody who wants to get into the distribution business. But he hasn't paid for it yet, and Pablo doesn't want it to disappear."

"Where's the car now?"

"Still at the arrest site." Poison named an intersection not far away. "The cops had to call for a tow truck. The towing service operator is a friend of ours, so he's delaying as long as he can. But he won't be able to hold off much longer, or they'll just call someone else."

"What about the driver?"

"He's already been booked. If you can get him out, fine, but he's not as important as the merchandise. Pablo wants to make sure the car doesn't get to the police garage, because they'll find it in no time. Twenty kilos is hard to hide in a regular car."

"How do you want to do it?"

"I don't know if you have enough seniority to take over the investigation," Poison said.

"No," Aguilar said. "Not nearly."

"Then we'll probably have to do it by force. Either there at the scene, or intercept it en route."

Aguilar considered for a moment. There would be more cops on the scene; having nothing more interesting to do, they'd have gathered together, smoking, trading the latest gossip. Once the car was on the way, though, they would lose interest. One car might follow the tow truck to the garage, but no more than that. Controlling the variables would be harder, because the vehicle would be on the move—meaning a greater risk of innocents being caught in the crossfire, including the tow truck driver. But the danger to himself and Poison would be lessened.

"On the way," he said. "Can we find out what route the driver will take?"

Poison tapped a radio receiver mounted on the motorcycle. "You have your radio, and I have mine," he said. "We'll know."

While they waited, they planned their attack as best they could. When the call came, they made some last-minute adjustments and headed out.

There would be a point on Avenida San Juan at which the tow truck would pass beneath a highway. The sides of the road were concrete walls there, usually covered in graffiti, which would minimize the danger to bystanders. And once the truck was in the underpass, it wouldn't easily be able to escape.

Poison raced through traffic on his motorcycle. When Aguilar felt he was falling too far behind, he switched on lights and siren and cleared the way ahead.

On Avenida San Juan, he spotted the tow truck hauling a yellow Toyota sedan, traveling in the center of three lanes. As he'd expected, a single police car rode behind with two officers inside. They were talking animatedly; he saw their heads bobbing like puppets. He killed the siren and lights before closing in, so he wouldn't alert them.

Poison had assured him that the truck driver

would be ready. When Poison passed him on the motorcycle and gave him a sign, the driver would slam on his brakes.

They got into position, with Aguilar four vehicles back, behind an ancient pickup truck piled high with what appeared to be all of a family's possessions. He could see the police car and the tow truck, but unless the officers in the car were more observant than he expected, they wouldn't be able to see him. Poison was alongside him, but at Aguilar's nod, he sped ahead. He took the inside lane and raced ahead of the other vehicles, then cut across until he was beside the tow truck. Catching the driver's eye, he gave a salute and shot in front of the truck.

The driver hit his brakes. The tow truck shuddered and skidded to a halt, its rear end fishtailing and blocking the left lane as well as its own. Behind it, brakes squealed as cars either lurched to a stop or slid into the rightmost lane, the only one still open. A couple of cars bumped across the median strip and into the oncoming lanes, then had to repeat the process to avoid head-on collisions.

The driver of the police car wasn't so lucky. Doubtless distracted by his conversation, he braked, swerved, and slammed into the sedan under tow, caving in his front end.

The car behind that managed to avoid the pile-up, but the pickup truck's brakes weren't up to the challenge. The driver tried to stop, but his truck slid sideways, clipped the rear fender of the police car, and tipped over. Chairs, bicycles, children's toys of every description, a dining table, three mattresses, and dozens of boxes spilled across all three lanes of traffic, some even winding up in the nearest oncoming lane.

Clothing scattered—women's, men's, children's—and, caught by the wind rushing through the underpass, fluttered and soared back across the mess. A pair of women's panties snagged on the twisted windshield wiper blade of the police car, causing Aguilar to wish he had brought Montoya's Polaroid.

His amusement didn't last long. The capsized truck blocked every lane, and he couldn't drive up to the tow truck. The idea was that once they'd dispatched the following officers, they would reroute the tow truck to someplace where they could recover the cocaine. Once they had it safely in Aguilar's Nissan, it didn't matter what became of the car itself.

Now, though, Poison was ahead of the tow truck, stopped and straddling his motorcycle, looking back at the wreck. The police car was tangled up with the sedan; Aguilar thought it might take a crowbar or a torch to separate them. But the pickup truck and its detritus had stopped all traffic behind it, so Aguilar couldn't get through. Traffic in the other direction was slowing down, as people moved over to avoid the far left lane and to observe the calamity.

He sat for a little while, trying to determine the best course of action. Finally, he turned on the lights and siren again, and slowly rolled up over the concrete median. Blaring his siren and horn at oncoming vehicles, he worked his way past the wreckage and cut back in front of the tow truck. Poison parked his motorcycle and joined him there. The two cops got out of their car and eyed Aguilar with relief.

"That damn driver," one of them said, gesturing toward the tow truck. "What the hell did he stop for? There was nothing in his—"

Poison cut him off with three quick shots, two to

the chest and one to the head. The other cop reached for his gun, but he hesitated. Aguilar recognized him; they'd been at the academy together, sometimes had coffee together in the mornings before class. "Jose, why—" the guy began. Aguilar drew and fired five rounds, four of which found their target. He couldn't remember the guy's name.

With both officers down, Aguilar pounded on the tow truck's door. "What are you sitting there for?" he asked. "Get out and help us!"

The driver scrambled down from the truck. Poison was already freeing rubber-wrapped kilos from the Toyota and stacking them on the road. Aguilar and the truck driver snatched them up and carried them to Aguilar's SUV, loading them into the cargo area. Around them, horns were honking and people were swearing, but Aguilar pointed to his badge and waved at them to stop. Someone went to the pickup and helped the family inside crawl out, dazed and bloody. The sight stung Aguilar like an arrow to the heart. *That should have been me*, he thought. *Helping the victims, not taking advantage of their anguish to further a crime.*

But life was too short for should-have-beens, or so Montoya might have said. Aguilar pushed that thought from his mind and moved the cocaine.

19

THE NEXT TASKS assigned to Aguilar were easier to accomplish, and attracted less attention. He was asked to make evidence disappear, to alter reports, sometimes to use police resources to locate people or to inconvenience them in some way. Nothing too complicated or dangerous, and he was receiving four times his police salary to carry them out from time to time.

But then there were the murders.

Escobar, it seemed, always had a list of people who needed killing. Police, judges, lawyers, bankers, merchants, drug dealers, informers, criminals, guerillas... it seemed endless. *El Patrón* preferred that innocents not be hurt during those assassinations, especially women and children. But if it couldn't be avoided, then that was okay. The important thing was to take out the targets.

At first, he thought he would never grow accustomed to killing. Each time he did it, he was shattered all over again. The look in the eyes of the person about to die, lying on the ground knowing they were breathing their last. The sobbing, the begging for life, for just one more day. Everyone who had time to speak seemed to have a family, wives and children who needed them, aging parents who relied on them.

But after a while, he realized those things affected him less and less. He could pop off a few rounds into a man kneeling before him, hands clasped together in weepy supplication, without feeling that pull at his chest that he had at first. He could move in close and gut someone with his knife, what Escobar called the Jaguar's Claw, and when the hot gush of blood and intestines drenched his hand, he could shake it off and be on his way.

As more time passed, he began to look forward to it. He came to appreciate the challenge: plotting the perfect hit, learning the target's habits, anticipating obstacles, and then carrying out the plan just so. He took a craftsman's pride in his work; anything worth doing was worth doing well. His father had tried to impress that upon him, when he was younger. Of course, he'd mostly been talking about fixing shoes, not ending lives. But the principle applied just the same.

He never saw his parents anymore, or Luisa's family. They all remained in the area, but he felt isolated from them, separated by circumstance and occupation. At the funeral, his father had taken him aside and tilted his grizzled head toward Escobar.

"Why do you have someone like that at your wife's burial?" he asked. "It shames us all."

"Don Pablo's a great man," Aguilar replied, almost believing it. "He's one of the richest men in Colombia. He's going into politics, and he'll probably be president one day."

"He's a gangster and a murderer," his father said.

"And everybody knows it."

"You can't believe everything you read in the newspapers, Father. His reputation is overblown. Sure, some of his methods are a little strange. But look at everything he's done for Antioquia. The clinics, the sports fields, housing for the poor. Would a gangster do all that?"

"He would if he worried about what people thought."

"You'll see, Father. When he leads Colombia, you'll be proud to say he spoke at your daughter-in-law's funeral."

His father shook his head sadly, looking at the ground. "The fact that you could even speak that sentence means you'll never understand," he said. "I don't know how you came to this."

He walked away, and they hadn't spoken since.

They could never comprehend what he did, and he couldn't even try to explain it. And because they hadn't experienced it for themselves—his parents had lived through *La Violencia*, but had never taken human lives—an unbridgeable chasm had opened between them. He didn't even see people he and Luisa had been friends with, or spend time with those he'd known at the academy.

His life dovetailed with Escobar's now. His only friends were Don Pablo's *sicarios*. But that was okay.

They understood him.

The weeks passed in a blur of blood and violence, fueled by liquor, pot, and adrenaline. Aguilar didn't sleep much. When he showed up for work, he was disheveled and distracted. It was only when he was doing jobs with Escobar's men that he felt like his heart was really beating, that his lungs were taking in breath. It was amazing how ending another person's life could crystallize one's own.

Finally, he went to Escobar with a request.

"I'm no good at work," he said. "I think they're going to fire me. They're not giving me any responsibility anymore, and I don't know if I can even be of any use to you there."

They were sitting beside the pool at one of Escobar's homes in Medellín. The mansion was surrounded by tall stone walls that looked as if they'd survived the centuries and could last for a few more. Spring flowers scented the air, which was alive with buzzing insects and chirping birds. Escobar listened patiently as Aguilar described the state he was in. "I thought this would happen," he said when Aguilar had finished. "I'm surprised it took so long."

"What took so long?" Aguilar asked.

"For you to become fed up with the straight life. Some call it the honest life, but to me, what's honest is living up to one's own capabilities. You were never meant to be a cog in some bureaucratic machine, Jaguar. The primary function of the police is to enforce the status quo. The police exist to protect the financial interests of the oligarchs. Protecting the people—the real people, like your family and mine—is always secondary to that. You see the protection that I have around me at all times, for the safety of my family— that's necessary because the police won't protect people like us. In Colombia, unless we're born into the right families, we have to take care of ourselves."

Escobar had just won a seat as a representative to Colombia's House of Representatives, running as an alternate to Jairo Ortega, who abdicated his seat immediately following the election. Aguilar had accompanied the guys to some of his many campaign appearances, and felt like this speech was just one more of those he'd delivered to adoring crowds over the last several weeks.

But for all that it sounded like Escobar's standard speech, it tugged at something deep inside Aguilar. The man was right. As a police officer, his duty had presumably been to serve all Medellín's citizens. But the truth of it had been far different. If a merchant who sold diamond rings to the city's wealthy was robbed, a massive police response resulted. That merchant would no doubt have insurance, and losing a day's profits would hardly bankrupt him. But if a street vendor was robbed of what might amount to all the money he would earn in a week, that hardly merited sending out a single officer to write up a report, with no follow-up. The murder of a socialite whose sole contribution to society was that she got her picture in the papers wearing fabulous gowns demanded action; the murder of a teenager from impoverished La Estrella barely raised an eyebrow.

"You're right," Aguilar said. "I see it every day. The police only serve the rich. Sure, they'll send us out to a crime against a poor person, but only if there are no rich ones needing us at that moment. As soon as one does, we drop everything else and rush to be of service. It's sickening."

"That's why I've earned the fortune that I have," Escobar said. "So I can spend it on those who would otherwise go without. The trees I've planted throughout the valley, the clinics and classrooms, the parks and soccer fields—they're all for the people.

The *real* people. The many, not the few."

"You're a good man, Don Pablo."

Escobar chuckled. "I wouldn't go that far. I try, but I have my failings, like anyone else."

"Anyway," Aguilar began. He swallowed, and continued. "I was wondering if I could quit the police and work for you. Full-time."

"Of course," Escobar said. "I've been hoping you would. But you had to choose when. You had to see that it was right for you, so I didn't push. When do you want to do it?"

"Right away," Aguilar said. "I guess I have to go in tomorrow, to tell them I'm quitting. They'll want my car back, and my gun, I guess. My badge."

"Keep your uniform if you can," Escobar said. "At least one of them. If they won't let you keep your badge, we have plenty you can use. Even if you're no longer a cop, there might be times when it's handy for you to look like you are."

"I'll try. Anything else?"

"Anything they'll let you have might come in handy. Try not to burn any bridges, in case we need you to use your contacts there from time to time. But don't be afraid to let the bosses know how you feel. There's nothing they can do to you now. The minute you don't need them anymore, you're the one with the power, not them. Always remember that."

"I will," Aguilar said.

"And one more thing. Welcome to the family. At last."

"At last," Aguilar echoed. Escobar grasped his hand and held it tightly, and Aguilar felt like he had come home after a long absence.

20

THREE NIGHTS LATER, Aguilar was playing *Galaga* with some of the guys in the mansion's game room when Escobar came in, something akin to panic on his face. "We have a problem," he said.

"What is it, *Patrón*?" La Quica asked.

"It's my niece—Tata's sister's little girl, Adriana. She's been taken. Kidnapped."

"By who? Guerillas? A cartel?"

"I don't think so," Escobar said, shaking his head. "No. No, this was a guy in a little blue car. She was walking home from school. A boy in her class saw her, up ahead of him. A man in a blue car stopped and the man said something to her, and she got in. He mentioned it to his mother when he got home, and she called Dayanna, Tata's sister. Dayanna was already worried sick because Adriana was late."

"Do you think he's some kind of pervert, boss?" Big Badmouth asked.

"I don't know, maybe. What other kind of man would snatch a little girl off the street like that? She's only nine."

"You should call the police," Trigger said.

"The police won't help us. They'll sit on their asses and laugh at our worst fears."

"He's right," Aguilar said. "The police won't do anything for this family. We'll have to do it ourselves. Do you know where she was taken from, Don Pablo?"

"I can find out."

"Good, do it now. Anybody have a good map of Medellín?"

"In my car," Sure Shot said.

"Grab it," Aguilar said.

Sure Shot ran from the room, right behind Escobar.

It hadn't even occurred to Aguilar that he'd been throwing orders around—including to Escobar himself—and that people were obeying them.

Soon, he had a map unfolded over the video game, and with a marker he blocked out different areas within a three-kilometer radius of the abduction site. "How do you know she'll be there?" Escobar asked. By now his wife, Victoria Eugenia Henao Vallejo—Tata to Escobar, Señora Escobar to everyone else—was in the room along with all the *sicarios* at the property.

"I don't," Aguilar admitted. "But look at it this way. The guy was in a small car. If he'd had a van or a truck or something, I would make the perimeter larger. But in a small car, with a little girl, I don't think he would want to travel far. She might make a fuss, and people would see through the windows. He wouldn't have grabbed her on a street where he's known, but I think he took her someplace close by."

Aguilar indicated different sections he'd marked.

"Four guys per section," he said. "One goes down the street in one direction, one in the other. Look inside every garage, if there are any. The third guy goes down the alleys behind those streets, doing the same. Be discreet—you don't want him to see you—but check every house or building. That car's somewhere, and wherever it is, Adriana is. When you find the car, don't go in alone. For one thing, it might be the wrong blue car. But if it's the right one, the guy might kill her to keep her quiet. Call here, and someone will dispatch backup to your location. Once enough guys are there to enter in force, through every door and some windows, then you can go in."

"What if it's the wrong fucking car?" Big Badmouth asked.

"Tough shit. Bad day to drive a small blue car," Aguilar said.

"Everyone, talk to everybody you know," Escobar said. "Every informant, every lookout, every would-be *sicario*. Somebody in the city must have seen something, besides that little boy. Let's find out who, and what they know."

Aguilar didn't think that would be as helpful as a thorough foot search, but he wasn't about to turn down the suggestion. He and Escobar quickly assigned teams of four to the different sectors, and the guys headed out to search. Aguilar stayed behind to coordinate the effort.

When it was just him, Escobar, and Tata in the room, Aguilar noticed that she was quietly sobbing. Escobar gently put his arms around her and pulled her into a hug. He eyed Aguilar over her shoulder. "It'll be okay, Tata," he said. "With Jaguar running the show, we'll find her." Then, to Aguilar, he added,

"You sounded just like a cop."

"I guess it's my training coming out," Aguilar said. "Sorry."

"No, it's good. Sometimes we need somebody who can think on his feet like that. The way you were bossing those guys around, for a minute you sounded like me."

Tata blinked away tears and managed a brief smile. "Thank you, Jaguar, for your efforts."

"You're welcome, Señora. It's the least I can do."

"Jaguar isn't your real name, is it? Pablo loves those silly nicknames."

"I'm Jose, ma'am. Jose Aguilar Gonzales."

She shrugged free of Escobar's grip and crossed to him, extending a hand. "It's good to officially meet you, Jose Aguilar Gonzales. I've seen you around. You seem different from most of Pablo's guys."

"It's because he has an education, and he had an actual job," Escobar said. "He was a real police officer, and a good one. Too good for Medellín, so I had to hire him before he arrested me for something."

Aguilar grinned, but didn't respond. Instead, he said, "I'm sure we'll find your niece, Señora. The guy won't have taken her far away."

"I hope you're right," she said.

"He'd better be," Escobar added.

The call came in two hours later. The team headed by Sure Shot had found a small blue car inside a garage, with a blanket thrown over it to hide it from anyone looking in through the little windows set high in the garage door. Dust on the passenger door had been smeared and there were smudges on that window, as if from tiny hands.

Aguilar called the three nearest teams and gave them

171

the address. It wasn't too far from the Escobar home, so he and Escobar got into a car and headed out to meet them. Escobar gave instructions not to move in until he'd arrived—he didn't want to miss the action.

Aguilar took the wheel of a silver Mercedes-Benz—the most expensive vehicle he'd been in, much less driven, even including the rented Corvette—and headed for the address. He was nervous about driving Escobar, anxious about driving the pricey vehicle, and worried about how it might all turn out. Escobar didn't think this was a political kidnapping, or one with a ransom as the goal. That only left one reason a random man would snatch a little girl off the street. Aguilar shuddered to think about it.

"You might be wondering why I'd go through so much effort and expense for a little girl I hardly know," Escobar said as they wended their way down narrow roads. "It's because she's family. Family is everything, Jaguar. Everything. All that I do—even if it's for the poor, for the people—it all comes back to family. I want my family to grow and live in a Colombia at peace, one where the poor have the same opportunities as the rich. Without Tata and little Juan Pablo and my mother, Hermilda, I would be nothing. I might have the world, but it would be meaningless. I know Dayanna feels the same way about Adriana. And Tata loves her sister. I'd burn this city to the ground if I had to, to get Adriana back safe and sound."

He was silent for a little while. Aguilar didn't know what to say; he had basically given up his family to be an adjunct to Escobar's. Maybe family was who you chose to be with, rather than necessarily who you were born to be with.

Then Escobar added, "Do you think we will? Get her back? Alive and unhurt?"

"It's been hours," Aguilar said. "Typically, when a child is abducted, it's rare for them to survive the first few hours. It's different if the goal is ransom, or leverage of some kind—then the abductor has a stake in keeping the child alive. Or if it's a parent. But stranger abduction... it's not good, Don Pablo. I won't lie to you. We can hope for the best, but..."

"But prepare for the worst. Yes, I understand. If that *pendejo* has laid a finger on her, he'll pay." He was quiet again, scowling. "He will pay," he muttered. "He will pay."

Aguilar came to a stop a half-block away from the house in question. He could see Sure Shot, La Quica, Blackie, Brayan, Royer, and a few of the other guys. Nine in all, plus him and Escobar. With eleven, they could breach every entryway and find the guy wherever he was in the house—hopefully without giving him time to hurt the girl, if he hadn't already.

The house was small, modest, and set back from the street. A carriage house converted into a garage sat up close to the road; it was through windows in the door that Sure Shot had spotted the camouflaged car. Lights burned inside two rooms of the house, which was a single story unless it had a basement. For a moment, Aguilar wished Montoya were here—this would be much like the approach they had used to grab Leo Castellanos, what seemed like lifetimes ago. The differences were that this time they had more men— and they had an innocent victim to worry about.

If Adriana had survived the abduction only to be hurt in the rescue, Escobar would hang his spotted hide on a wall and use it for target practice.

He huddled with the guys for a couple of minutes, laying out the plan and assigning stations. Sure Shot had already been around the house, counting doors and windows. There were two men for each door—front, back, and side—and one for each window. One of the windows was too small for an adult to go through; Sure Shot figured it was in a bathroom. But a desperate man could shove a little girl through it, so Aguilar wanted it covered, just in case.

He and Escobar took the side door; *El Patrón* had a Heckler & Koch submachine gun strapped over his shoulder, and Aguilar carried a handheld battering ram he'd kept from his police car, with his gun in a holster and his knife on his ankle. On the theory that having men crash through every opening in the house at the same time would be surprise enough, he didn't worry about trying to synchronize watches or anything like that. He gave everyone a minute to get into position, then shouted, "Go!" At that, he swung the ram into the door, right beside the lock. The jamb splintered and the door flew open. They charged into an empty kitchen. All around the house, he heard others crashing through doors and smashing out windows.

Then he heard screams—little girl screams as well as adult male ones. She was alive.

From the rear of the house, Trigger shouted, "They're in here! Stay away from her!" Aguilar and Escobar followed the voices and found themselves in a bedroom. La Quica had gone in through the window, and Snake-eyes and Poison had blocked the doorway.

The man was thin, almost emaciated. He had short, graying hair and an angular face, and he was wearing a dirty, grease-stained T-shirt with a cigarette pack in the breast pocket, and boxer shorts. Adriana was still wearing her school clothes: a red jumper with a white blouse, and pink sneakers. She stood beside a bed, wailing in terror, but at least the man had shut up. He was sitting on the edge of the bed, gripping the sheets tightly.

Escobar kicked him in the leg, hard enough to break the skin. "Did you hurt her?" he demanded. "Did you touch her?"

"I... I j-just wanted someone to p-play with," the man stammered. "I... I didn't want to h-hurt anybody!"

Escobar kicked him again, harder, and shoved the barrel of his gun against the guy's face. "Did you touch her?"

"Only a l-little," the man said.

Escobar turned to the girl and squatted beside her. His voice was suddenly tender. "Adriana, it's me, your Uncle Pablo. You're safe now. My men will take you home to your mother. She's been so worried about you, and so has Tía Tata. But you're fine now, okay?"

She seemed to recognize Escobar. The tears kept coming, but the wailing stopped, and she nodded.

"Who do you know?" Escobar asked. The other guys were crowding into the doorway now, and the girl scanned their faces before pointing out Poison.

"Poison and La Quica, take Adriana home. And call Tata, so she can call Dayanna and tell her you're on the way." To the girl, using his soft voice, he said, "These men will take you home. You'll be fine, okay? Uncle Pablo wouldn't let anybody hurt you. All right?"

"All right," she said, nodding again.

"You're a brave girl. Uncle Pablo loves you. You know that, right?"

She nodded once more.

"You'll have to come over and play with Juan Pablo soon. He misses you, too. Go with these men, now. They'll take good care of you, and they'll make sure you get home safely."

He locked eyes with Poison, then La Quica, as if to reinforce the message, then let her go. Poison took her hand and led her from the room. Escobar's tenderness with the girl surprised Aguilar; maybe he really meant what he'd been saying on the way over, about family.

Escobar was quiet, listening. When he heard car doors slam closed and the engine start up and drive away, he turned back to the man on the bed. He held out the machine gun, saying, "Somebody give me a pistol."

Four pistols were instantly proffered. Escobar took one and handed off the machine gun. "You think taking little girls off the street is fun?" he asked.

The man was trembling uncontrollably, his hands twisting the bed sheets into knots. "N-no," he squeaked. "I-I'm so s-sorry."

Escobar aimed the gun and fired a shot into the man's left foot. The man yowled with pain. Before he could do anything else, Escobar shot the right one.

"Do you know who I am?"

"Y-you're Don P-P-Pablo," the man said. Tears and snot ran down his face, and blood pattered onto the floor from his feet.

Escobar flashed a quick grin, as if pleased that he'd been recognized. Then he was back to business, his face stern. He fired twice, shooting the man in both legs. The man screamed, then jammed a hand into his mouth and bit into it.

"Do you see your mistake?" Escobar asked.

The man couldn't speak, but he managed to nod his head. Escobar fired again. Left knee, then right.

The man shrieked and started praying loudly, as if he might still be delivered from evil.

Escobar shifted his aim and shot him in the upper right arm. This time, the gun locked open. Empty. Escobar held it out, and someone snatched it away and gave him another. He fired again, into the upper left arm, then both elbows, and both wrists.

The man flailed around on the bed, only wordless screeches coming from him now. Every part of him was shaking. He'd filled his boxers and the stench rose in the room, making Aguilar glad for the gunfire smell that blocked at least some of it.

When that gun was empty, Escobar asked for the machine gun. He pointed it at the man's groin and emptied it. When he was finished, the man was dead, his crotch a smoking, smoldering mess.

"Everybody remember what you saw here," Escobar said. "Tell everyone you meet what happens to men who mess around with little girls. We'll make Colombia safe for children, if we have to kill every pervert in the land to do it."

He looked at Aguilar, his eyes suddenly weary. "Jaguar," he said, "take me home. I need to see my family."

21

"THAT WAS GOOD, Jaguar, what you did last night," Snake-eyes said. "Fast thinking."

"Thanks."

A steady rain was falling, and they were huddled in the guard shack at the estate's front gate. They should have been walking the perimeter, but neither one wanted to.

"How did you know to do that?"

"I guess it's from my police training. They teach you to take command of any situation. Assess it, make decisions, and carry them out. That's what I did."

"I just about shit when you started ordering Pablo around."

Aguilar laughed. "I did too, when I realized what I'd done. By then it was too late, so I just went with it. I'm glad it all turned out okay."

"How young do you think is too young for him?"

"What do you mean? For Don Pablo?"

"Tata's eleven years younger."

"That's not so bad. My mother is fifteen years younger than my father."

"But how old was she when they married?"

"Twenty-two, I think."

"I'm not sure how old Tata was, but young. Fifteen, maybe."

Aguilar shrugged. "If her parents approved..."

"I guess they must have. When we go out sometimes, for prostitutes, he always picks the youngest they have. Me, I like a woman with some meat on her, and some experience."

"You go for prostitutes with Don Pablo?"

"Sometimes. You will, too, one of these days. He likes to take some of the guys, pay for them. It makes him feel generous, I think, and he believes it makes us feel indebted to him."

Aguilar wasn't sure how he would feel about that. He had hardly thought about women or sex since Luisa's death. He'd always supposed a time would come when he would be interested in it again, but for now, he couldn't separate it from his loss. Luisa haunted his dreams, and sometimes he thought he saw her on the street. Being with anyone else would feel like a betrayal.

He saw Montoya, too, in nightmares. Saw the fear in his former friend's eyes, the pain racking his face as Aguilar cut him, the blood pooling on the floor. It was rare for a night to go by without those memories floating to the surface at least once. He tried to chase them away with thoughts of Luisa, but that was only sometimes effective.

"I'm not saying there's anything wrong with it," Snake-eyes clarified. "Just, you know, he got so upset with that guy last night, and Adriana is nine. I was curious as to what's too young for him, and what's just right."

"We'll probably never know," Aguilar said. "And that's as it should be."

"You're probably right. I'm glad he did what he did. People who prey on children like that—they should all have their balls shot off. Even that might be too good for them."

"Yeah," Aguilar agreed. "It's wrong, for sure."

"It messes a kid up," Snake-eyes said. "Makes him distrustful. Mean."

"Him?"

"It happens to boys, too, you know." His expression was curious, somewhere between bemused and sad, and he gestured toward himself in a way that Aguilar wasn't sure how to interpret.

"You?" he asked.

Snake-eyes shrugged. "I'm not ashamed of it. I couldn't control it. And when I got old enough, I found the bastard and blew his brains out. My second killing." He flashed a quick, uneasy grin. "The first was just practice, to make sure I could do it when I found him."

Aguilar wasn't sure what to say. He'd come to know Snake-eyes a little, working with him, but not that well. A revelation like this seemed premature, at best.

Still, he figured Snake-eyes was right. It wasn't anything he had done wrong, it was something that had been done to him, no doubt against his will. And he'd dealt with it appropriately, when he was able.

"I'm sorry that happened," he said. "But I'm glad you got payback."

"Yeah, so am I."

They were quiet for a little while, watching the rain and the occasional vehicle shushing up the street. Then Snake-eyes said, "Hey, don't tell anybody, okay?"

"Okay," Aguilar said. "No problem."

"I'm not ashamed," Snake-eyes said again. "But it's not something I want everybody to know about, either. I don't even know why I told you."

"It's cool," Aguilar said. "I can keep secrets."

"We can all do that, right? If we couldn't keep secrets, Pablo would have our heads."

They laughed, then were quiet again.

The rain kept falling.

After their shift, Aguilar had taken a hot shower and settled into a comfortable chair with a book. He had found a copy of Andrés Caicedo's posthumous novel *¡Que viva la música!* on a shelf in the mansion, and picked it up out of curiosity. Now he found himself gripped by the story of María del Carmen Huerta and the 1970s Cali that Caicedo had himself known. Some of the other guys were watching *Sábados Felices* and cracking up, but Aguilar had never found Alfonso Lizarazo that funny, and he was able to immerse himself in the book.

"Reading. That's good. I should read more."

Aguilar looked up from the book and saw Escobar standing beside him.

"I like to read," Escobar went on. "But these days, I mostly read newspapers and news magazines. Is that a good one?"

"I think so," Aguilar said.

"Sorry to bother you," Escobar said. "We're heading to Hacienda Nápoles. We're going to have an important visitor tomorrow, from North America. I want to entertain him there for a few days."

"Are we all going?" Aguilar asked.

"Most of us. Tata wants you to drive her. I usually ride in a separate car from her, Juan Pablo, and my mother. In case of trouble, you know."

Aguilar had already noticed that. "I thought she had a regular driver."

"She does. But she was impressed with you. Not *too* impressed, if you get my meaning, but impressed. I tried to discourage her—not that I don't trust you, but I've only ridden with you once, last night, and you didn't seem too comfortable with the Benz."

"I've never driven anything like that. So luxurious."

"Well, you'll take one of the Land Cruisers for this trip. I'll be following, about two kilometers behind. You'll have a radiotelephone, so if there's any sign of trouble, you'll be able to let me know."

"Anything you say, *Patrón*. Are we leaving now?"

"Soon."

"Can I bring the book with me? It was on a shelf downstairs."

"Of course. Just remember where it came from, and bring it back next time we're here."

Aguilar was surprised by that. Escobar was casual about so many things—like murder—but particular about others.

But then, he was learning that *El Patrón* was a complicated man, with layers upon layers to him. Just when he thought he had the man figured out, he learned something new and unexpected.

He guessed Escobar cultivated that, to keep people off guard. At least, he figured, it was probably what he would want to do, if most people in the world wanted to either kill him, arrest him, or take his money. *Better Pablo's problem than mine*, he thought. He was already making more money than he had ever expected to, but he would never have Escobar's kind of wealth. That was fine with him. From where he sat, being rich was far too much trouble.

Tata sat in the front passenger seat, with Juan Pablo and Hermilda in the back.

Aguilar knew the city well from his police work, but before they'd gone four blocks, Tata said, "Turn left up here, then right two streets down."

"Don't listen to her," Hermilda said, poking Aguilar's shoulder with her glasses. "Turn right up here."

"I know my way around Medellín, Hermilda."

"You never even left Envigado until you married Pablo. I've lived all over Antioquia—El Tablazo, Titiribí, Girardota, Rionegro, and different neighborhoods all over Medellín. I think I know my way around."

"Yes, but you still think of the city as it used to be. It's changed, and there's construction work ahead, and—"

Exasperated, Aguilar cut in. "I just need to know which way I'm supposed to turn. Otherwise, I'm going straight for another two kilometers, then cutting over to Calle 44."

"That will work, too," Hermilda said.

"Fine," Tata added.

He went straight.

After that, there were some strained attempts at small talk, then an uncomfortable silence, broken only by Hermilda correcting Juan Pablo's behavior. "Sit up straight!" "Don't pick your nose!" "Keep your hands away from your mouth!" "Sit still!"

Aguilar wondered how someone born to a woman so obsessed with appropriate behavior could have become a famous criminal and murderer. After a while, Juan Pablo fell asleep, and so did she.

Then Tata started asking questions, keeping her voice low so those in back couldn't hear. "I wonder what you must think of me," she said. "A woman like me being married to someone like Pablo."

"He's a good man," Aguilar said.

"He's a gangster. So are you, I suppose. But you know what he's like, what he does. What does that say about me?"

Aguilar kept his eyes on the unspooling blacktop ahead. "That you love him, I guess. I know he loves you. He talks about it all the time."

"Does he?"

"Absolutely."

"But he also has affairs. If he loved me like you say, wouldn't he be faithful?"

"I don't know about that." He didn't want to share what Snake-eyes had said about prostitutes.

"Was your father faithful to your mother?"

"I think so," Aguilar said. "I don't know for sure. I suppose if he had affairs, he hid them from the whole family."

"Pablo doesn't do much to hide his. He pretends to hide them, but I always know."

"I'm not really comfortable talking about that, Señora."

"Sorry, I didn't mean to make it awkward for you."

"That's okay."

"Tell me about you, Jose," she said. "You're not like the others. Most of his men are unschooled, barely out of their teens if they are at all. I've seen you at work, seen you reading books. You're intelligent."

Aguilar hoped the flush he felt wasn't visible. "Thank you."

"Did you go to school?"

"I finished upper secondary," he said. "At first I was on the technical track, but then I changed to the academic."

"Why?"

"I wanted to be able to get a good job, so I thought the technical track would be best. But one of my teachers told me that having a rounded education offered more flexibility, which would be appealing to different kinds of employers." He paused, wondering what that teacher would think of his current livelihood. "But then I became a police officer, which doesn't require that much rounding."

"But flexibility helps, I would think, in police work."

"Sure. There weren't many opportunities to discuss philosophy or literature with the people I arrested, though."

She laughed. "Probably not working for Pablo, either. He values those things in others, but he's never had time for them. To him, everything is about making money. His goal was to earn a million pesos by the time he was thirty."

"And he did, right?"

"More than. He had several million United States dollars before he reached thirty. Now I don't think he even knows how rich he is. He has money cached at most of his properties. He buries it in the ground, hides it in the walls, stores it in warehouses. Sometimes the rats eat it, or rain gets in and makes it moldy. Can you imagine having so much money that you could just throw it away when it goes bad?"

"It's never lasted long enough to go bad, for me."

"It never did for me, until Pablo."

"Do you like it? Being rich?"

"It's nice to not have to go without. To wear good clothes, to buy jewelry or art when I see something lovely. I don't need as much as he has—neither does he, or he wouldn't have to worry about where to store it—but he won't stop making more. We've all asked him to retire; he couldn't spend what he already has if he lived to be a thousand. But he worries about the future, about his parents, about Juan Pablo, and me. He wants to make sure all our needs are always met, and those of any descendants. He never wants there to be another poor Escobar."

"And he likes to give it away," Aguilar said. "To do things for the community. All the housing he builds, and the parks, the athletic fields and so on."

"He's very generous that way. He sees the rich sitting on their money, hoarding it, and the poor going without. He doesn't mind hoarding it, but he doesn't want the poor to need what they can't ever have. If there's a problem and money can fix it, he's willing to spend that money."

"Like I said, he's a good man."

"He's a good man, and a drug dealer, and worse," Tata said. "I love him, but it's not always easy. He's complicated."

"Everybody's complicated."

"True. But not like him. There aren't many like him."

"From what I've seen," Aguilar said, "there aren't *any* like him. There's only one Pablo Escobar."

Tata chuckled again. "The world couldn't stand two of them."

22

ESCOBAR'S DISTINGUISHED NORTH American visitor was Kyle Caldwell, who La Quica said had distributed at least ninety million dollars' worth of Escobar's cocaine in the Miami area. He and Escobar had met in person a couple of times, and enjoyed each other's company as well as having business interests in common, but this was his first trip to Colombia. Escobar wanted Caldwell to have a good time—whatever that took.

Gaviria took three of the guys and picked Caldwell up at the airport in Bogotá, then drove him to Nápoles. Aguilar was in the main house when they came in. Caldwell was tall and rangy, and he wore a silk shirt with a floral print, open to the fourth button, a brown leather blazer, jeans, and loafers with no socks. He had thick brown hair and a bushy mustache. Beneath sky-blue eyes was a nose that had been broken once or twice—the only flaw Aguilar could see in what was otherwise the most handsome man he'd ever met. Then he turned a little, and Aguilar noticed his left ear. Most of it was gone; he had a little flap left, but it was otherwise open to the elements. Aguilar wondered if that interfered with his hearing, or enhanced it.

When Gaviria introduced them, Caldwell said, "Great to meet you, Jaguar. I've heard about your knife work. We should compare notes later; I bet you could teach me a thing or two." Aguilar had taken English all through secondary school, and learned more from watching North American television shows. He was glad for the opportunity to practice.

"I don't know anything special," Aguilar said. "I just cut."

"Whatever works, man. It ain't about being fancy, it's being alive at the end that counts."

"Kyle," Gaviria cut in. "Sorry, Don Pablo is waiting."

"Yeah, sorry," Caldwell said. "Catch you later, man," he added to Aguilar.

Because the *finca* was too far from the city to drive in just to party, the party was brought to Nápoles. Sure Shot and Poison drove up in trucks carrying dozens of prostitutes. A helicopter landed and Colombian musicians spilled out; a second one brought their instruments and gear. More trucks showed up with food and liquor. Plenty of grass was already on hand.

A huge tent was set up outside one of the estate's additional houses, far from the main house. The word went out—no wives were invited to this bash; it was men only, except for the imported professionals.

Aguilar wasn't sure what to expect when he rode down in a Land Cruiser with some of the other *sicarios*. Everyone had dressed in their best clothes and splashed on too much cologne. Aguilar cracked his window a little, hoping that the rush of fresh air

188

would dissipate the cloying stink.

They arrived a little before midnight, and the party appeared to be in full swing—they could see a glow from behind the hills, and hear the music before the house came into view. Then they rounded a corner and there it was. Light gleamed through the tent walls and from torches on poles set all around it. Every light in the house seemed to be on, and the doors were open, with people coming and going between house and tent. As they got closer, Aguilar saw couples having sex beside the road, on the front steps of the house, and framed by some of the windows. Men were shouting and singing along with the band and occasionally firing guns into the air.

Inside was more of the same. Aguilar instantly felt out of place. He had a few beers, which helped a little, and he admired some of the nude or half-naked women. But he wasn't interested in being with them, and the guys were, for the most part, either completely hammered, stoned out of their minds, or busy chasing after them.

After a while, he saw Kyle Caldwell coming out of the house. His shirt was torn, shirttails out. He'd ditched the leather blazer somewhere, or lost it. He was grinning, his face flushed, but when he saw Aguilar the smile widened.

"My man Jaguar! What's the haps, brother?"

Aguilar wasn't sure what that meant, but he took it for a friendly greeting. "Hello, Kyle. Are you having fun?"

"So much fun you wouldn't believe it. These women, man, I'm telling you."

None of his English classes had covered material like this. Again, he got the gist, so he nodded and said,

"I'm glad. Don Pablo will be glad, too. This is all in your honor."

"He's quite the motherfucking host, old Pablo," Caldwell said. "You like working for him?"

"Yes. I used to be a police officer, in Medellín, but—"

Caldwell cut him off. "A cop? Righteous, brother." He threw an arm across Aguilar's shoulders. "Come on, let me buy you a drink."

"Don Pablo already paid for all the liquor," Aguilar said.

"Even better!" Caldwell laughed, and Aguilar joined him. The party had just gotten considerably more interesting.

Escobar never got up before noon. Sometimes he slept considerably later than that, then spent time smoking pot, reading newspapers, and brushing his teeth—he was notorious for the time and attention he lavished on those. Many of his crew had adjusted their own sleep schedules accordingly, but Aguilar had always been an early riser, unless he'd worked a night shift.

This day, he slept late because of the party, but by eleven he was up and in search of some breakfast. He scrounged a cup of coffee and some food in the kitchen, then was surprised to find Caldwell sitting at the dining room table in the main house, with an empty plate in front of him. Aguilar felt like he'd been dragged around by a truck, but Caldwell looked like he'd had a full eight hours of sleep.

"Morning, Jaguar!" he said.

"Good morning, Kyle," Aguilar said. He almost couldn't even find the words in Spanish, but he managed to pull out the English just in time.

"You have a good time last night?"

"Yes." He put down his plate and cup and scraped back a chair. "And you?"

"Those local *señoritas* are *más* sexy, brother."

Aguilar thought Caldwell had been with at least three of them during the party. He should have been exhausted and drained. "Colombians make beautiful women," he said.

"Fucking A," Caldwell said. "Your English is really good, man. Way better than my Spanish, anyway."

"I studied English all through secondary school."

"Is that like what we call high school, in America?"

"High school, yes. But this is also America."

"South America, though."

"Right, South America. And the United States, it's in North America."

"Back home we just think of it as America," Caldwell said.

"What about Mexico and Canada? They are also in North America."

Caldwell rubbed his chin, considering. "I guess. We sort of think of them as second tier, you know? They don't really count."

"Second tier?" Aguilar didn't understand the phrase.

"Never mind, man. Listen, I wanted to talk to you about your knife work," Caldwell said, suddenly changing the subject. "You have some free time?"

"Yes." Aguilar forked some eggs into his mouth, chased them with a sip of strong coffee. "As soon as I finish this."

"I'll be outside," Caldwell said. "Catching some rays. Join me when you're done."

Aguilar didn't know what "catching some rays" meant. When he had polished off the breakfast and drained a second cup of coffee, he went out into a grassy yard behind the house and found Caldwell, shirt off and eyes closed, soaking up sunshine.

Caldwell's eyes snapped open at his approach. "You got your knife?"

Aguilar tapped his leg. "Always."

"Can I see it?"

Was it an honest request, or a trick? Aguilar wasn't sure. What if Caldwell's first lesson turned out to be "Never give anyone your knife"?

But he trusted the North American. For some reason, the man had seemed to take an immediate liking to him, and Aguilar returned the feeling.

He freed it from the sheath and handed it over. Caldwell held it by the grip, made a couple of stabbing moves with it, then balanced it on a finger. "Nice piece," he said. "You keep it sharp."

"I try to. I work it every few days with a stone."

"A whetstone?"

"Right," Aguilar said with a chuckle. He hadn't been able to remember the English word.

"Do you have a tapered sharpening rod, for the serrations?" Caldwell asked. He demonstrated with his fingers, until Aguilar grasped what he meant.

"No."

"You need one." He thumbed across the serrated section. "These can dull, too. Get a rod that tapers to a point and figure out where it fits the serrations just right. And always use a good wax on the knife, not oil."

"No oil on the stone?"

"No. With a good whetstone, you won't need a lubricant. Get a good hard wax, not a liquid, like car wax. Wax your sheath once in a while, too. And use two stones, a coarse grit and a fine grit, on the blade."

"Where did you learn so much about knives?"

"I got some of it when I was a U.S. Marine in Vietnam," Caldwell said. He tapped his ruined left ear. "That's where this happened, too. Fucking VC who was faster with his knife than I was."

"Looks like it hurts," Aguilar said.

"It did, at the time. Now I pretty much forget about it, except when some foxy broad sees it and she gets that 'eww, gross!' expression.

"Anyway, I met a guy there—an old Special Ops hand, who was in country back in the late fifties, before anybody was officially there. His job was winning hearts and minds, and he mostly did it by cutting out hearts and scaring people out of their minds."

He gave Aguilar back the knife. "Show me a stab move."

Aguilar spread his legs for balance, held the blade vertical to the ground, and thrust it forward, putting his back and shoulder into it.

"Not bad," Caldwell said.

"Thanks."

Caldwell held out his hand. "May I?"

Aguilar handed the knife back. Caldwell took it, held it the same way Aguilar had, then gave his wrist a quarter-turn to the left. "In the Marines, they taught us to always stab with the blade parallel to the ground, not perpendicular to it." He demonstrated, making a move much like Aguilar's but with the blade striking its imaginary target horizontally instead of vertically.

"Then," he continued, "you give it a good twist, like so." He turned his wrist back to the original position, so the blade was once again vertical. "And then you cut down and across—left to right, or right to left—as much as you can before you pull it out."

He demonstrated slashing across an opponent's body. Aguilar saw at once how much more damage could be done using that technique, as opposed to stab-withdraw-stab again. "I understand," he said.

Caldwell gave the knife back, and Aguilar tried a couple of stabs using his technique. It felt awkward, but the advantage was clear. "This would slide between the ribs better, too."

"Exactly," Caldwell said. "It doesn't matter if you do it with your palm up or down, just be sure it's one of those. Then the twist and slash."

"Thank you," Aguilar said.

"Of course, the other guy's going to be trying to do the same thing to you, if he also has a knife. If he has a gun, your best chance is to get the hell out of there. Always go one better than the other guy. If he has a stick, you can use a knife. If he has a knife, use a gun. If he has a gun, get a bazooka or a motherfucking tank. There's no way, if you're in a knife-against-knife fight, that you're not going to get cut up, and it's going to hurt like a bitch."

"I've been lucky so far."

"Luck doesn't last. And fancy technique is for suckers. If you're in a combat situation, where it's your life or the other guy's, you want to hit first and hit hard. Try to drop him before he has a chance to do you any damage. If you can do that, you might survive."

Aguilar nodded. "Got it."

Caldwell showed him the stabbing motions several more times, with no knife in his hand. Palm down, then quarter-twist right. Palm up, then quarter-twist left. "Keep practicing that until it's second nature, and you'll be good."

"Thank you for the lesson," Aguilar said.

"No problem. We're brothers of the blade—we have to watch out for each other."

"Brothers of the blade," Aguilar echoed, laughing. "I like that."

"I like it, too, buddy." Caldwell clapped him on the back. "I like it, too."

23

CALDWELL STAYED FOR two more days of jet-skiing on the lakes, racing motorcycles, alcohol-fueled parties and hookers from Colombia and Brazil. Aguilar enjoyed his company. He was glad that he'd killed Montoya—honor demanded it of him, if nothing else—but he missed the kind of camaraderie they'd shared. Since his rainy-day confession, Snake-eyes had been spending more time with him, almost as if the sharing of that secret had bonded them, in a way.

But Caldwell was more gregarious, more demonstratively friendly, and more unusual. Snake-eyes was one more poor Colombian kid who'd chosen crime over the straight life. Caldwell was exotic—a North American, a military veteran who had smuggled heroin from Vietnam until he found that distributing Escobar's cocaine had a much better profit margin.

Even his damaged ear helped bring them together, as if they were kindred spirits, in a way. Caldwell's ear and Aguilar's spots.

When he left, Aguilar missed him more than he'd expected.

But he didn't have much time to worry about it.

During Caldwell's visit, a newspaper editor in Medellín had run what he promised would only be the first in a series of incendiary editorials, calling out the kingpins of the Medellín Cartel by name—Escobar, the Ochoa brothers, Carlos Lehder, and Gacha— and demanding that they be arrested or killed. The journalist's name was Juan Sebastian Osorio Benítez, and he had a large following, not just in that city but around the country.

The editorial was on the front page of the *Diario del Medellín*, under a blazing headline: COLOMBIA WILL NEVER KNOW PEACE WHILE KILLERS WALK FREE!

Its concluding paragraph was a call to action. "Every Colombian citizen must take the continued existence of these men and their criminal conspiracy as an attack on our nation, as surely as if some foreign power rained down bombs upon us. These gangsters own police, judges, and elected officials; therefore, it is up to us, to every honest, patriotic Colombian, to root them out. They must be imprisoned or killed, before we can ever call ourselves a free people. And I will not stop saying so, out loud, where I know they can hear. Join me, fellow Colombians. Stand up for yourselves, and demand that the authorities stand up, as well."

Escobar wanted him silenced.

When he saw the newspaper, he paced for twenty minutes, crumpling it in his fist and hitting his other palm, his thigh, furniture, whatever he could with it, as if Osorio himself could feel the blows.

"This bastard can't be allowed to write another

word," Escobar ranted. "He'll stir up the public against us, and they'll stir up the courts and the politicians."

He assigned Aguilar, Poison, and Snake-eyes to eliminate Osorio. It shouldn't be difficult, they reasoned. He wasn't an elected official or a police commander, so he wouldn't have protection from the military or law enforcement.

When they got to Medellín and staked out the *Diario* offices, they discovered their error.

Because he wouldn't be protected by law enforcement or the military, Osorio had organized his own defensive force. When he exited the offices, he was surrounded by a phalanx of armed men approximately the size of refrigerator-freezers. They escorted him into an armored SUV, which drove him home with another one in front of it and one behind, and motorcyclists flanking it. His home was similarly defended; in addition to the human guards, it had motion-sensitive lights, alarms, and a tall fence, and a team of Dobermans prowled the grounds day and night.

Osorio wasn't taking any chances.

A couple of days and the judicious distribution of stacks of money turned up an answer to one question—the men were mercenaries, hired from the United States, South Africa, Israel, and elsewhere. They knew their work and they'd done it before.

"Shit," Poison said when they gathered to discuss their findings. They had rented a small, furnished apartment two blocks from the newspaper office. There, they ate take-out food from local restaurants, and watched the newspaper building, keeping track of Osorio's comings and goings. They were sitting at a little wooden dining table, which they had pulled close to the window. It was covered with empty bottles and food wrappings. "He's got himself an army. He's as well protected as Don Pablo."

"Don't let him hear you say that," Snake-eyes replied. "He'll fire us and hire himself some outside mercenaries."

"Those guys are just in it for the money," Aguilar said. "They wouldn't lay down their lives for him, like we would for *El Patrón.*"

"You want to test that?" Poison asked. "Or approach them and try to buy them off?"

"If we could get to them," Snake-eyes suggested, "maybe we could. Offer them triple what he's paying them. He's just a newspaper guy, he can't be rich."

"No, probably not. But the owner of the *Diario* is an oligarch," Poison said. "He's not in Don Pablo's league, but he's a millionaire several times over. He's probably paying their salaries, not Osorio."

"Why would he do that?" Aguilar asked.

"Because big headlines sell newspapers. By taking on the cartels, Osorio has made himself the story— even TV journalists and other newspapers are reporting on his editorial. It's great advertising for the *Diario*, so it's worth it to the paper's owner to keep his money-maker alive."

"Well, if we can't get to him and we can't buy off his security," Snake-eyes asked, "what are we going to do?"

"You want to go back to Don Pablo and tell him you give up?"

"Hell no," Snake-eyes said. "It'd be safer to let those mercenaries kill me. At least they'd do it fast."

"Then we have no choice," Aguilar said. "We have to figure out how to get to him. And we should do it before he runs the next part of his series, or Pablo's going to be pissed." He sat there for a moment, looking at his comrades and shaking his head.

"What?" Poison asked.

"I was just thinking how strange it is to be sitting in a room trying to figure out the best way to kill someone."

"Not strange to me," Poison said. "When was the first time you killed a man?"

"I was fifteen," Snake-eyes said.

"For me, it was the night we got Costa."

Both of the others stared at him. "You're a newborn!" Poison said. "A murder-baby!"

"I guess. I never thought of myself as a killer. I guess I'm rethinking everything now. I'm a different person than I was—or than I thought I was—and that takes some getting used to."

"I was eleven the first time," Poison said.

"Eleven? You were a *real* murder-baby."

Poison shrugged. "My family was dirt-poor, but someone from our church gave me a brand-new bike. There was a bigger kid in the neighborhood, kind of a bully. He saw me riding it, the second day I had it, and he knocked me down and took it. I went home and got my father's gun from his drawer, and walked the streets until I found him. Then I shot him four times. I missed the first two times, but he was so scared he froze, with piss running down his leg, so I moved in close and put four rounds into his fat, ugly face."

"What happened?"

"I got my bike back." Poison grinned. "I wasn't stupid enough to do it in front of witnesses. At least, if anybody saw, they were smart enough to keep their mouths shut. Nobody was ever arrested."

"Did it bother you?" Aguilar asked. "Killing somebody?"

"Not even a little. I slept like a baby. From that day on, I knew if anybody ever fucked with me, I could take care of it. And I did. I started stealing bikes myself, then motorbikes, cars, whatever I could. Then I was recruited to be a lookout for Don Pablo. When I found out somebody would pay me for what I was happy to do anyway, it was the best day of my life. I never regretted a minute of it."

Aguilar found himself torn. He had willingly become a murderer—he'd known, even from the beginning, that the tasks he was accepting from Escobar would lead to that. But at the same time, he had once dedicated his life—however briefly—to protecting the public by fighting against people like Poison. He had always thought he had a moral code, but if he did, he'd broken it pretty easily, step by step.

"It still bothers me," he admitted. "A little, I guess. Not like I thought it would."

"Well, you're pretty good at it," Snake-eyes said.

"Thanks," Aguilar said. A little thrill of pride rushed through him. "It's the job, right?"

Poison glanced at his watch. "It's four-ten. He should be coming along any time now."

Osorio was a creature of habit; he arrived at the office at eight o'clock every morning, and left at ten after four every afternoon. He ate breakfast at the same restaurant, surrounded by his goon squad. He had lunch delivered to him in his newspaper office, and he had dinner at one of several restaurants he favored. He had no wife, no family, seemingly no interests other than his work. Once he was at home after dinner, he didn't leave until the next morning.

Sure enough, in a couple of minutes, the usual procession rolled into view. The armored Suburban in front, with gunmen inside it. Then the second, with Osorio and a couple of guards in it, and motorcycles keeping pace. Finally, the third Suburban.

From the apartment, they couldn't even be sure that Osorio was in the middle car, although they had seen him enter it and exit it on numerous other occasions and trusted that his routine was unchanging. He sat in the center of the rear seat, with a guard on either side of him. The windows were tinted. The angle from this window was all wrong; Osorio was invisible from here. They'd discussed trying to shoot from the apartment, but their bullets wouldn't penetrate the SUV's roof.

As the vehicles rolled past, Snake-eyes said, "One guy could shoot the driver of the first car from here, and the others could be waiting downstairs, on either side of the street. When the first car stopped, they'd open fire on the second one."

"Except the bulletproof glass would protect the driver," Poison said. "And those mercenaries would make hamburger out of the two guys on the street."

"Yeah," Snake-eyes agreed. "It was just an idea. I didn't say it was a good one."

"What about an RPG?" Poison asked.

"Do you know how to shoot one with enough accuracy to hit your target from up here?" Snake-eyes countered.

"I guess that would take some practice. Which we don't have time for."

But Aguilar, watching the vehicle roll up the next block, had a different idea. "Look," he said, pointing.

The next corner had a stop sign. The Suburbans came to a halt, then the first one started into the intersection. Once it had entered, it crawled through, and the second and third passed the sign without stopping. Horns blared, but nobody who looked inside the vehicles would dare make a fuss.

"Yeah, they're assholes," Snake-eyes said. "So?"

"So look—Osorio's car was stopped right next to that storm drain."

It was hard to make out from here, but a wedge of shadow indicated an opening in the curb. Aguilar had spotted it moments before the first SUV reached it, and noticed the second one brake to a full stop beside it. If there had been more traffic on the cross street, it could have been sitting there for thirty seconds or more.

"Okay," Poison said. "But even if someone could fit in there, he couldn't shoot through that armor."

"I'm not thinking about a gun," Aguilar said. "I'm thinking about a bomb."

A grin spread across Poison's face as he considered the idea. "That could work. A powerful enough bomb that close to the underside of the car would disable it, for sure. Maybe even destroy it."

"And we could be near enough to gun down anybody who wasn't killed by the blast," Aguilar said. "Maybe in that café across the street."

"What do you know about making bombs?" Snake-eyes asked.

"Nothing," Aguilar said. "But I know somebody who might know somebody."

"Can you trust him?"

Aguilar shook his head. "It's a her. And yes, absolutely."

24

JULIANA REMEMBERED AGUILAR, and when enough pesos had crossed her palm, it turned out that she did indeed know somebody who was good with explosives. His name was Oscar, and like Juliana, he did not care to divulge more than that.

They didn't give their names, either, or say who they worked for. Juliana had brought them together, and that was sufficient for purposes of trust. Oscar met them in the gravel parking lot of a mountain park. Plenty of other people were around, some outfitted for serious hiking and others just enjoying the cool spring day. Juliana had told them to look for a black van with no windows, and Snake-eyes brought their Land Cruiser up next to it.

The man inside was unshaven, heavy, slope-shouldered, with a massive brow that shaded small eyes. He looked them over from inside the van and, seemingly satisfied, opened his door and got out. He didn't smile.

When they emerged from the Land Cruiser, Oscar

indicated one of the hiking trails. "Let's go for a walk," he said.

"Thanks for meeting with us," Aguilar said.

"No problem."

"What we need—"

Oscar cut him off with a wave of his hand. "Not until we're on the trail."

Aguilar understood. He didn't want anybody eavesdropping or using listening devices. For all he knew, their SUV could be bugged. And for all they knew, his van could be.

"Right."

They hiked up into the trees. A soft breeze ruffled leaves and pine needles and scented the air. Birds called and flitted about. Finally, Oscar stopped. "Okay, what are you looking to accomplish?"

"We want something we can place in a storm drain," Poison said. "Strong enough to blow up an armored Suburban stopped beside it."

"Is the undercarriage armored, too?"

"We don't know."

"Then we have to assume it is. How much collateral damage is acceptable?"

"Collateral damage?" Snake-eyes asked.

"A charge that's going to take out the armored vehicle is going to take out a lot more than that. Whatever building is on the same side of the street as the storm drain will take some serious damage. It's not a hospital or a veterans' home or anything like that, is it?"

"Just some stores on that side," Aguilar said. "And a travel agency, I think. There's a café across the street."

"Okay. How long do you want to have it sitting in the storm drain? Minutes? Hours?"

"Minutes, I think," Poison said. "We know what

the car's schedule is, so we can place it shortly before."

"How will you make sure it doesn't fall down into the sewer?"

Poison and Aguilar locked eyes. "We hadn't thought about that, I guess," Aguilar said. "Any ideas?"

Oscar considered for a moment. "Get a box. Fairly flat, maybe fifteen centimeters high, but big enough that it won't easily fall in. Make sure it's beat-up, so it looks like you're trying to stuff garbage down the drain, but also make sure it's reinforced enough to support the device. Then coat the bottom of it with something like rubber cement, so when you set it in place it won't slide around as traffic goes past. If you place it right before the Suburban arrives, people probably won't go after it. If anybody does and it goes off?" He shrugged. "They shouldn't have tried to pick up somebody else's trash."

"Can you make the device?" Poison asked. "So it can be triggered remotely?"

"Would you be here talking to me if I couldn't?"

"No, I guess not."

"I can make it. Can you afford it?"

"How much?"

Oscar named a price. Poison pretended to think it over. "That's acceptable," he said. "If this works, our boss will be very happy. He might even have more work for you, down the line."

"It'll work," Oscar promised. "If you do exactly what I say, I can guarantee the results."

The device's manufacture took four days, during which time Osorio published the second in his series of anti-Cartel editorials. NEVER GIVE UP ON COLOMBIA!

the headline blared. The first paragraph said, "Not since Simón Bolívar expelled the Spaniards has the rule of the Colombian people been so threatened. For now, we have the vote and the power to choose our destiny. But with the extravagant wealth of the drug cartels growing daily—and with it their power over Colombian elected officials, law enforcement, and the military, the rights of the people and the power to choose are endangered species."

Escobar called and demanded to know why the fuck Osorio hadn't been dealt with yet. "We're working on it, *Patrón*," Poison told him. "We're told that the bomb will be ready tomorrow. By tomorrow night, Osorio will be nothing but a stain on the pavement and a bad memory."

"He'd better be!" Escobar replied, loud enough that Poison moved the phone away from his ear. Aguilar could hear him from across the room. "I didn't send you to Medellín so you could enjoy liquor and whores for a week!"

"We're not, *Patrón*. I swear. Osorio is too well protected, that's all. Then we came up with this plan, but it takes time to build it so it'll do what we need it to. Tomorrow night, we can drive back to Nápoles."

"Good," Escobar said. He sounded like he'd calmed down some, but his voice was still loud. "Get this taken care of, and get back here."

"Tomorrow, Don Pablo," Poison said. "For sure."

Escobar hung up. Poison put the phone back on the table, and said, "Next time, one of you guys answers the phone."

Finally, Oscar delivered the device. He left it with Juliana, who called Aguilar to tell him she had it. Aguilar and the others took her the second half of the money—half had been paid up front—and exchanged it for the device. Aguilar thought it looked crude: it was a big glob of some putty-looking stuff with wires enmeshed in it, and an electronic device with a softly glowing green light on the other end of the wires. "That's it?" he said. "I thought there would be dynamite or something." A separate item looked like a garage door opener.

"It's C-4," Juliana said. "There's a detonator in it. When you click this"—she indicated the door opener—"the detonator goes off and that's what blows the C-4. Otherwise, you can drop it, shoot it, set it on fire, and it won't go off. I wouldn't recommend any of those—especially setting it on fire, because the fumes are toxic. But it's perfectly safe and stable until it's detonated by a primary charge. Also, it's malleable, but don't mess with it. Oscar said it's in the shape you need for the result you want." She pointed to one side. "He said to be sure this side faces your target. The detonator's range is fifteen to twenty meters. Any closer and you'd be in danger, but any farther and it won't connect."

Snake-eyes had carried in the crumpled but reinforced box they would place it in, and Aguilar had brought in a briefcase full of U.S. dollars. He set the case on a table and opened it. Juliana riffled through a couple of stacks, appraising them. "Looks fine," she said. She gave Aguilar a quick hug. "Thanks for doing business with me. I hope to see you again."

"Me too," Aguilar said. He hadn't thought he would ever see her again after that first time, but it turned out that she was a handy person to know.

"Oh, how's that knife working out for you?"

"It's great," he said.

"You're the one who gave the Jaguar his claw?" Poison asked. "It's famous now. At least, in our world."

"Jaguar?" She smiled. "I like it. It suits you."

"Just because I'm spotted?"

"Because you're mysterious," she said. "And dangerous."

Aguilar liked the sound of that.

At four o'clock, Aguilar and the others strolled, seemingly casually, past the storm drain. Poison was carrying the box, and Aguilar had a gym bag over his shoulder with weapons inside. Just before reaching the drain, Aguilar stepped off the sidewalk and into the street. Poison followed. Aguilar paused beside the storm drain, turning this way and that, as if looking for something. On the sidewalk, Snake-eyes did the same. They were both trying to attract the attention of anyone who might otherwise notice Poison duck down and shove the box—rubber cement coating its bottom surface—into the drain.

A second later, Poison stepped back onto the curb, followed by Aguilar.

"Done," Poison said quietly. "Let's go to that place across the street and watch the fireworks."

They were seated by the windows facing the road, and had their coffee on the table before Osorio's convoy appeared down the block. Poison reached into the pocket of the light jacket he wore. The detonator, Aguilar knew, was in that pocket. Just seconds to go.

He took a sip of strong coffee, then set the mug on the table, bracing for the blast.

The front Suburban rolled to a stop at the corner. Behind it, the second one—Osorio's—obstructed his view of the storm drain. A terrible thought occurred to him: what if the SUV's armor blocked the radio signal from the garage door opener? Escobar would be furious.

Then a white flash drove all thoughts from his head.

Everything seemed to happen at once. Concrete soared into the air from the sidewalk above the storm drain. Windows in the nearest buildings shattered, and the front wall of the closest building buckled, stones dropping to the street. The Suburban lifted off the ground—and the pavement along with it—flipped a quarter-turn in midair, and crashed back to earth with the side facing the blast torn to shredded steel. All of it was accompanied by a deafening roar and a yellow-white fireball that seemed to shoot six meters into the air, then balloon out.

The windows of the café blew in, sending shards of glass into the patrons. Aguilar covered his face, but too late; he was vaguely aware that he'd been cut. He saw another shard jutting from his right upper arm—instinctively, he yanked it out, and blood spurted from the wound. He clapped his left hand over it, to stanch the bleeding.

Only then did he realize three things: he had been cut worse than he thought—not only the arm but his face was bleeding from multiple wounds, and his chest was bleeding through his shirt; he could barely hear anything other than a pronounced ringing in his ears; and gunmen were pouring from the front and rear Suburbans, looking for somebody to shoot.

And a fourth thing—a couple of the mercenaries went to Osorio's overturned vehicle and helped two survivors out through what was now the upper door.

"Shit!" Snake-eyes shouted. His voice sounded distant, as though he was speaking from somewhere beneath the ocean. "That's Osorio!"

Aguilar didn't have to hear him to know it was true. Osorio lived, despite their efforts.

That was why they'd brought the guns. Aguilar hoisted the bag from the floor, set it on the table, and unzipped it. Each man snatched up a Mini Uzi and two extra magazines. Poison said something Aguilar couldn't hear and stepped through the wreckage of the café's windows. Aguilar and Snake-eyes followed.

The scene was chaos—thick smoke and flames and onlookers rushing toward them and Osorio bleeding from dozens of wounds—which kept the mercenaries from noticing them at first. They were just three more of the blast's victims, disoriented, walking toward its epicenter. When the guns came up, the mercenaries realized their mistake and reacted, but they were too late. As they had arranged, Poison targeted Osorio while the other two raked their fire over the mercenaries. Osorio's head exploded under Poison's barrage.

Three of the mercenaries ducked behind the armored vehicles and returned fire, but with Osorio down, Aguilar and the others were already sprinting for the motorcycles they had left down the block. Aguilar fired over his shoulder, and when Poison reached his bike, he aimed a covering spray back toward the Suburbans.

Snake-eyes was slower to reach the motorcycles, and Aguilar saw that he was dragging his left leg. His jeans were drenched with blood. "Come on, man," Aguilar shouted. "You're almost there!"

Snake-eyes looked up, met his gaze—and a burst from the mercenaries' guns tore through his back, ripping his chest into bloody chunks. He flopped forward onto the street.

"Let's go!" Poison shouted. "He's done!"

Aguilar didn't want to leave Snake-eyes—the closest thing to a real friend he had among the *sicarios*—but Poison was right. Osorio was dead, and it was too late to do anything for Snake-eyes. If they weren't all to die here, they had to get going. He started his bike and took off. In case of pursuit, they'd planned to take different routes back to the apartment, so he made a right at the next corner while Poison peeled left.

The cost was high, but the job was done.

To *El Patrón*, that was the only thing that really mattered. The rest of it was details.

25

Escobar had tired of Hacienda Nápoles, or believed for security reasons that it was time to move to another of his many residences, or had simply arbitrarily decided to change locations. At any rate, in the week since the deaths of Osorio and Snake-eyes, preparations were made to leave Nápoles.

It was no simple matter. Household staff, a landscaping crew, and security personnel had to stay at Nápoles. The property had an airstrip, which would remain in use for outgoing shipments of cocaine and incoming ones of cash. Even with those people remaining behind, a small army would move. Trucks were loaded with personal possessions, equipment, and men. A separate convoy of vehicles carried cash and weapons, and the *sicarios* required to keep those safe. Finally, Escobar and his family had to be transported, in multiple vehicles, with *their* personal belongings.

In the midst of the bustle, Escobar found Aguilar supervising the loading of a truck. "Tata wants you to drive her and Juan Pablo," he said.

"Okay."

"I know you'll drive carefully."

"Of course."

"She trusts you. Likes you."

"She's a great lady. You're a lucky man."

"I know it," Escobar said. "She's more than I deserve."

Aguilar didn't know how to respond to that, so he left it alone. Escobar added, "There's something else I need for you to do."

"Anything, *Patrón*."

"I need to know that she's faithful."

"I'm sure she is."

"So am I. But still, it's in my nature to be suspicious. I don't have reason to think she's not, but I need to know. I want you to find out. Subtly, of course. Don't let her know that I told you to ask her, or anything like that. Just bring it up somehow, and try to draw her out."

"I'll try."

"If I thought she was sleeping with anyone else... I don't know what I would do. With her, I mean. I know what I would do to the man."

Aguilar had the impression that it would be painful indeed, and memorable for whatever brief length of time the man might live.

But he also had the impression that Escobar might indeed suspect that Tata was sleeping with someone— and that the "someone" in question was him. This wasn't just a request for information, it was a warning.

"I'm sure she would never be unfaithful, Don Pablo," he said. "She loves you; that much I know for certain. She told me so."

"And I love her," Escobar said. The unspoken

context was clear—although he loved Tata, he'd had many other lovers since they'd been married. Tata wasn't like that, Aguilar believed, but he didn't know how to convince Escobar of it. People often projected their worst qualities on those around them, and Escobar was a master.

"I'll bring it up casually," he promised. "She'll never know you were asking."

"Good," Escobar said. "And take care of her and my son."

"Always."

Once again, Tata sat up front, next to him. Juan Pablo was sleepy, and stretched out in the back seat. Aguilar was glad he wouldn't hear the conversation, but he couldn't think of a good way to introduce the topic. He made a couple of half-hearted attempts, then gave up. He would tell Escobar that she had sworn eternal fidelity and she was living up to that vow. Escobar would never ask her about a conversation he'd insisted had to be subtle and never traced back to him.

Almost as if she could read his mind, or found his silence uncomfortable, she raised a subject of her own. "I know you lost your wife," she said. "I'm so sorry for that. What about the rest of your family? Tell me about them."

"There's not much to tell. My mother fixes people's clothing. She made my clothing, when I was little, but she never thought she was good enough to make things for anyone outside the family. But if someone had a tear, or needed a patch or some pants made a little longer, anything like that she could do and nobody would ever know it had been mended. Sometimes she sold lottery tickets, too, for extra money, but not anymore. My father is a cobbler. He can practically rebuild a pair of shoes. I guess they both fix things that people need but that wear out or can be damaged, and they do it more cheaply than buying new things. I never thought about it that way before."

"They sound like good, hardworking people."

"They are. They were good to me."

"Mine were like that, too. Simple, good people."

"Do you see them much?" Aguilar asked.

"My father's gone. My mother, sometimes. My father never approved of Pablo, but my mother was willing to let me make my own decisions. How about you? Do you see yours?"

He hadn't, for ages. Since Luisa's funeral, and his father's comments there. He sent money and gifts, but without including a letter or a message of any kind. "Not often," he said.

"You should. After we get settled in at the ranch. It's not so far from Medellín. Ask Pablo for a few days off so you can visit them. Or I can ask him for you."

Aguilar worried about what Escobar might think if his wife asked for time off on his behalf. "No, that's okay. Thank you. I'll ask him, but you don't need to trouble yourself."

"It's no trouble, Jose."

"It's better if I ask myself, though. I will, I swear."

"All right. I'll give you two days, after we're moved in. If you haven't by then, I'll ask him myself."

"I will," he said again. *Sicarios* were often hesitant to ask Don Pablo for special favors, he had noticed. He had also seen Tata take it upon herself, as if she knew she could get away with things the men couldn't. But Escobar had confessed his suspicions to Aguilar,

216

and he didn't want to do anything to direct those suspicions toward him.

"Two days. That's all."

Settling in was as large an effort as moving out had been. Escobar had properties all over the country, some little more than hideouts he could escape to at a moment's notice, if the law or professional enemies came after him. But when he was planning to stay for a while, with his family and most of his organization, it was like moving an army. The trucks needed to be unloaded, a place found for everybody and everything.

This ranch was in the hills above Medellín. The property was considerably smaller than Nápoles, with only a few houses and a big barn on it. Most of it was open pasture, on which long-horned cattle grazed. The air smelled like cows, morning, noon, and night.

Aguilar wasn't sure he wanted to see his parents. But he had promised Tata. And after a couple of days of smelling cattle, he was ready for a change. He asked Escobar for permission—he'd already assured the man that Tata was absolutely faithful to him—and Escobar told him to go.

So he drove down the hill and into the city. His old neighborhood hadn't changed, that he could see. It still smelled of sewage and the paper mill. The same small shops lined the main street, with the same small houses on the streets behind that. He even saw old Pedro, the drunk, sitting on his usual bench outside the butcher shop. He couldn't say for sure if Pedro had ever been off that bench, or if perhaps he was glued to it.

Nothing had changed, and that remained true even

as he approached his parents' home. The trees along the street were green and full, the houses that had flowers blooming in front were the ones that always did, and the houses that looked like they should be torn down had somehow managed to stay upright, but in no better condition.

His parents' house was in between; neither of them had time or energy to plant and care for flowers, but the house was solid. It needed paint—it had been blue once, now faded to a pale gray—but structurally it was sound. Aguilar's father did most of the work on the house himself. It was, he said from time to time, much like fixing shoes, only on a bigger scale. The principle was the same: keep the wearer warm and dry and keep the weather out.

Aguilar parked and sat in the car for a few minutes. He had a suitcase in back, in case he stayed for a few days, but he didn't think he wanted to take it in at first. No one had invited him. He didn't even know if they were home, or if they had plans. Except that they were always home, and outside of working they never seemed to have plans. He had no reason to believe that anything inside the house had changed any more than the exterior had. Anyway, it was almost six; his mother would be preparing dinner and his father would be complaining about the wait.

Finally, he told himself to stop delaying. They were his parents, they'd be glad to see him. They would welcome him, probably want to serve him a big dinner, and would want him to stay for as long as he could. No sense putting it off.

He got out of the car, leaving the suitcase in the trunk for now, and walked up to the front door. It was locked, so he knocked on it. After a little while, he heard muttering on the other side, then it opened and his father stood there. The man had changed; he looked older, his cheeks sunken in, his hair grayer and sparser on his head. He had a streak of boot polish on his nose and cheek.

"Hello, Papa," Aguilar said.

"Oh, it's you." His father turned to shout inside. "Sofia, it's the boy!"

He looked at Aguilar, without expression or another word, until she came to the door. "Get out of the way, Gilbert," she said. "Let me see my son."

"Hello, Mama."

She brushed past her husband with her arms out, and drew Aguilar into them. She smelled of the chili peppers she had probably spent much of the morning roasting, and she was soft and warm. "It's so good to see you!" she said. "You've been away so long!"

"It's good to see you, Mama," Aguilar said. "You too, Papa."

"You might as well come inside," his father said. "Dinner's late as it is."

"I can take you out someplace," Aguilar offered.

"Nonsense," his mother said. "There's plenty. And Gilbert is wrong, it's not late, because you weren't here yet. It'll be ready in no time."

"I don't want to be a bother."

"Then you might have called first, or not come right at dinnertime."

His mother punched her husband's arm, hard. "Gilbert! This is our only son! He's a grown man, a serious man. A police officer. Treat him with respect." Still gripping Aguilar, she led him inside the house and kicked the door closed.

"I'm not with the police anymore," he said. He

followed his mother down the narrow hallway and into the small kitchen. It smelled like home.

"With that gangster, then?" his father asked. "Do you read the *Diario*? Did you hear the editor, Osorio, was murdered by those thugs?"

Aguilar didn't want to lie to his parents. But he didn't want to tell them the truth. When his father mentioned the killing, he remembered his last glimpse of Snake-eyes, bleeding out in the street but still alive, his gaze locked on Aguilar's, beseeching. Could he have been helped? Maybe. But the mercenaries' rounds had torn through his back and out his chest; severe organ damage was a certainty. It would have taken an immediate medical response to have any hope of saving him, and with the mercenaries still gunning for them, that was impossible.

Osorio's death wasn't his concern. He'd known when he called out Don Pablo that he was taking his life in his hands. Snake-eyes had known that, too, but he'd just been doing a job. Osorio had been a glory-seeker, trying to inflate his own position by tying himself to the cartel.

"Osorio had plenty of enemies," Aguilar said. "He's been making them his entire career. You can't blame Don Pablo for that."

"I do. Who else would have attacked him in such a way? Seven innocent bystanders were also killed, in the street and the nearby buildings, in addition to Osorio and his bodyguards."

Aguilar hadn't heard about that. Oscar had warned them about what he called "collateral damage." They'd dismissed his concerns. Escobar wanted Osorio gone; anyone else who got hurt was just in the way. He sat at the little kitchen table, shrugged.

"Their bad luck, I guess."

"So Luisa's death, that was also just bad luck?"

Was it? Montoya and the others had attacked the restaurant to eliminate an enemy of Escobar's. Aguilar had taken her death very personally indeed, and Montoya had paid the ultimate price for it.

In the end, though, Luisa was also collateral damage.

"I guess, in a way."

"Can we talk about something less sad?" Aguilar's mother asked. "Thank you for all the gifts you've been sending. Your father gripes, but he enjoys watching the big color television."

"It's a good set," Aguilar's father admitted, eyes downcast. Aguilar saw some of the gifts he'd sent in the kitchen: a brand-new coffee maker, an expensive blender, a set of pans.

"How are you eating, Jose? You look like you've gained weight."

"I'm eating well, Mama. It's not your cooking, but it's good, and there's always plenty."

"Of course there is," his father said. "Escobar likes to pretend he's a man of the people, but he always makes sure he has the most of everything."

"He is a man of the people. He's been very generous. You can see it all over Medellín."

"Sure, if there are news cameras in the area. Charity is charity if it's done quietly. If it's done in the press, it's publicity."

"I guess there's nothing I can say about him that you won't complain about, Papa."

"Since I thought we raised an honest man, that's true."

Aguilar turned away from the bitter disappointment in the man's eyes.

His mother rescued the moment by bringing plates of *bandeja paisa* to the table. The aroma yanked Aguilar back to his childhood, and after grace—he crossed himself and spoke the words, though he hadn't been to Mass in months and thought God had turned His back on him—he happily dug in.

During dinner, conversation was minimal. His mother brought him up to date on neighbors and relatives, and made a couple of pointed references to the eligible daughter of a family friend. Aguilar had no interest in her; he remembered her as silly, flighty, and dumb, so he made sure not to express any interest. He was able to avoid speaking much by keeping his mouth full. He noticed his father's disapproving glances, though, and the way his mother's gaze drifted back and forth between the two men, as if ready to intervene at any time.

After the meal, Aguilar helped his mother with the dishes, then said, "Well, I need to get back."

"You can't stay? Even for the night?"

"The master whistles," his father said. "The dog must obey."

Aguilar resisted the impulse to turn and look at his father. The man still sat at the table, arms folded over his chest, a dour expression on his face. "I'm sorry, Mama. I have too much work to do. It's a busy time."

"Do whatever's best," she said. "Just take care of yourself. Make sure you're eating right and getting enough sleep and going to Mass."

"I am," Aguilar lied.

"I wish you could stay for the night."

"Me too." Another lie.

His father muttered a few words in parting, and then Aguilar was out the door. Relief washed over him like a summer breeze on a hot day.

He had grown up with those people, in that house. Why didn't he feel like he belonged there? He had felt like a visitor from another planet, who had nothing in common with the residents of this one.

It had been claustrophobic in there. The rooms had been tiny, close. Underlying the odor of his mother's cooking had been the stench of his family's failures. They'd never done anything with their lives. His father still fixed shoes for other people, and wore the stains of polish on his face like some kind of badge of honor. His mother repaired clothing. They'd lived in the same house for all their married years, raised one son, and they would probably die there without having accomplished anything to be remembered for.

He was glad he hadn't taken his suitcase inside. Spending a night there would have driven him mad. He might have had to kill himself, if his father hadn't killed him first.

He started the car and headed for the ranch, without looking back.

26

"DON'T UNPACK YOUR bag," La Quica said when Aguilar got back to the ranch building they were using as a barracks.

"What? Why?"

"*El Patrón* wants some guys to go with him to Miami. He said if you got back in time, he wanted you to be part of the group."

"Miami? In North America?"

"That's the only Miami I know of," La Quica said. He ran a hand through his unkempt mop of dark hair. "You speak English, right?"

"Some. I could talk to Kyle when he was here."

"That's why he wants you, I think. So are you in?"

"Don Pablo wants me to go?"

"Do you have beans in your ears?"

"Hell yes, I'm in!" Aguilar had never been out of Colombia. The trip to Cartagena was the farthest from Medellín he'd traveled. He'd never been on an airplane, either, and always wondered what it would be like. Would the people on the ground look like ants?

Then he remembered a problem. "I don't have a passport, though."

"Don't worry, that'll be taken care of."

"When do we leave?"

"Day after tomorrow," La Quica said.

"That soon?"

La Quica walked away, shaking his head and muttering. Aguilar thought he heard "Fucking beans in his ears," but he might have been mistaken.

The next day, he had a new passport with his picture and his real name in it. It looked official, and for all he knew, it was. Passports ordinarily took time, but when Don Pablo wanted something done, it was done quickly and without fuss. He imagined some poor sap in the passport office had stayed up all night, preparing one for every member of the team. That person would be exhausted today, but he would have received a hefty cash bonus, or been relieved of some personal obligation, or both.

That afternoon, Escobar came into the room he was sharing with Trigger, Jairo, and Sure Shot, all of whom were also on the team selected for the Miami trip. He and Jairo had their suitcases open on their beds. Aguilar had just put his Beretta in his.

"*Patrón*, can I bring my MAC-10 as well?" he asked.

"You can't even bring the pistol," Escobar replied.

"I can't?"

"Too much trouble at Customs. We're businessmen, flying to Miami for meetings on a commercial airline, and that's what we have to look like. That goes for all of you," Escobar clarified. "No guns. We'll get some on the ground there, for the length of our stay." He looked back at Aguilar. "You can bring your knife, just keep it packed in your suitcase. If anyone asks in Customs, tell them it's a gift for an American friend."

"What are we going to Miami for?" Trigger asked.

"Business," Escobar said. "We'll have some fun while we're there, so bring some clothes for going out at night. I'll explain more when we get there."

They had an early morning flight out of Bogotá, so spent the night before in a hotel near the El Dorado International Airport. Aguilar could barely sleep, and in the morning he was up before the alarm, showered and ready for the flight.

Escobar had a window seat in first class, with La Quica on the aisle beside him. The others were in coach, but that was fine with Aguilar. He took a window seat, with Trigger in the center seat and Jairo on the end, and Sure Shot across the aisle from Jairo.

"Have you ever been in a plane?" he asked.

"Not me," Trigger said. He was still in his teens, and Aguilar doubted that he'd been out of his neighborhood before Escobar hired him.

"I have," Jairo said. "But not a big one like this. I flew with a shipment to Panama once, when Don Pablo was worried that the guys on the ground there were ripping him off."

"Were they?"

"Yeah. We took care of it, though."

Aguilar knew what that meant. He briefly wondered how many people had died to further Escobar's business interests. He didn't stress about it, though; he was too excited to be in an airplane on his way to the United States.

The stewardess for their section was a black woman with long legs and a brilliant, toothy smile. Aguilar watched as she demonstrated the seatbelts and pointed out the emergency exits, and wished she would just stand in the aisle for the whole flight, looking pretty.

Then the airplane started to move, and his heart jumped. He clutched his armrests. "We're going!" He looked out the window. "We're still on the ground, though."

"We have to taxi out to the runway," Jairo explained. "Then probably sit and wait until it's clear. Then we taxi some more, faster and faster, until we take off. Don't worry, you'll know when we're airborne."

Jairo was right. It took another fifteen minutes before they had a clear runway, then the plane started forward. Aguilar listened to the engines race as it picked up speed, staring out his window at the scenery whipping past. When it left the ground, he swallowed and crossed himself, just in case. As they rose above the city, he was too excited to be worried, watching Bogotá pass by. They gained altitude quickly, and soon were over the mountains, then banked and flew almost due north. The seatbelt light blinked off, and the no-smoking light, and soon smoke wafted throughout the whole cabin.

The flight took about four hours, during which time the friendly stewardess brought drinks and lunch in a plastic tray, and scowled when Jairo pinched her ass. When they dropped down toward Miami, Aguilar thought his eardrums were going to burst out of his head. He distracted himself by watching the glittering ocean and the tall buildings growing larger and closer with every second. Finally, they were on the ground. He shook his head, trying to clear his ears, and waited to deplane.

Customs took an hour, but they got through it, and Lion met them on the other side. Aguilar had heard about him, but had never met him. He was handsome, with his brown hair slicked back away from his forehead and a neat beard and mustache. He wore what looked like an expensive silk T-shirt, white jeans, and leather loafers, and had gold jewelry at his neck and wrists. When Escobar saw him, he threw his arms around the man in a warm embrace.

"Lion!" he shouted. Still holding on, he looked over his shoulder at the others. "Boys, this is the Lion, my main man in Miami. He's been in charge here since day one." He introduced Lion to the others.

When they got outside, the air was humid and heavy, settling over Aguilar's skin like a hot, wet blanket. But there were palm trees and shining buildings all around, and taking it all in made Aguilar forget the weather. The airport seemed to be right in the middle of the city.

"Where are we staying?" La Quica asked as they walked through the parking lot. "I've heard good things about the Mutiny."

"The Mutiny's a dive for drug dealers," Lion said.

La Quica laughed. "Sounds perfect! That's what we are!"

"I mean, they have a box in the champagne cave where you can lock up your guns. It's fun, but it's not classy. Don Pablo's a class act, so he needs a nice place."

"So where are we?"

"I got you the penthouse suite at the Fontainebleau," Lion said. "It's the classic Miami Beach landmark. You'll love it."

"I already love it," Escobar said.

"It's in the heart of the Millionaire's Row district."

"Now I love it even more."

"Have you guys ever been to Miami?" Lion asked. "I know Pablo has."

None of the others had. They told him that, and as they reached his convertible Trans Am, Lion said, "I would have brought the Ferrari, but all of you guys wouldn't fit in it. As it is, you'll have to be friendly back there. I'll take you down Tamiami Trail and we'll cruise through Little Havana. It's not home, but it's closer to it than Miami Beach is."

"Lion's from home," Escobar explained. "He knew Gustavo there, growing up. But he's lived in North America for a long time. Poor bastard."

"You guys will like Little Havana," Lion said. "But you'll love Miami Beach. Sun, sand, bikinis, and the most beautiful women in the world. Including Colombia."

"No way," La Quica said. "Prettier than Colombian ladies?"

"You'll see."

Lion was true to his word. Little Havana looked and smelled much like Medellín, albeit with Cuban and American variations. After a little time there, they headed for what Lion called the causeway, which took them over the narrow channel of Biscayne Bay, past fishing boats, pleasure yachts, and enormous cruise ships. After briefly passing across a small island, they shot out over the water again. Massive cranes to the right indicated the seaport. Escobar waved toward them. "We've moved so much product through there, you wouldn't believe it," he said. "Miami has been very good to us."

Then high-rise buildings loomed ahead. "Almost there, boys," Escobar said. "Our home for the next few days. I think you'll enjoy it."

"I started enjoying it as soon as we got here," Trigger said. Aguilar liked him—he wasn't the sharpest tack in the box, but he was almost always in a good mood. For a killer, he was surprisingly optimistic. And although some of the *sicarios* were valuable because they were willing to kill, Trigger was actually one of the better shots among them, and sometimes gave marksmanship lessons to the rest.

When the causeway ended, Lion stayed on Fifth Street and took them into South Beach. "This is where the fashion models hang out," he said as he made a left on Ocean Drive. "You won't believe how tiny bikinis can get until you see them on the girls here."

It looked like heaven to Aguilar. To their left were buildings housing high-end hotels, restaurants, and bars. To their right, only a grassy park and a few trees separated them from glorious white-sand beaches and the Atlantic Ocean. On the sidewalks and sitting in the open-air bars were women who must have been some of the fashion models Lion had mentioned.

Finally, they pulled up to the sweeping white façade of the Fontainebleau. Bellmen were at the car before they could even get out. "Checking in?" one asked, wheeling a gold cart up to the trunk.

"Yes," Lion said. "My friends are." He opened the trunk and supervised the unloading of the bags onto the cart. When there was only one bag left—which hadn't come with them from Colombia—he picked it up. "I'll carry that one."

The penthouse suite was on the thirty-seventh floor. Aguilar had never seen such luxury, even in Escobar's homes. Each man had his own bedroom, with a huge TV and a bathroom—and each bathroom had its own telephone! The floors were marble, the beds like tethered clouds, the views practically infinite.

After everyone had picked his room—Don Pablo, of course, had the largest, most sumptuous—they met in the suite's huge foyer. Lion put the bag he'd carried on the table and unzipped it. "I brought Walther PPKs for everyone. If you need something more sophisticated, let me know, but I figured you could carry these easily without anybody noticing. This isn't Colombia, and you won't be able to get away with anything you want just by mentioning Pablo's name, so you don't want to get picked up carrying a piece if you can help it."

"I have my knife, too," Aguilar said.

Lion grinned. "I've heard about that knife," he said. "Caldwell told me about you."

"Caldwell's cool," Aguilar said.

"About that," Escobar said, his expression suddenly grim. He sat down heavily. "Kyle Caldwell is why we're here."

"What's up, *Patrón*?" Jairo asked.

"He lost a shipment. A hundred and twenty kilos. He called and said the Miami cops seized it, but he got away without getting busted."

"Except Lehder and I have been watching the newspapers," Lion said. "A seizure like that would have made the news, but this one didn't."

"So what do you think happened?" Trigger asked.

"I think he's selling it himself, freelance, and pocketing the whole take," Escobar said. He sounded sorrowful. "I trusted him. He makes millions, but he's never been satisfied with that. Always wanting more. It's a sickness with some people."

"I can't say I never expected it," Lion added. "He

231

complains a lot. He spends a lot, and he gambles. You can't trust a gambler."

"Where is he?" La Quica asked.

"We don't know," Lion said.

"He'll meet with us tomorrow to discuss things," Escobar added. "Today... let's have some fun."

27

THEY DONNED SWIMMING trunks and went to the beach, where Lion arranged a private cabana for them. There, they drank good liquor and splashed in the waves. Lion's promise of beautiful women in tiny bikinis was true. Luxurious yachts and massive cruise and cargo ships cut across the horizon. Aguilar assumed that a city as large as Miami would have its share of poverty, but he hadn't seen it—even Little Havana appeared fairly well-to-do. Back home, it was everywhere, but here, if it existed, it was kept carefully away from public view. The lives he saw looked charmed, all sunshine and good times.

Later, half-drunk, they had a huge dinner at one of the hotel's ritziest restaurants, washed down with yet more alcohol.

After dinner, they sat in the suite for a while, drinking and swapping stories. Finally, Lion announced that it was time to go out. Aguilar went back to his room and dressed in the nicest clothes he'd brought: a pastel Gianni Versace suit with a flowered silk shirt left open to his midsection, a couple of thin gold chains around his neck, and Bruno Magli loafers with silk socks. He spent some time in the bathroom working on his hair, before finally deciding there was nothing more he could do about it. Besides, with his skin, most people didn't even notice that he had hair. He looked as good as he was going to look, but he was sure all the other guys—the ones without jaguar skin—would attract women before he did.

For that matter, he wasn't sure he was ready to be with another woman. Everyone expected to bring somebody back to the suite—that, after all, was one of the reasons for all the separate bedrooms. In theory, the idea appealed to him. It had been a long time, and a man had needs, after all.

But the long shadow of Luisa lay over all thoughts of intimacy. Would he be able to make love to someone without thinking about her? He supposed if he were drunk enough, he might. But then how would he feel in the morning? Relieved that he'd gotten through it, or wracked with guilt?

He determined to just go with the flow and see what happened. If there was a woman that he found attractive, and she wasn't repelled by his scarred flesh, maybe the questions would answer themselves.

When they met up again in the foyer, Escobar was the only one who hadn't changed. He had on the same white jeans, sneakers, and the striped shirt he'd worn on the airplane. He looked over the others. "You look good," he said.

Aguilar supposed that was a sign of the confidence that came with vast wealth and power. Escobar didn't have to dress up. The very fact that he didn't would draw people to him, because they would know that he was *someone*. The other guys would be competing with every other man in the club, each of whom would have dressed in his finest, while *El Patrón* would just sit back and watch the cream of the crop gravitate toward him.

Lion had hired a white stretch limousine almost as long as a soccer field. When they showed up in it, Aguilar knew, they would attract attention. And it would provide plenty of space in which to take women back to the suite, later on. It seemed Lion had thought of everything.

When they arrived at the club, Aguilar could feel the bass notes booming through his bones. A line waited outside, and a crew of burly bouncers vetted people carefully before letting them in. Some walked away dejectedly and others sat on the curb crying, having been denied entrance.

Lion swaggered up to the nearest bouncer and spoke into his ear for a minute. Aguilar couldn't tell if he also slipped the man some cash, but the man threw Escobar a wide grin and beckoned them all toward the door, bypassing the line completely. People in line watched with puzzlement, admiration, or scorn. Lion's strategy had worked—everyone in line saw them exit the huge white limo and be waved straight inside. By now they would be objects of curiosity and interest, and when these people got inside—those who were admitted—they'd be itching to satisfy that curiosity.

"He's a good host, Lion," Aguilar said to Trigger as they reached the door. Trigger replied, but his words were lost in the roar of music swelling forth when the door swung open for them.

Inside, the place was rocking.

Bodies gyrating to a disco beat jammed the dance

floor. He saw people he recognized, movie stars and musicians. He had never paid much attention to celebrities, so he couldn't come up with any names, but he knew the faces.

What light there was bounced all over the place, never still but flashing, moving, multicolored. Various smells—tobacco and clove cigarettes, pot, sweat, cologne, perfume—battled for supremacy. A hostess led the party to a large, private booth, where champagne bottles waited in ice-filled buckets and fluted glasses were already in position. The men took seats and the hostess—young, slim, possibly one of the fashion models Lion had mentioned—opened a bottle and poured champagne for everyone. "Enjoy yourselves," she shouted. She touched her nose with a knuckle and sniffled before whirling around and disappearing into the crowd. *Great*, Aguilar thought, *our hostess has a cold*.

La Quica drained his first glass and poured himself another. Sure Shot was close behind. Escobar, Aguilar noted, only sipped at his. He sat back in his seat, smiling, looking out at the scene before him. *He looks like a king*, Aguilar thought, *watching his court. Deciding who'll share his bed tonight and who'll lose their heads by morning*.

Aguilar drank his, not gulping it down but not sipping. Trigger had barely touched his, but Aguilar had noticed that he didn't drink much. After his second round, La Quica slammed his glass down on the table. "I'm dancing!" he announced. "Anybody else?"

"Dancing with who?" Aguilar asked.

La Quica laughed and gestured toward the dance floor. "Everybody!"

Aguilar's back was to the dance floor. He swiveled

in his seat and saw what La Quica meant. There were few visible couples or partners; most people simply moved, many with their eyes closed. They were staying with the beat of the music, or not. Many seemed lost inside themselves, involved in a kind of communal orgy of solitude.

He wondered if he could reach that state. Self-consciousness had been a constant since childhood, as a result of his burns and the knowledge that wherever he went, everyone noticed him. The dancers before him seemed to have left self-consciousness behind. They looked good, they knew, but they didn't care who was looking. Maybe that was a quality reserved for the beautiful.

While he pondered, La Quica and Sure Shot moved onto the floor. Right away, they were dancing, drawing nods or smiles from women who could have escaped from magazine covers or centerfolds. As quickly as those silent acknowledgements were made, they were withdrawn; eyes closed again or gazes blank, empty, as if to say, "Feel free to dance near me, but you're not dancing *with* me."

That might feel like dismissal, Aguilar thought. On the other hand, it didn't judge. He polished off his glass and said, "I'm dancing, too."

"I'll come," Jairo said.

Trigger, Lion, and Escobar remained at the table, happy for now to drink and observe. Aguilar and Jairo went to the edge of the dance floor. It seemed hotter here, more humid, louder, the bass notes rising up through the floor and making Aguilar's teeth ache. He started bobbing his head, connecting to the beat, then moving his hands, then giving himself up to the music. He lost track of Jairo, and everyone else. As

237

he eased into the midst of the crowd, he bumped into people and they ran into him, and each was forgiven with a quick smile or nod. A gorgeous brunette locked eyes with him and matched his steps for a minute, then spun away.

The songs blended into one another. He didn't recognize any of them, but that didn't matter. Here, it was about the beat, about letting the music take control of legs and arms and torso. It was loud enough to drive most conscious thought from his mind, and the alcohol he had consumed throughout the afternoon and evening helped deal with the rest. He was barely aware that self-consciousness had fled. Maybe he looked like a fool, trying to keep up with these beautiful people although he had jaguar skin and didn't know any of the right dance steps. He didn't care. He was here, he was alive, he was flesh and bone and muscle, drive and ambition, strengths and fears and weaknesses, but he was one with the music and with the bodies moving around him.

He felt the almost hypnotic spell break when he saw a stunning young woman in a slinky dress open a kind of locket hanging on a slender chain around her neck. She raised it to her right nostril, plugged the left with a thumb, and snorted. She seemed to disappear into herself for a moment, then almost forgetfully closed the locket, and broke into a grin. She kept on dancing, but grabbed onto the guy nearest her— Aguilar couldn't tell if they were together, but the guy accepted her overture with a smile—and pressed herself against him.

Cocaine.

He almost never saw it used, back home. Sure, there was a small market for it, but not among the people he knew. Escobar frowned upon its use by his people—every gram snorted was one not sold for a profit. As far as Aguilar knew, Escobar had never even tried the stuff that had made him a billionaire. Aguilar never had, either.

Once he was aware of it, he saw more and more. When people dabbed at their noses, he realized, it was because they'd just taken some. The hostess didn't have a cold, she'd snorted before they came in, or maybe even while leading them to their table. Dancers carried small containers of it in their pockets and offered it to those around them, or sniffed it up themselves.

It wasn't the music that drove these dancers. Not community, or sex—though that was certainly part of it—or freedom. It was coke, most or all of it brought to Miami by Pablo Escobar. Was that why he sat up there like a conquering hero? Did he know that his product was everywhere here, that if all the cases and vials and containers were opened at once, a snowstorm would result?

Suddenly, Aguilar felt less like dancing. He needed to get off the dance floor, but not back to Escobar, not right now. He needed to pee anyway, so he figured out where the restrooms were and worked his way in that direction. It took a little while to navigate through the bodies, but soon enough he was in a tight, dimly lit hallway. A few people leaned against the walls, taking a break from the dancing, he guessed, or waiting their turn. One of them was a girl of more than surpassing beauty, with a figure that could have landed her a centerspread in any nudie magazine Aguilar had ever seen. She offered a wan smile as he squeezed past.

In the men's room, a guy in tight pants and an open shirt leaned over the little steel counter above the sink, a rolled-up dollar bill in his hand, snorting thick white lines. Other men stood at the urinals, including one propped up with one hand against the wall, head drooping as if he could barely stay awake. "Save some for me, Nicky," he said.

The guy at the sink poured more powder out on the counter and used a razor blade to divide it into straight lines. When he handed the bill over to the second man, Aguilar saw that it was a hundred dollars, not a single one. "All yours," the second man said, tilting his head toward the urinal.

Aguilar took his place there and unzipped. Behind him, he heard loud snorting, followed by, "Fuck yes, that's better."

When he was finished, there were already men at the other urinals and some waiting in line. A couple of them were sniffling or rubbing their noses, actions Aguilar thought he would forever associate with cocaine use from that day forward.

Back in the narrow corridor, the woman he'd noticed before was still there. She had turned to face the men's room, and when she saw him coming, a shy smile crept across her face and she moved away from the wall, half-blocking his way.

"Hi there," she said.

"Hello."

"Oh, what a cute accent! Where are you from?"

"I'm Colombian," he said.

She pursed her lips and narrowed her eyes. "Ooh, mysterious Colombia! Are you a gangster? Some kind of narco kingpin?" She laughed at herself, and he joined in.

"Is that all you think of when you hear Colombia?" he asked. "We have a great culture. Writers, artists, engineers, architects, everything you have here."

"I was teasing," she said, clutching his arm. "I'm sorry. I just thought you looked cute and I wanted to get to know you."

"Cute?" he echoed. "Me?"

"Handsome, I mean." She batted her eyes, a little too obviously, he thought. If this was flirting, she wasn't that good at it. Maybe she'd never had to be, with that face and that body.

"You're blind. Beautiful, but blind."

She squeezed the arm tighter. "No, I'm not. Maybe we can find someplace quiet and get to know each other better."

"Quiet? In here?"

Still holding his arm, she pressed the back of her other hand against his crotch and licked her lips. "Maybe outside there's an alley. Or in your car? I could make you feel really good."

"I'm sure you could," Aguilar said. This had suddenly turned strange. Girls in Colombia weren't this aggressive.

Unless they wanted something.

"What are we waiting for, then?" She was standing so close that her breasts pressed against the arm she was holding onto. He could feel her breath against his skin. He wanted her; he could feel himself growing hard under the pressure of her hand.

"What do you... what do you want?" he asked, not sure of how to better phrase it in English.

"I just need a little something to get me through the night," she said. She released his arm long enough to tap her nose. "A little toot?"

"Cocaine?"

"Shh!" She laughed. "Not so loud!"

"It's not exactly a secret in this place, is it? Or hard to find?"

"I thought you looked nice. And like you might be fun, and maybe generous."

"I don't have any drugs," he said.

"But you can get some."

"No. No, I really can't."

She arched her back, pushing her breasts against him with more force. "You're sure?"

"I'm sure," he said.

She let go of him and her face went hard. "Your loss," she said. Then she turned away, back toward the restrooms. Waiting for somebody else, he figured.

He needed to get out of here, needed some fresh air. Suddenly, this place had become suffocating.

He pushed his way through the dance floor crowd again, this time bothered by the elbow jabs and knees and people stepping on him. His mood had turned sour, and he didn't think he was getting back the temporary high he'd felt before, when he had given in to the throbbing music and the undulating masses of flesh. People at tables and booths on the perimeter were cutting lines right on the tables and snorting them. At the door, he nodded to the bouncer, to be sure he would be readmitted when he was ready to go back in.

Outside, the night was still warm. Balmy. He had to walk halfway out into the parking lot before he stopped feeling the music vibrating through him. Here, it was calm, quiet. He realized he was sweating; inside, it had been barely noticeable, but now it was like he'd just stepped from the shower.

Aguilar held his shirt open, trying to let the faint breeze dry his skin, when he heard what sounded like sobs mixed with curses. The voice was vaguely familiar. One of the guys? No, the words he heard were English, he was certain. An American. Lion spoke English like an American, and Kyle Caldwell was American. One of them, then? He followed the sound to a silver Maserati. The front door was open, the interior light on, but he couldn't see anyone.

Stepping around the car, he found a man on his knees in the parking lot, shoulders and head inside the car. He wasn't Lion or Caldwell, but he was clearly in a bad state. The curses and sobs were louder. Maybe he was sick. "Hey, do you need help?" Aguilar asked. "You maybe need a doctor or something?"

The man drew himself out of the car and Aguilar was astonished to find that he recognized him. He couldn't remember the name—one of those North American names that all sounded the same—but he was a movie star who'd appeared in five or six action movies that Aguilar had seen. With his wavy dark hair, square jaw, and weightlifter's build, he was the guy who beat all the villains, saved the day, and bedded the girl in the end.

Now, though, the hair hung in damp strings around his face. His cheeks were slick with tears and mucus, and dark threads were stuck to it. "What?" he asked.

"I wanted to know if you needed a doctor or something. Are you okay?"

"I spilled my stash on the floor," he said. "I'm just trying to—"

He stopped mid-sentence, as if speaking took too much of the energy better spent on other things. Then he stuck his head back into the car. Aguilar heard snorting, and realized the man—rich, famous, extraordinarily handsome—was snorting coke out of the carpet where his feet went when he drove.

"Hey," he started. But he watched the movie star's back ripple as he sucked up the drug, and he decided not to finish.

The man had other things on what was left of his mind.

28

NOT YET READY to go back inside, Aguilar walked around the building. There was an alley running behind it, as the woman inside had said. Illumination was scant; a couple of lights mounted high up on the building, and the faint glow of nearby streetlamps. It smelled like piss, vomit, and booze. Aguilar felt glass crunch under his feet. He almost turned around, but then saw a shadowed form halfway down the alley. It looked like a man, in seeming distress. He was reaching out, hands against the wall. Maybe just puking, but Aguilar wanted to make sure he was okay.

Then he saw the woman. On her knees in the filthy alley, in front of the man, her head bobbing. He couldn't be sure it was the one from the hallway, but in the dim light, it looked like her. So she'd found someone to supply her needs after all.

He turned away, disgusted with himself and the entire human race. He roamed the parking lot until he found the white limo, and the driver let him inside. He sank into the rich leather seats. This whole thing—the trip, the luxurious limousine, the over-the-top hotel room—had been paid for by cocaine money.

He'd never seen so much of it in just a few minutes. Less than an hour, and he had encountered seemingly dozens of people using it, or looking for more.

The luxury? The limousines and hotel rooms, the paychecks and bonuses he got from Don Pablo? He liked those. He was making more money every month than his parents had in their entire lives. He was living in a manner he would never have believed. Sure, he'd had to rearrange his principles, adjust his moral code. But that had happened one step at a time, little by little. He had seen it happening, and made the choice at each step.

This, though—it hit him like a club to the head. He'd thought that cocaine pumped people up, helped them function, made them feel more confident and alive. And maybe it did that. But its effects were more extreme than that, more pernicious, and he hadn't understood that until tonight. He had thought there was something glamorous about it. That glamor was gone.

He was still sitting there when the others came out of the club. Six women came with them. They were uniformly gorgeous, but "women" was a stretch in some cases; although he understood that the legal age to be in the club was twenty-one, two of them looked as young as fifteen or sixteen. Those two flanked Escobar when he took his seat, the others clung to La Quica, Poison, Sure Shot, and Jairo. Trigger looked dejected.

"We wondered where you were, Jaguar," Escobar said.

"I had a headache," Aguilar said. "The loud music, the smoke— I had to get out."

"Sorry you didn't get a date. Maybe you guys can

share yours with Jaguar and Trigger."

Poison squeezed the sumptuous breasts of his woman. "Sure," he said. "There's plenty to go around."

Aguilar didn't want to take advantage of that offer, but also didn't want to say so here, in front of everyone. If the offer was made later, in private, he would decline. He had too much to think about; having sex with Poison's playmate, especially after Poison had already taken his turn, was a giant step too far.

Aguilar grabbed a bottle of bourbon from the bar and took it into his room. There, he locked the door and turned on the TV to drown out the sounds that he was already hearing—laughter, squeals, slaps—and those that would doubtless follow soon. He undressed and climbed into the bed, which was more comfortable than any he'd ever been in, and drank until he couldn't keep his eyes open.

He didn't stir until a loud banging on his door woke him. Sunlight streamed in through the windows; he'd forgotten to close the curtains. Groggy, his stomach turning flips, he staggered to the door.

"What is it?"

"Open up." The voice was Jairo's. Aguilar braced himself against the jamb and cracked the door.

"What's up?"

"Get some clothes on," Jairo said. "Take a quick shower if you have to. There's coffee and breakfast in the dining room, and we have a meeting in an hour."

"A meeting? With who?"

"Caldwell."

"What? Where?"

"He has an apartment here. Come on, get busy. We don't want to be late."

"Are your whores gone?"

"They weren't whores," Jairo said. "Too bad you missed all the fun."

"I'll be out in a little while," Aguilar said. He closed the door, and heard Jairo walk away.

In the shower, he wondered how the meeting would go. He liked Caldwell, and the guy had always been friendly to him. He hoped there was a good explanation for the missing product. They could settle this quickly, maybe spend some more time on the beach, and go home.

Caldwell's apartment was on the third floor of an Art Deco building in South Beach. The building was pink, the apartment huge, open, and sun-splashed, with a view onto Ocean Drive and the beach beyond. Caldwell had a telescope on the balcony, aimed down toward the beach instead of up at the stars.

He opened the door with a grin, and greeted Aguilar, Jairo, and Poison with hugs and back-slaps. He wore jeans, a silk T-shirt, and sandals. "It's great to see you guys," he said in Spanish. "I hope you're having a good time here."

"Great time," Poison said. "Miami women are delicious."

"Yes, they are," Caldwell said. He ushered the visitors into plush leather chairs arranged around a glass-topped coffee table, and took a seat in one on the end. "I love visiting Colombia, but I have to say, Miami has its advantages."

"Don Pablo appreciates the years you've put in working with him here. You've made him a lot of money."

"He's done the same for me. I love Pablo."

"He loves you," Poison said. On the way over, they'd decided that Poison would be their primary spokesperson, with the others chiming in only as necessary. Everybody was strapped, and they had to assume that Caldwell was, too, and probably also had guns hidden around the apartment. "But he's disappointed. You know why we're here."

"Yes, yes, of course. An unfortunate situation."

"Yes," Poison agreed. "That's a lot of product to misplace."

"It wasn't misplaced, man. It was seized. Confiscated."

"That's a lot of product to be seized, then. Tell us what happened. Why was that much all together in one place?"

Caldwell sucked in a deep breath, blew it out. "You guys need a drink or anything?"

"No," Poison said. "Let's just talk."

"Okay. Here's the deal. I have great contacts in Miami, as you know. I've moved literally tons of product for Pablo here. But it's a finite market, you see what I mean? Pablo keeps sending more and more here, and Lion and I have to figure out how to unload it. But there are only so many dealers we can work with. We have to stick with people we know and trust, right?"

"Of course."

"So a guy I knew here who moved to Kentucky—you know where that is, couple states north of the Florida Panhandle?"

"I know where Kentucky is," Poison said. Aguilar doubted that he did. Aguilar had completed secondary school, and even he had only the vaguest sense of U.S. geography.

"Okay, cool. So this guy says he's trying to meet a strong demand for product in Kentucky, and could I hook him up? I thought, this will work. I can provide him with a good-sized supply to get started, and that way I'd expand my marketplace outside of Miami. If this guy can move enough in Kentucky and maybe shift into some other states in that area, then I can keep taking in whatever Pablo sends and increase everybody's profits."

"That makes sense," Poison said. "So what went wrong?"

"What went wrong was that my buddy fucked me over," Caldwell said. "Turned out he'd gone over to the cops. He was wearing a wire, and he'd tipped off Vice to our meet. I showed up with the hundred and twenty kilos he asked for, and he showed up with the money. But as soon as the cash changed hands, cops swarmed in."

"And they grabbed the product and the money?"

"Exactly!"

"Then how did you get away?"

"I got lucky as hell," Caldwell said. "I saw them coming before they reached me. We'd met in a swampy area, where I knew we wouldn't be disturbed. When I saw the cops, I ran—and accidentally ran straight into the swamp. Well, you can't really run in that kind of place, but I figured, what the hell, I'm in it now. So I swam. I just lit out for open water. I know I swam right past an alligator—we startled the hell out of each other—and probably a few water moccasins. But like I said, I got lucky. The cops were splashing around looking for me, but I was mostly underwater. Then they saw that big fucking gator and I guess they thought I couldn't have gone that way. So they started looking in other directions, and I kept going until I hit dry land. Then I hitched a ride back to the city with a trucker, and here I am."

"Incredible story," Poison said.

"Yeah. Sometimes the most incredible ones are true. That's what this one was."

"Did you get in touch with your Kentucky friend again?"

"Hell no. I don't want to give him another shot at me. If I call him or write to him, he'll probably turn that over to Vice or DEA. That dude is dead to me."

"And you were alone when you met him?"

"Of course. I trusted the guy. I knew he wouldn't try to rip me off. I just didn't think he'd ever cooperate with the law."

"So there's nobody who can back up your story?"

Caldwell's eyes started darting around from one person to another. "I don't know why I would need anyone to back me up. I've never lied to Pablo. I've been a loyal soldier, and I've made him a shitload of money. Why would I need a witness? What are we doing here? Is this a friendly visit, or what?"

Aguilar had hoped it would be a friendly visit, but it wasn't hard to see the problems with his story. No witnesses. A major police operation and a huge seizure that hadn't been reported to the press. And a very valuable supply of product, disappeared.

No, he didn't see how things were going to stay friendly. He could see from Poison's posture, upright in the chair, hands on his knees, muscles tensed, that Poison didn't, either.

"It was," Poison said. "But I think you know how this sounds. You're going to have to come with us, and explain things to Don Pablo in person."

"Yeah, sure," Caldwell answered. "Glad to. At your hotel? Where you at?"

"Not at the hotel," Poison said. "At a safe house we have in town. It's cool, he just wants to hear it from you."

Caldwell licked his lips. He looked nervous.

Aguilar didn't blame him.

A safe house?

That didn't sound good at all.

29

THE SAFE HOUSE was at the end of a cul-de-sac in a rural neighborhood. They weren't too far from the city center, and Aguilar was surprised by how quickly they had moved from an urban landscape to one with thick forest and lots of green foliage. The house was surrounded by tall trees, dripping with moss. The closest other house was some distance away, and had a FOR SALE sign out front. It looked abandoned.

So did the safe house, although as they approached it, Aguilar saw that the door was sturdy and there were multiple locks on it. From the street, a passerby would think nobody lived there, but anyone trying to break in would have more trouble than he expected.

The exterior was stucco, like so many houses in Colombia. It had been painted yellow, but that had faded almost to white in some places, and moss or mold had darkened the walls near the bottom. The roof was flat, and tree branches stretched out over it like friendly arms offering shade.

Behind the wheel, Jairo parked in the cracked,

weed-choked driveway, and they walked to the front door. It opened before they reached it, and Trigger stood inside with an AK-47. Apparently Lion had indeed been able to provide the heavier firepower he'd hinted at.

"He cool?" Trigger asked.

"We frisked him," Poison assured him.

Aguilar nodded to Trigger as he passed. Nobody else spoke until they got into the house's living room. Mold had seeped in here, too, drawing black dots and streaks on the walls. The smell was musty, unhealthy. But the sparse furnishings looked clean enough. Escobar sat in one of the chairs, looking none the worse for wear for his undoubtedly busy night with the two young women.

He didn't get up when Caldwell walked in, with Poison, Aguilar, and Jairo behind him. Aguilar considered that a pointed statement in itself.

"Kyle," he said. There was no expression in his voice, none on his face.

"Pablo," Kyle said, sounding much more friendly. He moved forward, hand extended. Escobar's hands remained folded over his stomach. Caldwell got the message and drew his hand back.

"It's like that, huh?" Caldwell said.

"Sit, Kyle."

Kyle sat in the other chair. The four *sicarios* remained standing. Aguilar wondered where La Quica was, but didn't ask.

"I told you what happened when I called," Caldwell said.

"You did."

"And I told these guys today. Didn't I, Poison?"

"He did," Poison said.

"Look, I know it sucks," Caldwell said. "Believe me, it sucks for me, too. I can't afford eight million dollars, but I know that's what I owe you."

"Closer to eight and a half," Escobar said. "But let's not quibble."

"I'm rounding," Caldwell said. "Point is, you can absorb that kind of loss. I can't."

"And yet, you're the one who lost the product."

"I am. I freely admit that. Maybe I can spend a few hundred thousand and see if I can get it back from an evidence warehouse somewhere."

"But you haven't done that yet," Escobar said.

"I didn't know you'd want me to."

"I don't like losing product," Escobar said. "More than that, I don't like being lied to. And I hate being stolen from."

"Pablo, if I stole it, I'd have sold it. Then I'd have the money, and I'd be able to pay you. I'd be stupid not to."

"Unless you already spent it. Or lost it gambling. Or promised it to someone you fear more than you fear me."

Caldwell held his hands out, palms facing Escobar. "Pablo, there's nobody. No one I respect more than you. It's not about fear, it's about respect and a long-time, profitable partnership."

"I'm curious about something," Escobar said.

Caldwell lowered his hands, seemingly glad for the change of subject. "What?"

"Why wouldn't the Miami police have publicized a seizure of this size? I've seen pictures in the newspapers when they get their hands on three or four kilos. This would have been international news."

"I've been wondering that very thing," Caldwell

said. "I just can't figure it out. After you asked me on the phone, I talked to the reporter for the *Herald* who covers that kind of thing."

"Mr. Arnold?" Escobar asked.

"Right. Harry Arnold."

"And what did Mr. Arnold say?"

"He told me it's going to run in the next few days. Like, today, tomorrow. By the end of the week, anyway."

"Harry Arnold told you that?"

"That's right."

Escobar was quiet for a full minute. "That's funny," he said.

"What's funny?"

Finally, Escobar heaved himself from his chair. Floorboards squeaked under his feet. "Come with me."

"Yeah," Caldwell said. Flop sweat broke out on his brow, and dark circles had formed under the pits of his silk T-shirt. "Sure."

Escobar led the way out of the living room and down a hallway toward the back of the house.

At the end of the hallway was a closed door. As they approached, it swung open, and La Quica stood there. He had an AK-47 of his own. Sunlight glowed from inside the room.

"Hey," La Quica said.

"Hey, La Quica," Caldwell said.

Escobar stopped and stepped to the side of the door. He gestured Caldwell inside. "After you."

"You sure?" Caldwell asked.

"Of course."

La Quica moved out of the way and Caldwell went into the room.

He paused just inside the door and made a noise deep in his throat. Aguilar thought he was going to be sick.

"Go on," Escobar said. "Say hello to Mr. Arnold."

A prod from La Quica's gun barrel moved Caldwell farther into the room. The others crowded in behind him.

On his side, on the room's sole piece of furniture—a bed—lay a man, or what was left of one. His head had been wrapped with duct tape, discolored by blood that had seeped through the edges or run out the holes left for him to breathe through. Where there was no tape—above the forehead to his crown and around the ears—his flesh was swollen and discolored, so what should have been a head was shaped more like an oddly distended melon.

The man's hands had been taped together behind his back, and from the looks of his arms, they'd been dislocated at the shoulders. He was naked, and nearly every centimeter of his torso was bloody and bruised. His genitals had been mangled. His legs were similarly bruised.

The man didn't move, and Aguilar realized that he was dead.

Caldwell breathed heavily, almost panting. He was trembling so hard that Aguilar could feel the floor shake.

"This is the Harry Arnold you were talking about, yes?" Escobar asked. "Of the *Miami Herald*?"

Caldwell didn't respond.

La Quica shoved the barrel of his AK into Caldwell's kidneys, hard.

"Don Pablo asked you a question, *puta*."

"I can't see his f-f-face," Caldwell managed at last. "B-but it could be him."

"It's him. He told me he hadn't heard about any such seizure," Escobar said. "I asked him about you, specifically. He said he had heard of you, but had never spoken to you."

He paused, as if waiting for a response. Caldwell stood there, shaking, but didn't answer.

"By the end," Escobar added, "I believed him. He had no more reason to lie. You, on the other hand... Kyle, I think you're lying to me. And I hate it when people lie to me."

"P-Pablo, n-n-no!" Caldwell said. "I *love* you, man. I would *never* lie to you. We've made so much money for each other. You can't— You can't let this..."

His words trailed off, as if he had run out of things to say, or realized that nothing he said would help him.

Aguilar's curiosity finally got the best of him. He was standing beside Sure Shot, so in a low voice, he said, "What's the duct tape around his head for?"

"Holds it together," Sure Shot whispered. "So you can smash it up more before it kills him. Just putting it on scares the shit out of them, and then the damage you can do is intense. Plus, they can't scream."

"Let me ask you a question, Kyle," Escobar said. "Are you in a position to pay me my eight and a half million dollars today?"

"I can get it," Caldwell said quickly. "N-not today, but... three, four days. No p-p-problem."

"Not today," Escobar said. "You steal from me, you lie to me, and then you want me to wait around while you leave town? Do you really think me so stupid?"

"No! It's not— That's not what I—"

Escobar dismissed his argument with a wave of his hand. "It isn't about the money anymore, Kyle. If I let you steal from me and survive, what message does that send to others?" He looked over at the *sicarios*, bunched up in the doorway, and his gaze met Aguilar's.

"Jaguar," he said, "do you have your claw?"

30

AGUILAR'S KNIFE WAS in its usual spot, strapped to his ankle. He nodded.

"Good," Escobar said. He looked at Poison. "Tape this bastard's mouth. I don't want to hear him scream."

The roll of duct tape that had been used on Arnold lay on the floor. Poison picked it up. Caldwell moved to run or fight—Aguilar wasn't sure which, and it didn't really matter—but Sure Shot, Jairo, and Trigger held him still. He struggled against them without much spirit, as if in his mind he'd already surrendered. La Quica rammed the gun barrel into his kidneys a couple more times, as punctuation.

Poison approached the quivering American and pulled a long strip of duct tape from the roll. He covered Caldwell's mouth and wrapped it around the back of his head, then made a couple more turns to secure it.

"Take off your clothes," Escobar ordered.

Caldwell shook his head.

"If you don't, we'll do it for you."

Caldwell just stood there, shaking his head. Poison grabbed the neck of his T-shirt and yanked, tearing the shirt off him. Trigger undid his belt and tugged down Caldwell's jeans and underwear. He tossed aside the man's sandals and pulled the pants and underwear over his feet, one leg at a time.

"Get that guy off the bed," Escobar said. "Kyle needs it."

Caldwell started shaking his head again. Poison rolled Arnold's corpse from the bed and let it fall to the floor, then shoved it out of the way.

"Wrap his wrists and ankles," Escobar said.

The others pushed Caldwell onto the bed. Poison snatched up the tape again and did as he was told.

Caldwell thrashed around, tried to speak through the tape, but the others held him. Escobar caught Aguilar's eye again. "The Jaguar's Claw, please," he said.

Aguilar bent over and drew the knife from its sheath. He reversed it so he was holding it by the blade, and offered it to Escobar. *El Patrón* shook his head. "You do the honors," he said. "Just make sure his death is slow and painful."

"Me?" Aguilar asked.

"Is there a problem?" Escobar said.

He didn't like to give an order more than once, Aguilar knew. And he didn't like his orders to be questioned. Given the mood he was in, he was as likely to order Aguilar tortured and killed as to repeat himself.

"No problem," Aguilar said.

"Then please proceed. Slow and painful."

Aguilar turned the knife around again, held it by the grip. He remembered killing Montoya, remembered how sick he'd become of causing his one-time friend pain and how he had just gone ahead and finished the man off. And he'd hated Montoya at that moment.

But Kyle Caldwell had never done anything to hurt him. He'd liked Caldwell, and the feeling seemed to be mutual. They'd shared drinks and laughs and a fondness for knives. They were both disfigured, in their own ways, and had felt a bond over that.

Caldwell lay helpless before him, naked and terrified. He'd wet himself and the bed.

"Well?" Escobar said. He wasn't known for his patience, and it was clearly running out.

"Yes, *Patrón*," Aguilar said.

The other guys moved out of his way. There was no one between him and Caldwell. Caldwell looked out at him over the duct tape, his eyes moist and pleading.

Aguilar wanted to refuse the order, but he didn't dare. In a way, he was as much a prisoner as Caldwell. Both had entered into relationships with Escobar of their own free will, and profited handsomely from it. Now they were locked into this dance, partnered by fate and the hand of Don Pablo.

He met Caldwell's terrified gaze, tried to say *I'm sorry* with his own.

And he started cutting.

First on the ankle. Caldwell jerked his legs away. "Hold him," Aguilar said, willing his voice to be steady and strong.

A couple of the guys grabbed him, and one held his feet. "It'll be easier if you're still," Aguilar said. He cut again. These were small cuts, not deep. They drew blood but did no serious damage. Escobar wanted Caldwell to suffer, not to bleed out too quickly.

Caldwell wouldn't stay still. He tried to writhe and thrash, and even with the men holding him it was hard for Aguilar to slice as precisely as he wanted. He cut both of Caldwell's legs in several places, working his way up to the thighs, then started in on his trunk. He kept hoping the man would die, that his heart would seize up and he could end this.

It didn't happen. Caldwell whimpered and tried to twist away. Aguilar kept cutting, inflicting pain, teasing out blood. His stomach churned and he had to swallow back stinging bile. The bed turned spongy with blood, urine, and sweat.

He was making a careful slice across Caldwell's chest when a hand on his shoulder startled him. He jumped, almost dropping the knife, but managed to catch it by the blade without cutting himself.

Escobar stood close behind him. "Give it to me," he said.

For a moment, Aguilar didn't know what he meant. Then he saw Escobar's open palm. "The knife?"

"Yes, the knife. Your claw."

Aguilar placed it in Escobar's hand, hoping his boss didn't want to use it on him.

"Out of the way," Escobar said.

Relief washed over Aguilar. He straightened, all his muscles complaining because he'd been hunched over the bed or kneeling on the floor for so long, and moved away.

Escobar put his left hand over the duct tape, holding Caldwell's head still, and with his right, slashed deep across the man's throat. Caldwell sputtered behind the tape and blood gushed from the wound. Escobar wiped the blade twice on the mattress and handed it back.

"We're losing beach time," he said. "Let's get out of here."

* * *

Back at the Fontainebleau, Escobar rented jet skis for everyone and they spent a couple of hours carving through the surf, splashing one another and racing back and forth parallel to the coastline. A couple of the guys picked up women on the beach and took them for rides. Fighting to control the powerful craft almost allowed Aguilar to forget—briefly, at least— the hour or so he had spent using his knife on a man he had considered a friend.

Later, Lion took them to a Cuban restaurant in Little Havana. They took a private room there, and during the course of the meal, people from the local community—Colombians, Cubans, and others— came in to pay their respects. Some brought gifts for Escobar, others dipped their heads or knelt on the floor and kissed his fingers, as though they were meeting a pope.

After dinner, they returned to the suite for rest and drinking, then shortly before midnight, they all piled back into the stretch limo for a trip to what Lion swore was Miami's top strip club. The parking lot was vast, the building huge, with purple neon that could be seen glowing into the night sky from blocks away.

In the limo, Escobar gave each man a stack of twenty hundred-dollar bills. "Have a good time, boys," he said. "Tomorrow we fly home, but tonight, we party."

The club wasn't as loud as the dance club the night before, but it was loud. There were multiple stages, with groupings of tables and chairs between them and naked women on each one. Flesh was everywhere; there must have been a hundred women working, Aguilar guessed, and few of them were wearing more than filmy negligees, if that. A young woman escorted their group to a section of tables reserved for them, set away from most of the others. "There's also a champagne room," she said as they took their seats. "It's six hundred each, but it's full service."

What "full service" meant wasn't made clear, but Aguilar had a guess.

Walking from the door to their reserved tables, he had seen customers and dancers both cutting and snorting lines of coke. The other guys seemed excited by the idea of nude women and liquor, but he wasn't sure he felt the same way. The hectares of flesh intrigued him; he hadn't seen a naked woman in quite some time. At the same time, the lust they inspired felt disrespectful to Luisa's memory.

In the end, he crossed the line as he always did, step by step. Watching women on stage, dancing, gyrating, some performing genuinely athletic feats with nothing but their own muscles and a stage-to-ceiling pole. Then a close-up table dance, then a full-contact lap dance, in which he was assured that nothing was out of bounds. That was followed by a spell in the champagne room, which was almost pitch-black and communication was all touch and whispers.

The one he took back to the hotel was as unlike Luisa as he could find. She was a skinny blonde woman, older than most of the other dancers. She called herself Trixie; he didn't bother to ask her real name. She spoke no Spanish and her English was thickly accented—when he asked, she said she was from a place called Waycross, Georgia. Her hair was short, cut off at her jawline, and she had a tattoo of a spread-winged butterfly at the base of her spine.

When, halfway through the night, she asked for cocaine, Aguilar went to Jairo, then Sure Shot, who had some. Eventually, wrung out, he fell asleep. He woke up with the sun shining through his window and Trixie gone, along with all the money in his wallet.

Escobar laughed and said, "Then I guess you had a good time." As usual, he had found the youngest and loveliest girl at the club and brought her back, and in the morning had a taxi brought around to take her home, with five thousand dollars in her purse. He gave Aguilar a few hundred to tide him over. Their flight left Miami shortly after noon, and they'd landed in Bogotá by five.

Aguilar had some free time the next day. He took a walk around the ranch, watched the cattle graze in a meadow, sat in the dirt inside the barn listening to the skittering of mice in the rafters.

Later, in the kitchen, he ran into Tata. "Did you have a good time in Miami?" she asked.

"Sure," he said.

"That's not very convincing."

"It was... I don't know how to describe it. Strange."

"I'm not surprised," Tata said. "When he travels with me, with the family, Pablo behaves himself, for the most part. But I hear stories, of course, when I'm not along."

"He takes care of his people," Aguilar said. "He made sure we were entertained, and that we ate well. He rented jet skis and we played in the ocean. The beaches there are beautiful."

"Yes, they are. So are the women."

"I suppose."

"You don't have to pretend with me, Jose. I know what you men are like when there are no families around. And I know Pablo better than anyone. Hermilda thinks he's a saint, and Juan thinks he's a god. I'm the only one in his family—maybe the only one anywhere—who sees him as he truly is."

Tata was young—Aguilar knew by now that Escobar preferred his women that way—but she was different than the ones he had seen Escobar with on the trip. Those girls were, in some way, more worldly. Tata had been a sheltered, small-town girl before she met Escobar, and he sheltered her even more. But she was bright, observant. She knew what he was like, knew how he had built and protected his empire. She was a strange combination of innocent and wise beyond her years. Aguilar didn't know why Escobar had chosen her to be his bride, of all the young women he'd ever met. But he had made a good choice. In many ways, Tata was his equal. In others, Aguilar suspected, she was far more perceptive than Escobar even knew, and probably smarter than he was.

"Some men are like that," Aguilar countered. "I won't say I'm an angel. I've done things I never thought I would. But I—" He was about to say, "I have my limits," but midway through the sentence, remembered that he had exceeded every limit he'd ever set for himself. "Never mind, you're right. I'm just as bad as the rest."

"No," Tata said. "You're not. You might have done things you believe are wrong. Every human sins, after all. But you recognize right and wrong, and that sets you apart. You're a rare one, Jose."

She never called him Jaguar, although by now everyone else had adopted Escobar's nickname for him. He liked hearing his given name once in a while.

"As are you, Señora. A rare one, indeed. An orchid in the midst of brambles."

He wasn't sure, but he thought she might have blushed. At any rate, she turned and busied herself in a cupboard, and he took his leave.

31

THE NEXT DAY, Aguilar was on bodyguard duty. Escobar's bodyguards stayed close, so they could react to any attack against *El Patrón*—but in the absence of danger, they were expected to fade into the woodwork, hovering around the edges of conversations without listening in or taking part.

Escobar and Gaviria went to an upstairs balcony of the ranch house to smoke pot and discuss next steps, and the balcony wasn't big enough for Aguilar to entirely disappear. He stood at the doorway, preventing anyone from walking in on the discussion. But in so doing, he could hear every word.

"Caldwell said some bullshit about opening a new market in Kentucky, and possibly in other states in the American South," Escobar was telling Gaviria. "If it was true, he was trying to open that market without our involvement, selling product stolen from us. Or it might have been a lie he made up on the spot. Either way, though, it's not a bad idea. I talked to Lion, and he's approaching some connections he has, to see what can be done."

"Some of the best ideas come from the dead," Gaviria said. He held up his joint. "Take marijuana— whoever discovered it is long dead. But that man was a genius!" He started laughing, and Escobar joined in.

Once they'd brought their laughter under control, Escobar continued with his pitch. "The thing is, if we can open those markets—and if anyone can do it, Lion can—we're going to need to boost production."

"We're already at full capacity," Gaviria said. "Round-the-clock shifts at every plant."

"Then we need to expand capacity," Escobar countered. "There's plenty of room around our jungle lab in Caquetá, no? And a local work force in San Vicente del Caguán that would probably love some good jobs."

Gaviria shuddered. "I hate it out there, *hermano*. All those bugs. The snakes. Everything's wet all the time."

"I'm not saying we have to move there. A few weeks, maybe, to oversee the expansion. It won't be so bad. We'll bring in some whores to keep us and the workers entertained." Escobar looked over his shoulder at Aguilar, standing there pretending he wasn't listening. "Even Jaguar appreciates a good whore, don't you, Jaguar?"

"I suppose," Aguilar replied.

"Have you ever spent time in the deep jungle?"

"My father used to take me camping in the forest, but never the real jungle."

"Well, you'll come with us, then. It's an incredible place, the jungle. You might even see a real jaguar or two."

"Thank you, Don Pablo."

"When are we doing this, Pablo?" Gaviria asked.

"As soon as we can. Once Lion has the arrangements ready, I want to be able to start pumping out product right away."

It took most of a month to gather the necessary equipment and supplies and get it all loaded onto a caravan of military-style trucks with canopies over the beds. But Escobar was true to his word, and when the expedition eventually started out, Aguilar rode in the third truck, along with some of the other *sicarios* and several crates of laboratory equipment. Several times in the intervening weeks, he had thought about contacting his father, to remind him of his childhood fascination with Tarzan and jungles. But every time he started to, he remembered how their last encounters had gone, and he changed his mind. His father didn't want to hear from him—he would probably hope that Aguilar would go into the jungle and never return.

The journey was a long one. Highways led through Bogotá and decent, paved roads carried them all the way to Calamar. After that, though, most roads were unpaved. Bridges over the many rivers and streams were in various states of disrepair. More than once, trucks had to be unloaded and cargo carried across by hand, to avoid overstressing them.

The deeper into the jungle they went, the more Aguilar realized why Gaviria hated it. The insects really were far more numerous than in populated areas. And huge—he saw a spider bigger than his hand dangling from a web strung between three trees. Biting bugs, mosquitoes, and others were everywhere, and no amount of repellent could keep them off. The humidity increased deep in the trees; sweat poured off him in waterfalls, and he had to keep drinking water to stay hydrated. It was never quiet; the ripe, pungent air was full of sound every moment of every day.

At one point on the ride, with every irregularity in the road bouncing him and making his muscles ache, he managed to fall asleep in his seat. He dreamed that he was riding a horse. It was in Colombia's old days, and he worked for a ranch, and a big cat—cougar, jaguar, something—had been preying on the cattle and sheep. He was tracking it, but instead of a .44 rifle, an AR-15 lay across his saddle, and instead of reins he held onto ropes of fire that didn't burn his hands. He woke before he found the cat, but not before the sensation of being watched raised the hairs on the back of his neck.

Finally, they reached the jungle lab. Escobar and Gaviria had flown in that morning on a small plane; the lab had an airstrip that could be quickly disguised with potted trees, in the event of a military or government flyover, but it wasn't big enough for cargo planes.

The lab was crude at best. The equipment was sophisticated—lots of steel and copper and glass—but it was set up on cheap folding tables standing on a crude wooden floor, underneath a roof constructed of corrugated tin, tree limbs, and rope. Monkeys skittered around in the trees. Lean, dark-skinned men worked shirtless, wearing only shorts and maybe sandals of some kind. Most had bad teeth; all were dripping with sweat.

When the trucks rolled into the clearing, Escobar, Gaviria, and a third man, short, bespectacled, and lighter-skinned than those laboring under that roof, stepped out of the house that would be the only structure seen from the air. Each wore a broad smile, as if greeting long-lost relatives. The rumble of multiple generators filled the air, and the smell of their exhaust mixed with the odors of ammonia and kerosene—presumably from the lab—obscuring the jungle's usual aroma of life and decay.

"You made it," Escobar said as the travelers exited their trucks. "No problems?"

"A couple of police checkpoints," La Quica said. "Nothing that couldn't be fixed. And three flat tires."

"Good. Everybody will sleep in the house, so move your personal things in there, then you can work with the locals to get the trucks unloaded." He pointed to an area next to the existing lab that had been cleared of trees. Poles had been erected to support a roof, but the sheets of tin were leaning against one of them, not yet in place. The wooden floor had been laid out. "That's where the new lab equipment goes. This," he added, indicating the smaller man, "is Camilo, our chemist. He'll show you where to stage everything, and where to put it once we're ready."

"Okay, *Patrón*," La Quica said. He clapped his hands. "You heard him! Personal items in the house! Ten minutes to take a piss, then get back out here to help unload the trucks!"

Men scrambled to meet La Quica's arbitrary deadline. No one had heard the words "ten minutes" issue from Escobar's lips, but La Quica was, if not the head *sicario*, at least something like that, and his commands were understood to be *El Patrón*'s wishes. The only one who could have challenged La Quica for position in the *sicario* hierarchy was Blackie—a longtime friend to Escobar—but he had stayed back to protect the ranch and the women.

The house had three big bedrooms, empty but for stacks of pillows and light blankets. Aguilar figured the regular laborers either lived at home and traveled to work, or camped out in the jungle nearby, because the *sicarios* would fill all the available space. The line for the two indoor toilets was too long, so Aguilar hurried outside and melted into the trees away from the house. While he was going, he heard several other men who'd had the same idea, splashing away.

When the ten minutes were up, everyone was back at the trucks, and laborers from the lab had shown up to assist. The work was hot, grueling. Camilo's help was limited to pointing and the occasional, strained, "Be careful with that!"

"I didn't sign on to do manual labor," Aguilar grumbled at one point.

"You signed on to do whatever Don Pablo says to do," Poison reminded him. "But if you want to renegotiate terms with him, feel free. It's easy to make bodies disappear in the jungle."

Poison was right; there had been no contract laying out duties, no limitations set. When you worked for Pablo Escobar, your job was to follow orders, no matter what they were. Aguilar understood.

That didn't mean he had to like it.

Finally, everything was unloaded, the crates and boxes stacked on pallets laid out on the damp earth. Aguilar hoped they were finished for the day. He was so hungry he thought his stomach was going to eat him from the inside out, and he had sweated away what felt like ten or twenty kilos.

"That's a good start," Camilo said, observing their progress. "Time to get the canopy up. It'll probably rain tonight, and we can't have all this getting soaked."

The groans weren't just from Aguilar. He held his tongue this time, and let others complain. It would do no good, anyway.

The tin was lashed to the existing poles with sturdy rope. Once it was in place and secure, branches from the trees that had been downed to create the clearing were tied to it, to disguise the installation from the air.

"Why bother?" Pancho asked while they were fixing the branches in place. "Cocaine's going to be legalized anyway, isn't it? That's what Don Pablo says."

"*Maybe* it will be," Aguilar answered. "But that's still only a possibility. For now, it's not legal. There are factions in the government that have it in for Don Pablo and the other cartel heads, and they'd love to find his labs."

"When he's in the legislature, things will change," Sure Shot said. "He hasn't spent all that money on politicians just to have them walk away from him once he's sitting there with them."

His term was due to begin in a little more than a month. Aguilar wondered how their lives would change then. Would he give up the cocaine business and focus on governing? That seemed unlikely—the salary of a legislator was a fraction of what Escobar made now. But could he do both? When the spotlight of public life was upon him, when every journalist in the country would be watching his every move, how could he function?

Aguilar hoped it would mean more time spent in Bogotá. It was a thriving city, without all the emotional resonances that Medellín had. He wouldn't have to worry about running into relatives or old friends, wouldn't pass by landmarks that reminded him of his former life, or of Luisa.

The sun was getting low in the sky. As it did, the sounds of the jungle grew louder, and even more insects buzzed around the men. Aguilar was sure he'd already lost a liter of blood to the mosquitoes.

But still, the work wasn't finished. Camilo wanted the new folding tables set up and the equipment unpacked and arranged. He generously declared that connecting pipes and tubing and electricity could wait until morning, but everything else had to be in readiness tonight.

Finally, working in the light provided by generator-powered bulbs, they got things organized to Camilo's satisfaction. Scratching at new bites, hungry, and exhausted, the men headed into the house, where a meal had been laid out for them.

On the way to their rooms, after dinner, someone mentioned the absence of the prostitutes that Escobar had promised. Most of the others shouted him down; they were beat, filthy, ready to sleep. Aguilar kept quiet. He wasn't interested in the women, anyway— or didn't think he was. But if they had been available, he would probably have taken advantage of the offer. This way spared him the decision.

This is what I've become, he thought. *Instead of choosing between right and wrong, I'm relieved to not have to face the choice.*

When his head hit the pillow, he was still trying to figure out who was more responsible, himself or Escobar. He was asleep in seconds, with the question still unresolved.

32

IN THE MORNING, Camilo took the men who were assigned to hook up the equipment on a tour of the existing lab, so they would understand how the process worked. The labor had gone on all night, and the air under the tin roof was thick with fumes that made Aguilar feel lightheaded.

"We buy coca leaves directly from the farmers who grow it," he said. His voice was high-pitched, and he spoke fast, as if the words were trying to break free from his throat before he was ready. He waved an arm at several burlap bags of leaves stacked beside the pile. "We could buy paste after it's been manufactured from the leaves, but it's much more expensive that way. The leaves we get cheap. They have to be stiff, like paper, brittle, or the paste is no good. The farmers deliver them to us as whole leaves, and we mulch them in this shearing machine."

The shearing machine was rusty, with an intake at the top and a trough at the bottom where the leaves came out. He hoisted one of the bags, showed a fistful of leaves to the *sicarios*, then dumped the bag into the machine and flicked a switch. It shook and rumbled like an enormous coffee grinder, and in a couple of minutes, chopped-up leaves tumbled down the trough and into a bin.

"We sprinkle the mulched leaves with powder cement, as a binding agent. From here, it's washed—soaked and stirred in fuel and ether, three times—which releases the product from the pulp." He indicated the big steel drums in which the coca was presumably soaked, then walked them down the production line as he explained the steps. "After the washing, the residue is pressed and the liquid is wrung out, leaving a solid mass of coca. We let that dry, then cook it down over the fire until it's creamy and white, and we let that harden. Now we have the paste, which is what we're really after. We purify it with a bath of sulfuric acid and potassium permanganate, which produces manganese dioxide. We filter that out, and impurities with it. Diluted ammonia neutralizes the sulfuric acid. When that's dried, under the heat lamps, then it's crushed and packaged in the waterproof casings you've all seen."

"It's a complex process," Gordo said.

"Sure," Camilo agreed. "But simple people can be trained to master it. We'll have to hire more workers, to staff up this new section. And we'll have to expand the airstrip to accommodate bigger airplanes. Don Pablo says there are backhoes and bulldozers on the way, over the next few days, for that part."

"Do the workers here have any idea how valuable the final product is?"

Camilo looked over his shoulder, making sure that none of the laborers were listening. "They won't if you don't tell them." He grinned, as if he'd just told a joke, but his tone was serious. "Now you see how things have to work. Get it all wired and plumbed as it is on this side, and let me know when you're finished."

"Which means he's going back inside," Jairo whispered. "And leaving us out here with the bugs."

"He's the chemist," Royer replied. "He's the most important person here. Besides Don Pablo and Gustavo, I mean."

"He sure thinks so," Aguilar added, watching Camilo walk back toward the house.

"He's the one who knows how to mix the chemicals, who trains the workers," Royer said. "I don't like doing this shit either, but we know what we're here for. We're the hired muscle. Don Pablo doesn't want the laborers doing this work—the jobs they're already doing are too important, and he doesn't want to interrupt the supply. And the new ones haven't been hired yet. That leaves us."

When the lab was set up and Camilo had inspected all the connections, checking to make sure the power was hooked up right, the men were given a light lunch. Then four of them—La Quica, Aguilar, Gordo, and Jairo—were told to take a truck into the nearest village and hire some workers. Escobar gave them some cash to hand out, and instructed them not to come back until they had twenty men willing to work shifts around the clock.

They had passed briefly through the nearest village on their way out. It was a sleepy place, with a church on the main plaza, a small gathering of houses, a handful of shops, a dentist's office. At that early hour, the only person in the plaza had been asleep on a bench, but three goats had been happily munching on grass.

Now, in early afternoon, it was considerably busier. Vendors had set up carts or stands selling fruits and vegetables and *paletas*, lottery tickets, and newspapers. The aroma of strong coffee leaked out of a tiny restaurant. Old men sat in chairs, playing cards or chess. Dogs wandered freely, and children, naked or nearly so, played in the grass where the goats had been.

La Quica parked the truck in front of the church and climbed onto the bed. The canopy had been taken down and the bed left open. He took a pistol from his hip and fired a shot into the air. All conversation ceased; even the children turned to stare.

"I'm here to offer good jobs," La Quica began. "We have a laboratory, a few kilometers out in the jungle. We need good workers, people who can stay on their feet for hours at a time, doing hard physical labor. Nobody sick or weak, just people who can keep up with a fast pace." He put the gun away and pulled bills from his pocket, ruffled them in the air. "We pay well."

A few of the younger men approached the truck, hesitant to get too near. "Come on over," La Quica said. "I'm serious. Good jobs, good pay."

"Doing what?" one of the men asked. They were indigenous, dark-skinned, with straight black hair gleaming like spilled ink. The man who'd asked the question scratched at his lean stomach, lifting the fabric of his light T-shirt with his hand. There was a round scar there, as if he'd been bitten by a wild animal. This was the jungle, Aguilar remembered, so perhaps he had. The man's four upper front teeth were clad in gold, and judging by his hollow cheeks, they might have been the only teeth he had.

"Nothing dangerous," La Quica said. "Working in a lab."

"A lab?"

"They must be from the coca lab," another man said.

"That's right. You all know people who work there, right?"

"I know people who live on scraps," the first one said. "While the bosses get rich and fat."

"That's not how it is," La Quica argued. "The people who work there are happy to have good jobs."

"You don't even know them," another man pointed out. "Can you name even one? They're our friends, our families. They work day and night, for next to nothing."

"That's not what they tell me."

"You have the guns. Ask them when they're armed, too."

"Look, if you don't want jobs—" La Quica began.

The first man cut him off. "Maybe we should take over your lab. We could run it ourselves, sell the cocaine to your boss. Make some real money. This is a poor village, and all the wealth from our coca plants goes to people living like kings in Bogotá, Cali, and Medellín."

Curiosity had quickly turned to anger. Aguilar was glad that Medellín had come last on the young man's list; he didn't know that it was Escobar's lab, but blamed some nameless, faceless millionaire for his region's poverty. It was, he thought, not unlike Escobar's constant blaming of the unnamed oligarchs for Medellín's slums.

More young men came into the square and toward the truck, drawn by the increasingly loud voices. Some of them carried machetes, and a couple had pistols.

La Quica rested his hand on his gun. Jairo and

Aguilar climbed out of the truck, each holding an AR-15. Only Gordo, sitting in the center of the bench seat, remained inside, but he had a pistol in his hands.

"We came to offer paying work," La Quica said. "If there's nobody here who wants to work, that's fine. We'll try another village. But if you do want work, don't let these troublemakers scare you off. Come forward, and you'll have our protection."

There were a few tense moments of silence, then four men—scrawny, unhealthy-looking—stepped toward the truck. "I'll work," one said.

"Me too."

"Climb up here," La Quica said. "We're glad to have you. But understand: you won't be able to come back here. You'll be blindfolded on the way out, and as long as you work for us, you remain in the jungle."

"No problem," one man said. The others nodded their assent.

La Quica banged twice on the roof of the cab. "Gordo, you drive," he said. "We'll go to the next village."

Gordo slid over behind the wheel. Jairo and Aguilar got back into the cab before he pulled away, and three more men darted through the crowd, jumping onto the truck.

Seven, at this first stop. There were two more villages along the road, and eventually the larger municipality of San Vicente del Caguán. Escobar and Camilo wanted twenty men, so they were off to a decent start.

They made it all the way to San Vicente del Caguán before they had their twenty. When they did, they turned around and drove back through all the villages they'd passed, and the men from each of those villages ducked down as they went by, so they wouldn't be seen.

"What's the problem with these people?" Escobar asked when La Quica and Aguilar briefed him on their progress. "Don't they want to work?"

"They feel like they're not paid enough," La Quica said. "They're not Stone Age people, and they know that cocaine makes lots of money for a few people. They think they could take over the labs and keep all the money."

"Don't they know it takes a distribution network? Bribes to cops and customs officials? Airplanes and ships? The manufacture is the easiest part of the process."

"They know just enough to be dangerous," La Quica said.

"Dangerous? Do I have to worry about this, now? There are already paramilitary groups in some of the jungles, demanding protection payments. They haven't found this lab yet, but they could."

"The crews work all night, right?" Aguilar asked.

"Yes."

"Are there guards out?"

"One," Escobar said. "But he's mainly watching out for jungle beasts. The light and noise keeps most of them away, but there's always the possibility, if a worker steps away for a piss or something, that he'll be bitten by a snake or attacked by a big cat, something like that. So they have a man on duty who patrols with a light and a gun, driving off the animals."

"We might want to add more security for a little while," Aguilar suggested. "Some of those guys sounded angry. Threatening."

"Are you volunteering, Jaguar?"

Aguilar realized too late that he shouldn't have

opened his mouth. Still, guard duty might not be so bad. "How long will we be here?"

"Another week, at least. We have to get the airstrip expanded, and I want to be sure this new crew is working out before we go."

"Then I guess I could do some shifts on guard duty."

"Good. Get me five more volunteers, and we'll make a schedule."

The good thing about guard duty was that Aguilar was allowed to sleep during the hottest part of the day. And the bedroom wasn't crowded, so he could stretch out and use as many pillows as he wanted.

The bad part was the guard duty.

The jungle at night was like a living beast, fanged and many-eyed and dripping with malevolence. Beyond the reach of his flashlights and the bulbs strung along the tin roofs of the twin labs, the darkness was complete; no moonlight penetrated the dense canopy overhead. The only noise was the perpetual buzz of insects, so whenever a creature larger than a mouse moved through the brush, it sounded enormous.

Rain fell on two of his patrol nights. The first hint was a sound like the rush of an oncoming train, as the storm moved across the jungle toward him. Then it hit the upper canopy with a roar like a waterfall, followed by an almost musical progression as it ran from leaf to branch to branch to leaf, coming ever closer. Finally, it reached the ground, soaking him in an instant.

He patrolled with his AR-15 tightly gripped, finger beside the trigger and ready to slip onto it at any instant. His flashlight was mounted to the barrel, and he kept extra flashlight batteries in a pocket. The last thing he wanted was to be out of sight of the house without a light.

There were two guards on duty at all times, walking overlapping patrols. Their instructions were to make sure nothing—animal or human—presented a danger to the workers. But equally important, if less obvious at first blush, was to make sure that no one left the premises without the proper permission. The lab was involved in the production of a highly profitable and illegal substance, and the workers couldn't be allowed to leave. Once they were here, they were stuck. The only provision for terminating that employment was a bullet to the head and a shallow jungle grave.

Aguilar was nervous that first night, but when dawn brought a faint glow to the jungle he lost himself in its beauty. The trees, the vines and drooping branches, the underbrush with broad leaves and flowers of every shape and color, the glimpses of color as birds moved about—all of it merged into a living, breathing impressionist painting.

After his shift, he slept for a couple of hours. Then trucks bearing the heavy equipment needed for the airstrip expansion rolled in, waking him. Groggy, he went to the kitchen for some coffee and wandered outside with his mug. La Quica was watching the big vehicles roll off the trailers.

"Do those operators get killed when they're finished?" Aguilar asked.

"They've been blindfolded since San Vicente del Caguán," La Quica said. "There aren't any landmarks here but trees, and in the middle of the jungle they all look alike. They'd never find their way back here."

"Don Pablo doesn't like taking chances."

La Quica shook his head. "He takes chances every day. He just likes to improve the odds whenever he can. You'd do the same, in his position."

"I'd never be in his position."

"He's unique, isn't he? One of a kind. Not many men have the combination of vision and ruthlessness to pull off what he has."

That was probably a good thing, Aguilar believed. Men like that were bound to clash, sooner or later. So far Colombia's various cartel heads were able to coexist, because the markets were open enough that everybody could own different territories. That wouldn't be the case forever, he was sure. Like feudal lords fighting for power and territory, none of the men running cartels would be satisfied with a piece. Each would want the whole, and bloodshed on a massive scale would be the necessary result.

He remembered the old men in the village plaza, playing chess. That was Escobar, the Ochoas, Gacha, and the heads of the other cartels, moving their pieces across the board, seeking the advantage, taking out the opponent's pieces whenever possible.

Sooner or later, a war would come. *And I'll be a pawn in that war*, Aguilar thought. *A triggerman, a disposable soldier. Cannon fodder. If I live that long.*

He sipped his coffee and watched the big machines tear at the earth.

33

LATER, AGUILAR WAS outside again, watching the new workers trying to master the craft of manufacturing cocaine. Escobar and Gaviria were there as well. Camilo was explaining the various tasks to five men who would work a shift together. One of them kept asking questions that Aguilar thought were stupid ones—demanding that Camilo go back over things he had just covered. The man was young, still in his teens or just out of them, but that didn't excuse his inability to grasp an idea. And he was nervous, trembling.

Finally, he tripped over his own feet or someone else's, and knocked a bottle of ammonia off a table. It hit the wooden floor and shattered, and the fumes washed over everyone present.

Escobar had seen enough. "Give me your gun, Jaguar," he snapped.

Aguilar handed it over, assuming Escobar would use it to make a point of some kind.

He did, but not the kind Aguilar expected.

"You!" Escobar said, addressing the man, still trying to regain his footing.

The man looked at Escobar, gave him a sheepish grin. "Sorry."

"Yes, you are," Escobar said. He leveled the gun at the man and put a bullet between his eyes. The man collapsed like an empty sack, bleeding into the dirt.

"Get him out of here," Escobar said. "Dump him in the jungle somewhere. And if there are any more idiots among the workers, let them know the same thing will happen to them."

He turned and stormed toward the house. Gaviria shrugged. "He has a tooth that's been bothering him," he said. "He's been in a foul mood all day."

"There's a dentist in the nearest village," Aguilar said. "I saw the office yesterday."

Gaviria's eyes brightened. "Come with me. I'll see what he wants to do."

Aguilar was glad of that, because it meant he didn't have to be the one to dispose of the body. Gaviria went into the house, Aguilar at his heels.

Inside, Escobar sat at the dining table with his chin on his palm, rubbing his jaw with two fingers. Aguilar's pistol rested on the table before him. When Gaviria and Aguilar entered, he looked up.

"I forgot to give you back your gun, Jaguar. This fucking tooth is killing me. Here it is."

"Thanks," Aguilar said. He picked up the weapon and holstered it.

"That's not why I brought him in," Gaviria said. "He says there's a dentist in the village."

Escobar arched an eyebrow. "You think I need a dentist?"

"You have a toothache that's making you miserable,

Pablo. I can ask Camilo for some pliers and yank it myself, if you want."

"I don't want your hands anywhere near my teeth."

"Camilo, then. He's a chemist, maybe he can make some toothache powder or something. The marijuana didn't help?"

"Not enough."

"A little cocaine, maybe?"

Escobar shook his head, scowling. "I don't use that stuff." He pondered for a few moments. "Jaguar, do you know anything about this dentist?"

"Not a thing," Aguilar replied. "We were in the plaza and I saw the office, that's all. There was a light in the window. I could take you there."

"I'm not going into town. On that road? The bumps would kill me. Take one of the other guys and bring him here, with any equipment he'll need."

"Blindfolded?"

"Of course, blindfolded. We might need him again; I don't want to have to kill him."

"Yes, *Patrón*. Anything else?"

"No," Escobar said. Then, "Yes. Make it fast! This thing's killing me."

Gaviria walked Aguilar out, stuffing a wad of bills into his hand. "Hurry," he said quietly. "I'm afraid he's going to kill all our workers if his tooth isn't taken care of."

"I'm on my way," Aguilar assured him.

He went into the bedroom and found Trigger sitting on a pillow, staring out the window. "Trigger, come with me," he said.

Trigger blinked a couple of times, then seemed to focus on him. "Come where?"

"Into the village. We need to pick up a dentist."

"A dentist? What dentist?"

"I'll explain on the way. Come on, it's an emergency."

"Do you ever think about after?" Aguilar asked.

Trigger was chewing on his lip and looking at his fingernails. Aguilar, driving the big truck, was afraid to take his eyes off the narrow road for more than a second or two. Jungle pressed in on either side; it would be easy to run into the trees and maybe be stuck there. He didn't know what would happen if another vehicle came along, going the other way.

Well, yes he did. He would refuse to budge, and he would gun down the other driver if he had to.

"After what?"

"After this."

"We go back to Medellín, I guess. Or to the ranch, or someplace. Sleep in a bed again."

"I don't mean after this here. I mean, after being a *sicario* for Escobar."

"What after is that? It's all I've ever been."

"How old are you?"

"Nineteen," Trigger said. "Well, seventeen. Almost."

"How many *sicarios* have you seen over twenty-five? Over twenty?"

"You're over twenty."

"Because I went to university, and became a police officer."

"That doesn't make you better than anyone else."

"I didn't say it did," Aguilar said. "It makes me older, though. My point is, most of the guys are young. You can't be in this life forever. There are no fifty-year-old *sicarios*."

"Fifty?" Trigger laughed. "Before I started working

290

for Don Pablo, I figured I'd be lucky to live to twenty."

"And now?"

"Now I'll still be lucky to live to twenty. But before I die, I'll have taken out plenty of other motherfuckers."

"That's all life is to you? Killing and then dying?"

"And getting laid. Don't forget that. You think Don Pablo's ever going to bring up the whores he promised?"

"If we can't get this dentist to take care of his tooth, you can forget about the whores," Aguilar said. "While he suffers, we all suffer."

The dentist's office was in a small, one-story stone building with a flat roof. When Aguilar and Trigger went in the front door, a little bell tied to the handle rang. They found themselves in a small lobby with a desk on which rested a telephone and a big appointment book. Aguilar heard the sound of a drill from behind a wall.

"Be right there!" a female voice called.

"The dentist is a girl?" Trigger asked.

Aguilar shrugged. "I guess it could be."

The drilling continued, accompanied by pained shrieks and groans. "I'm almost finished here," a male voice said. "Just relax."

"Relax?" another man answered. "I'm not sure how much more of this torture I can bear."

"Maybe that's why Don Pablo wants a dentist," Trigger whispered. "He wants to learn new torture methods."

"Hush," Aguilar said. He didn't want the dentist to be scared off before they even met him.

Finally, the drilling stopped and the male spoke in reassuring tones. While he worked, the woman came out into the lobby area.

She was gorgeous.

Her hair was like liquid butterscotch, hanging to her shoulders and curling slightly at the ends. Her eyes were large, brown but with hints of green in them. Her smile was an arrow to the heart.

"Can I help you?" she asked. Her blue scrubs didn't show much of her figure, but Aguilar liked what he could see.

Aguilar could barely find his voice. "We need the dentist," he managed. "It's an emergency."

"He's almost finished with his patient," she said. "What's the problem?"

"It's a toothache."

"Which one of you?"

"Neither of us," Aguilar said. "Out in the jungle, about six or seven kilometers."

"Oh," she said. "I'm sorry, Dr. Mesa has a full schedule today."

"Not anymore," Aguilar said.

"I'm sure he'd be willing to go out in a day or two."

Aguilar took the cash Gaviria had given him from his pocket and held it out to her. "This is just a start. When Dr. Mesa helps our boss, there'll be more."

Trigger drew back his T-shirt, showing her the gun at his belt. "Explain to him that he can either make some money, or he might need a doctor himself. *Plata o plomo*."

Aguilar waved a hand at him. He hadn't wanted to put it that way to the dentist. Especially now that he'd seen the dentist's helper.

"My friend exaggerates," he said. "Still, it would be best if he comes with us. Right away. He should bring whatever he needs to take care of a toothache."

"There could be all kinds of reasons for that," she said.

"Then he should bring all kinds of things to fix it. Will he need help?"

"A dental assistant?"

"Sure, a dental assistant. Is that what you are?"

"That's right," she said. "I'm trained and certified."

"Then you can come with him."

"I'm not sure I want to go anywhere with gunmen."

"I told you," Aguilar said. "My associate gets carried away. You're in no danger."

"Unless you don't cooperate," Trigger said.

"Trigger, enough."

"His name's Trigger?"

"Nickname," Aguilar said. He realized that probably didn't help.

"What's yours? Coffin?"

"He's Jaguar," Trigger said. "Show her your claw, Jaguar."

"You have claws?"

"His knife."

"Trigger, that's enough," Aguilar said again. "You're scaring the lady. There's no need for that."

"I think I should call the police," she said.

"In this little village?" Aguilar asked. "There are police here?"

"Of course."

"How many?"

"Fifteen," she said. "They're very well armed, too."

"Fifteen, in a village this size?"

"All right, one. And he's probably drunk. He starts drinking between breakfast and lunch, but by the time lunch is over, he's usually out until well after dinner."

"That sounds more like it," Aguilar said. "Come on, tell your boss to hurry up."

She went back into the other room. Aguilar listened

from the doorway and heard her explain the situation. He was afraid she would try to persuade him not to go, or perhaps to call the village's drunk policeman, but she didn't.

A minute later, he came into the lobby. "Maribel tells me there's an emergency that can't wait."

"Yes," Aguilar said. "Our boss is a very important man, and he's in a lot of pain. That makes him grouchy, and when he's grouchy, people suffer."

"I have patients here who are suffering, too."

"They can't pay you what this one can."

"Maribel showed me the money you gave her. Your boss, he's wealthy? An oligarch?"

"Wealthy, yes. But no oligarch. He earned his money the hard way."

"Good," Mesa said. "I hate oligarchs."

"Then you and he will have a lot in common," Aguilar said. "Are you finished in there? We need to hurry."

"Two minutes," the dentist said.

"Two minutes," Aguilar agreed. "After that, we're tossing your patient out of here."

Five minutes later, having gathered the supplies Mesa said he would need, they walked out to the truck. "We're riding in that?" Maribel asked. "Don't you have something a little more modern? Like a horse and buggy?"

"Tell me, Dr. Mesa," Aguilar said, "has she always had a smart mouth, or is it just around me?"

"Always," the dentist said. "As long as I've known her."

"And you haven't fired her?"

"You've seen this village. It's very small. Where would I find another trained dental assistant?"

Aguilar took the man's medical bag and the small

box of supplies Maribel carried and set them on the cab floor. "Don't be afraid," he said. "But we're going to blindfold you now."

"Blindfold?" Mesa repeated. "Why?"

"You can't know where you're going," Aguilar said. "You'll be blindfolded on the way back, too."

"Will I have to work blindfolded, as well?"

"Of course not." Another moment passed before Aguilar realized it was a joke. "Now I see why you keep her on. You're just as bad."

"When you live and work in a village like this," Maribel said, "you have to take your amusements where you can find them."

Aguilar pulled the rags he would use for blindfolds from the seat. "I'll put these on now."

"And if we refuse?" Mesa asked.

"Where would this village find another trained dentist?"

"Go ahead, then." Mesa clamped his lips together and raised his chin proudly. He was short but sturdy, with wiry black hair and a distinguished mien. He still had on his white lab coat over a suit and tie. Aguilar thought he might like the man, under other circumstances. Then he thought about how long it had been since he'd seen a dentist—two or three years, at least. Maybe he should correct that.

Maybe he would see this dentist, if only to have an excuse to see Maribel again.

He put the blindfold on the dentist, then one on Maribel. She was trembling slightly, but trying not to show fear. She smelled like citrus and flowers and something smoky, and Aguilar thought he could breathe her in all day long.

"You'll sit beside me," he told her. "Then Dr. Mesa,

then Trigger. So nobody has any ideas about jumping out the door."

"Four people in there?" Maribel said. "Is it big enough?"

"We rode all the way out here from—" Aguilar began. He caught himself, and continued, "—from a distant city with four men in the cab. It's tight, but it'll be fine."

Mesa and Maribel protested a little more, but they climbed into the cab and sat where they were told. Aguilar had realized that the protests were mostly for show, to bolster one another's courage in an unusual situation. They would go along and do whatever needed to be done. By now, curiosity about their patient probably outweighed their fear. He wished Trigger hadn't shown Maribel the gun, but no real harm had been done.

34

WHEN HE REMOVED the blindfolds from the captive dentist and his assistant and walked them into the house, Aguilar could hear Escobar complaining before the door even closed. He hoped his boss would let the dentist examine him and not simply shoot him on sight.

It turned out that Escobar did allow the examination, although he complained every time his mouth was free from intrusive hands and instruments. He had broken a tooth, irreparably, and Mesa had to extract it and perform a root canal. In less than ideal circumstances and without his proper chair, it took almost two hours. Aguilar tried to stay out of shouting range for the duration.

Then it was over. Hearing that, Aguilar came in to check on him. Escobar whined about the pain, and immediately lit a joint to help dull it. Dr. Mesa assured him that in a week or two, he would forget that the tooth had ever existed, except when his tongue found the hollow spot at the back of his mouth.

"You're saying it'll hurt like this for a week?" Escobar demanded.

"A little better every day, Señor," Mesa said. "I can prescribe painkillers if you'd like."

"I don't need drugs," Escobar said. "I need a competent dentist."

"I assure you," Mesa replied, "that I've done for you what any good dentist would. The source of your pain is gone; what's left is residual. It will fade in due time."

"You'll fade in due time," Escobar said. Eyeing Maribel, he added, "You, perhaps not so much."

Maribel didn't crack a smile. "We should get back," she said. "There are other patients."

"Fine, get out of here," Escobar said. "Jaguar, take them home."

"Blindfolded?" Mesa asked.

"Of course," Escobar said. "Why would we blindfold you one way but not the other? It's for your own good. If I were you, I'd keep my eyes closed under the blindfold, just in case."

"Let's go," Aguilar urged. If *El Patrón* didn't start feeling better in a hurry, he might start shooting after all. Aguilar didn't want Mesa harmed, but he felt especially protective of Maribel. She had maintained her biting humor all the way to the lab site. It was probably her defense mechanism, he thought. She was afraid—anybody would be, in that situation—but rather than showing fear, she kept up a brave front.

He blindfolded the pair and put them in the truck. Trigger had wandered off somewhere—maybe back into the bedroom, staring at nothing again—and Aguilar didn't see either of the captives as a threat. He could handle them.

"Where's your little friend?" Maribel asked when it

was obvious that Trigger wasn't joining them. "Back to primary school?"

"He's not that young," Aguilar said.

"Chronologically," Maribel said. "Maturity and intelligence-wise, I'm not sure he's advanced that far yet."

"He's a poor kid from a poor neighborhood. He didn't have your advantages. Leave him alone."

"What makes you think I had any advantages?" Maribel snapped. "Or Dr. Mesa? I'm not even from a poor neighborhood, I'm from a poor village that only had the one neighborhood. None of us had any money. We struggled for everything. But I wanted to get out, so I worked and fought and earned my way to dental school."

"And then you moved to a similar village," Mesa said. "Proving that some people don't have sense enough to go in out of the rain."

"I wanted to help my people! What's wrong with that?"

"Nothing, dear," Mesa replied. "I'm only teasing you."

"You should talk," Maribel said. She turned toward Aguilar, which was a little comical considering she was blindfolded and couldn't see him anyway. "He came from Bogotá's worst *comuna*. Like me, he had to scrap every centimeter of the way, but he got out and became a respected dentist. Then he moved to the village because he knew the city had plenty of choices, but no one was taking care of those deep in the jungle. He works from dawn to dusk. He's paid in chickens, in coca leaves, sometimes in nothing but words of thanks, but he stays at it. Dr. Mesa's a hero."

"My boss is a hero, too," Aguilar said. "He helps others out of poverty. He's built entire developments for people who had nothing, who were living in junkyards. He's created clinics and hospitals where there were none, provided free soccer fields and parks for the poor. He's a great man."

He stopped, thinking he might have already said too much. Of course, unless national news didn't penetrate this far into the jungle, they had likely recognized Escobar. His political campaign had put his picture on front pages and news broadcasts in every city in Colombia.

Then again, what did it matter? *El Patrón* had enemies everywhere, but he was surrounded by friends, *sicarios* who would give their lives for him. And even if Mesa or Maribel meant him harm, they had no idea where in the jungle he was, only how long it took to reach him.

"You should know," Maribel said after a little while—almost as if she'd read his mind. "There are people in our village, and others nearby, who resent your boss. He's buying coca leaves from farmers in the area, and paying next to nothing. Meanwhile, they've stopped cultivating other crops, because earning that paltry amount is easier than hauling produce to some market in a far-off city and possibly dealing with unsold goods, or bandits, or damages. So the people are short on food because the farmers have stopped growing it, and the farmers are being cheated out of what they should earn for the coca. Some think if we ran the cocaine labs ourselves, we could all make more money. Why should all the profits go to Medellín instead of staying here, in the community?"

He had suspected that she had known, but this confirmed it. "So you knew all along."

"Of course," she said. "Who else but a gangster's

henchman would come into a dentist's office with guns and fat wads of money, demanding immediate service? And everyone around here knows that Pablo Escobar runs a cocaine lab in the area."

"Do you know where it is?"

"Only generally. I know the basic direction it's in, twenty-five kilometers or so from the village. Everybody knows that."

"But the blindfold..."

"That's your charade. We went along with it to humor you, but we were just being polite."

"Well, I appreciate that," Aguilar said. "But you could have told me earlier."

"Why? You weren't going to kill us; your boss was in excruciating pain. Dr. Mesa could have made his pain much, much worse, but instead he acted like a professional, and helped him. We aren't your enemies, Jaguar."

"You can call me Jose," he said.

"You can call me Señorita Restrepo."

"Not Maribel?"

"Are we friends?"

"I thought, in some small way..."

"You kidnapped us—*Jaguar*. Yes, you were a gentleman about it. But you're carrying a gun, and you threatened us. That's a strange basis for a friendship."

"I didn't threaten you, Trigger did. And I told him not to."

"Not all threats are explicit," she said.

"Well, I'm sorry if you felt threatened. That wasn't my intention. And I did pay you well."

"Yes, you did," Mesa said. Aguilar had almost forgotten he was in the truck as well. "And Señor Escobar gave us more. People in the village will eat well for a few weeks."

"You'll share that money?"

"Of course," Maribel said. "If we hoped to get rich, we'd be working in a city. Our basic needs are met; beyond that, we try to help our people."

"I guess you're both heroes," Aguilar said.

"Hardly. Just human beings, doing what people do." She paused, then added, "Some people."

"But not me, you're saying."

"I don't know you well enough to say either way, Jose." He noticed that she didn't call him Jaguar. The sound of his name coming from her lips sent a jolt through him.

"You could."

"Are you living here now, or just visiting?"

"Visiting, I guess. But I'm not sure for how long. A while longer, I think."

"Maybe, then."

"Maybe what?" he asked.

"Maybe you can call on me. But no guns, no blindfolds. If you want to get to know me, it'll be as a person, not as some gunman."

"Do you really mean it?" Aguilar asked. "You two aren't…?"

Mesa laughed. "Us, a couple? Thank you for the compliment, but no. I'm far too old for her, and far too crotchety. And my wife would object, as well."

"His wife's lovelier than him, anyway," Maribel added.

"I just wanted to make sure you were serious."

"Don't push her, son," Mesa warned. "She made the offer. She wouldn't have if she didn't mean it. But I can tell you from experience, if you act like a fool, she'll retract it."

"He knows me too well," Maribel said.

"I'm with you—what did you say? Dawn to dusk, every day. Of course I know you well."

Aguilar made a turn, and they were at the plaza. The dentist's office sat just ahead. He considered driving around the village a few times, just to spend a few more minutes beside Maribel. But smells from the plaza's food vendors had begun to permeate the cab, and he feared they would catch on.

Instead, he braked the truck beside the office. "We're here. You can take off the blindfolds."

They did. Maribel looked at Aguilar, blinking in the sudden late afternoon light.

"Thank you for the ride, Jose. And for not taking advantage of us. You had money, guns, blindfolds... many men would not have acted so honorably. That—not your silly nickname, or your reasonably handsome face, under the spots, or your position in the employ of a drug lord—is why I've agreed to see you again. If you would like."

"I would. Definitely."

"Find me at the office, then. If I'm not there, I'll be at home. Everyone in the village knows where that is. I'll pass the word to cooperate if you ask for me."

Mesa climbed out of the truck before Aguilar made it around to his door. Maribel was just getting out, so he extended a hand to help her down, and she took it. She graced him with a smile, and said, "I hope I'll see you soon."

Then she was gone, inside the office. Aguilar closed her door, feeling almost dreamlike. Had that really happened? A woman he'd essentially kidnapped, on Escobar's orders, had invited him to see her again? He practically floated back to the driver's door, grinning.

Before returning to the lab, he drove through the

villages and all the way to San Vicente del Caguán before he found a motorcycle for sale. He paid what the owner asked and a little more, made sure it worked and was full of gasoline, and put it in the back of the truck.

If he was going to make regular trips to the village, he didn't want to do it in a big flatbed truck.

35

THUS BEGAN A period of Aguilar's life that felt charmed. He patrolled at night, slept for a while after his shift, and whenever he had time off, rode his motorcycle into the village to spend it with Maribel. She seemed to like him as much as he did her. By their third visit, they were holding hands. One night he took her to dinner in San Vicente del Caguán, and after, in front of her door, she kissed him—a kiss that lasted a long time, and was rich with the promise of so much more.

After three more visits, including another dinner, she invited him inside. There, she put a cassette tape in a portable player—classical music from Spain, she said, her favorite—and took him in her arms. He didn't know much about dancing this way, but she held him and they moved together, and the warmth of her and the smell of her filled him. She felt it too, and before long they were kissing, touching, grasping, then urgently tearing off their clothes and lowering each other to the floor and making love in a white, blinding heat, and then lying there on the floor holding each other as the music ended, listening to each other breathing and the hiss of the empty cassette.

She talked about books and films, and she made strong, dark coffee, and she didn't have much money but she spent some of what she had on good wine. Making love with her was like the symphonies she preferred, long and complex, with crescendos that took his breath away.

Sometimes she walked him into the jungle or rode on the back of his bike to faraway spots, and taught him about the natural world. She showed him passionflowers and native palms, the red heliconia flowers she called lobster claws, the rubber trees. She took him to a lake almost entirely carpeted by Amazon water lilies; they shed their clothes and jumped in, splashing amidst the lilies and hiding under them for as long as their breath would hold, then making love by the shore. She introduced him to pink bananas and bromeliads and to what seemed like a thousand different types of orchid.

She knew the wild creatures, too. She showed him the cat-sized tamarin, the sword-billed hummingbird, and the pink river dolphin. Together they spotted jaguarundis and boas, venomous banana spiders and a golden dart frog, and, on a weekend trip to the high country, a spectacled bear and a crested eagle.

One day, just before twilight brought a curtain of darkness to the jungle, they were walking less than a kilometer from the village, on a path they'd followed several times before.

"I'm worried," she was saying.

"About what?"

"The people of the village. Ours, and the next. They're getting more upset about the lab. About the workers who went there, their brothers and fathers and sons, and who haven't come back."

"We can't exactly let them travel back and forth," Aguilar said. "Then everybody would know what it is, and where it is."

"What makes you think they don't?"

He smiled, and she squeezed his hand, then let it go. "They're serious, Jose. They're hungry. They feel like they're not only losing their land, they're losing their history. They're losing *everything*, and when people have nothing left to lose, they become dangerous. You need to take precautions. Make sure Escobar understands the threat."

Before he could answer, Maribel grabbed his arm. "Do you feel that?" she asked, her voice hushed.

"Feel what?"

"Something's watching us."

"Something, or someone?"

"I don't know," she said. "But I don't like it."

She hated that he went everywhere armed, and had made it clear that no long-term relationship could survive if he continued living as a criminal. Now, though, he was glad he had his knife at his ankle and a pistol at the small of his back. "Who's there?" he asked.

Nobody answered. A moment later, the brush parted and a jaguar stepped onto the path. The beast was long and sleek, solidly muscled, with a tawny spotted coat and golden eyes with round pupils. Those eyes blazed with intelligence. It opened its mouth, showing a pink tongue and sharp, long canine teeth. "He uses those to bite through the brains of his prey," Maribel whispered. Always the teacher. "Death comes instantly. No struggle. No other big cat does that."

"We're not prey," Aguilar said in a loud voice that

he hoped projected confidence. "You don't want to mess with us."

"Of course not," the jaguar said. "I'm not even here."

Aguilar was stunned. Jaguars could talk? He had never seen one in person before, not even in a zoo, but he thought somebody would have mentioned that. He froze. Maribel's hands tightened their grip on his arm. She heard it, too, then.

"I just came by to tell you that it's time to decide," the jaguar added. "Once and for all. Who are you, brother? What are you? You can't just drift through life, you know. You have to set your own course, and follow it."

"What do you know about—" Aguilar started to say. But then the jaguar was gone. For an instant, just a flash, he thought he saw a spider monkey riding on its back. But it vanished in less than a heartbeat, without even rustling the brush beside the path.

"Did you… did you see that?" he asked.

"See what?" Maribel replied.

"Don't joke around."

"I don't know what I saw," she said. "If anything. It was like I was here, with you, and then I wasn't, and then I was back. It all happened so fast."

"The jaguar," he said. "The talking jaguar. And the monkey."

"It's getting dark," Maribel said. "Hard to see anything, or to know what you saw. Let's go back to my house and make love."

That was an invitation Aguilar couldn't refuse.

After, they lay on her bed, half-covered by a damp sheet, legs twined together.

"He's right, you know," she said. "You have to choose."

"Choose what?"

"Your path. Your future. It's up to you to decide what it'll be."

"Then you did see it!" He punched the pillow behind his head. "You did!"

"Did I ever say I didn't?"

The next night, he was no longer sure he had seen anything at all. A talking jaguar was impossible. A monkey riding a jaguar was just as unlikely. It had been a trick of the fading light, or of his imagination.

But the point it had made—and which Maribel had underscored—was a good one.

She was an honest woman. He thought he loved her, and that she loved him. Even Luisa hadn't made him feel like this, like he hated to be out of arm's reach, that when he was away from her all he could think about was getting back.

Luisa had been comfortable. Safe. He had needed that, then.

But Maribel challenged him. He had to work to keep up with her blade-sharp wit and fiery intelligence. He needed that, now.

Needed her.

For her part, she told him that the supply of interesting men in the village was vanishingly small, particularly since so many around her age had gone to work at the lab. Aguilar had initially been a curiosity, but he had become something much more valuable: a friend, a companion, a confidant, and a lover.

But she wouldn't—couldn't—make a life with someone who lived with violence as a daily prospect. Things had been peaceful, these last weeks since

Escobar's tooth had healed. The airstrip expansion was going well, the new workers were catching on, production was up. Escobar had even brought whores in, as promised, though Aguilar had no interest in them. Everyone was happy, and for a time, it had almost seemed like his job wasn't one of murder and torture and death.

But it was. This was a respite, that was all. It couldn't last.

More and more, though, it was his romance with Maribel that he wanted to last. And it wouldn't, unless he broke with Escobar.

He couldn't have both.

He was thinking about these things as he patrolled the next night. The memory of the jaguar encounter— imaginary though it might have been—was so vivid he felt he could still smell the beast, although he hadn't smelled anything at all after it had gone.

And it hadn't really told him anything, just prodded him to examine his life. It had undoubtedly been his subconscious, bringing to the forefront of his mind a reality that he had been trying hard to push away.

He wanted Maribel.

He wanted a life with her. A peaceful, decent life, even here in the jungle. He had money put away, and she said she didn't need much. Her home was simple but comfortable, and when he was there with her he felt like he belonged.

He had been disgusted with himself ever since Miami, when he saw the devastation caused by cocaine, and he'd been forced to torture his friend. Maribel offered a second chance, a way out.

He had never been a proper *sicario* in the first place. He had always questioned everything, doubted

310

himself. You couldn't take a man who'd always been a butcher and turn him into a ballerina. He had been a student, a cop, middle class or close to it. The *sicarios* were poor kids, with no hope and no prospects. He wasn't a good fit.

With Maribel, he fit just right.

She could keep her job with Dr. Mesa, and he could find some kind of work. He could become a farmer, a hunter.

First he had to leave *El Patrón*, though.

That wouldn't be easy. Escobar didn't take defection lightly. He would believe that Aguilar knew too much to simply let him walk away. He would want to end Aguilar's career with bullets.

Unless…

Unless he could convince Escobar that he had always been loyal, always faithful, and would remain so.

Escobar had no reason to doubt him, after all. He had always followed orders. No matter what Escobar had demanded of him, he'd found a way to do it. He had become one of Don Pablo's most trusted, valued men.

He would appeal to the man's reason. "I'm getting old," he would say. "I'm tired of running around, killing people. I just want to settle down someplace, raise a family. You're a family man, you understand that."

Escobar had always been fair with him. He had appreciated Aguilar's service, had treated him almost as a member of the family. As had Tata, and if Escobar did anything to hurt him, she would be furious.

He had been worrying for nothing, he decided. He would finish up this shift and sleep for a while. When Escobar woke up, he would explain his situation. There would be a brief discussion, and then Aguilar would climb on his new motorcycle and ride out of the jungle, probably with a gift of several thousand pesos in his pocket.

He trained his flashlight on his wrist to check his watch. He had almost lost track of the time. Twice an hour, the two patrols were supposed to check in with each other. They had prearranged spots where their routes intersected, and he was late getting to the nearest.

He hurried. The jungle seemed especially close tonight, especially dark, and even the insects seemed to have hushed, for a change.

When he reached the small clearing, he saw Trigger, sitting on the trunk of a fallen tree, facing away from him.

"Trigger," Aguilar said. "I'm here, man. Sorry I'm late."

Trigger didn't move. Had he fallen asleep? Aguilar wasn't *that* late. A few minutes, that's all.

He crossed the clearing and touched Trigger's shoulder.

Trigger flopped over backward, falling off the trunk. Aguilar clicked on his flashlight to check him.

Where his face should have been was a bloody, pulpy mess. His eyes dangled from their sockets, the bones of his nose gleamed white, his teeth looked huge. Only the flesh was missing.

No jungle beast had done that, he thought. Terrified, he whipped the flashlight around the clearing, in case whoever had attacked Trigger was still here.

And there it was, pinned to a tree with a knife.

Trigger's face.

36

AGUILAR FIRED THREE shots into the air, the prearranged signal for trouble. He tried to pick the shortest route back to the house, but he'd become turned around in the clearing, and wasn't thinking straight. He ran for several minutes, not seeing the lights from the labs or the house, when he found himself at the edge of the airstrip. He'd gone in entirely the wrong direction.

But from the airstrip, it was a straight shot back to the house. He raced in that direction, and fired three more shots for good measure.

Then he heard more gunshots, many of them.

The lab was under attack.

He shut off the flashlight. Showing his position would only get him killed, either by the attackers or by his own men, if they thought he was the enemy.

The path from the airstrip to the lab was wide and well traveled, so moonlight shone down, illuminating his course. He moved quickly but quietly, keeping an eye out for anyone, friend or foe.

He was almost at the original lab—he could see

the bare bulbs hanging from the tin roof through the trees—when he spotted three men moving toward it. They were crouching, carrying old rifles with beat-up wooden stocks. Villagers, he thought. Maribel had been right; they had come to take over, without realizing what they were up against.

He brought the AR-15 to his shoulder, sighted in on the man on the left, and opened fire, drawing the gun from left to right as he squeezed out round after round. All three went down without returning his fire.

From the direction of the lab, someone started shooting at him. He threw himself to the ground, then raised his head enough to shout, "It's me! Jaguar! I just shot some attackers!"

Nobody answered, but the shots stopped coming his way. The lights at the labs went off—someone had finally been smart enough to pull the plugs. Aguilar risked showing himself again. Nothing. He clicked on his flashlight and heard voices raised in alarm, so he shone it on himself. Then he heard a shout of welcome, and he pushed through the brush until he reached the lab.

Most of the other *sicarios* had been awakened and rushed into the night in their underwear, pausing only long enough to grab guns that were always loaded and ready.

La Quica was in the lead, sprinting across the open space toward the lab. A villager lunged from the darkness, his machete flashing in the moonlight. Aguilar fired by reflex, and the attacker tumbled in the dirt and was still.

"For a second I thought you were shooting at me," La Quica said. "You saved my ass, man. I owe you, big time. I didn't even see him."

"I could tell," Aguilar said.

"Who are these guys?" La Quica asked. "What did you see?"

"They got Trigger. The bastards took his face off and stuck it to a tree. I killed three of them, over there. They had old guns, rifles. I think they're from the village."

"The village? They're not from some other cartel? I thought they were trying to take our lab."

"They are, but for themselves." He remembered Maribel's warning, which he had passed on to Escobar, but hadn't shared with all the other guys.

"How many are there?" Shorty asked.

Before Aguilar could answer—not that he had any idea—the sharp cracks of rifle fire split the quiet and rounds smashed into the lab equipment around them.

Aguilar and the others ducked, scanning the dark for muzzle flashes. When they saw them, they sprayed rounds in those directions.

"If they want the lab for themselves, they shouldn't destroy all the equipment!" Pancho said.

Then more rounds came in, from another direction, closer to the house. "Is anyone in there with Don Pablo?" Poison asked.

"I think somebody stayed back," La Quica said.

"I'll check," Aguilar said. He had his own reasons for wanting Escobar's approval right now. He made a dash toward the house, running hunched over, firing into the dark whenever a muzzle flash offered a target. Bullets whined past him, but none struck home.

Approaching the house, he saw a shadowy figure in the doorway. At first he thought it was someone else coming out, but then realized it was someone going in. He didn't recognize the man from behind, but clicked on his light. The man was a stranger—not a laborer or a *sicario*. He carried a revolver and a machete. At the sound of the flashlight, he started to spin around, but Aguilar pumped three rounds into him and he fell. Aguilar dragged him away from the door, still alive but probably not for long, and kicked the machete and gun away from his side.

He went in. "Don Pablo!" he called. "Gustavo! Camilo! Are you here?"

Escobar emerged from his room. He was wearing boxer shorts and a strapped undershirt and had a pistol in each hand. "Jaguar! What's going on out there?"

"The villagers," Aguilar said. "Like I told you, they've come to take over the lab. Who's in here with you?"

"Nobody. Gustavo and Camilo, I guess."

Gaviria came into the hall carrying an AR-15. "Camilo's under his bed," he said. "I emptied a magazine out my window, but I don't know if I hit anyone."

"Go to the bathroom," Aguilar said. "Lock the door and get in the tub. I'll be here at the door to make sure nobody gets in."

"You think I'd run from a fight?" Escobar asked.

"I know you wouldn't," Aguilar said. "But you're the most important of us. I need to keep you safe, and that's the safest place."

"Come on, Pablo," Gaviria said. "He's right."

Escobar scowled. Aguilar thought part of him really wanted to stay and do battle against the invaders. But there was another part that was more than willing to seek safe harbor. He relented and followed Gaviria into an interior bathroom.

Aguilar went back to the doorway. The house had windows all around it, and he couldn't defend all of those alone. But he could keep anyone from coming through the door. He switched off the light in the entryway so he wouldn't be silhouetted against it, and looked outside.

The battle was fully joined. *Sicarios* defending the labs had spread out, and villagers fired on them from the cover of the trees. Aguilar dropped to a crouch and brought his AR-15 to his shoulder, scanning for a glimpse of a target. Whenever he saw one, he sighted and put a round there. The occasional pained cry told him that he found his mark at least some of the time.

But there were cries from the labs, as well. Some of Escobar's men had been hit. He wondered how many villagers there were, and whether enough *sicarios* remained to hold them off. There would be a certain sick irony in being killed right before he told Escobar he was quitting.

Then a pack of villagers broke from the trees, rushing the house, shooting. Wood chips flew into his face, cutting him, and one round scraped across his leg. Aguilar scrambled back inside, firing as he did.

The entryway was an open space with a small iron-legged table against one wall, where Camilo left his keys and hat when he went inside. It opened into the dining room and a sitting room on one side. The door to the kitchen was behind those, and on the other side was the bathroom door and the hallway to the bedrooms.

No real cover anywhere.

Aguilar ducked under the table, which had a glass top. Its legs were thin and wouldn't block many bullets, but it was the best he could do and still be able to watch the door.

When attackers crowded into the doorway, he opened fire. He let the barrel drift up as he shot. There were so many people trying to come in, he could hardly help hitting something with each round.

The group thinned out more as *sicarios* rushed it from behind. Aguilar wrenched himself out from under the table and darted to the door, kicking guns away from the dying and finishing off the wounded. At the doorway he looked out, seeing only his own people. He heard a few last gunshots, and gradually silence returned, except for the moans of the injured and the hushed voices of *sicarios*.

"Is everyone okay?" he asked. He dragged bodies away from the door, his nostrils filling with blood and sweat and urine. One of them he recognized as the man who'd made so many objections, that day in the plaza. The guy with the gold teeth.

"Shorty and Royer are dead," La Quica said. "Sure Shot's hit, but not too bad. The labs are trashed, though."

Aguilar remembered his leg. The heat of the moment had caused him to forget it. He put down the AR-15, turned the lights on, and dropped his jeans. Blood had glued his pants leg to his flesh, but he peeled it away. Just a scrape, with fibers from his jeans embedded in it.

He was lucky. They were all lucky, except for poor Trigger, Shorty, and Royer.

Behind him, Escobar and Gaviria came out of the bathroom. "Are you playing with yourself, Jaguar?" Escobar asked.

Aguilar whirled around, a blush already rising on his face. He pointed to the bloody patch on his leg. "I was hit," he said. "I'm just checking it out. It's just a flesh wound. But Royer, Shorty, and Trigger are dead."

"That's all?"

"That's all I've heard about."

"What about the laborers?"

They slept in a camp on the far side of the house from the lab. As far as he knew, they had stayed on their bedrolls through the whole thing. Or joined in. "I don't know. La Quica said the labs are just about destroyed, though."

"Damn!" Escobar said.

"We'll have to rebuild," Gaviria said.

"Which means more weeks here. We'll have to bring in all new equipment. Probably new chemicals as well. And we'll have to hope the laborers are okay, and willing to keep working. Remember, I'm due to take office in Congress in less than a month."

"It won't take that long, Pablo. And if it does, you'll go to Bogotá and I'll stay here and finish up."

La Quica and the other *sicarios* straggled inside, two of them helping Sure Shot, who was bleeding from a wound at his ribs.

"How bad is that?" Escobar asked.

"Not too bad," Sure Shot said, grimacing with pain. "I'll live."

"Damn it," Escobar said. "They've put us back weeks. Are we sure it was people from the village?"

"I recognized one of them," Aguilar said. "He challenged us, that day we went to the villages to find workers."

"You're sure it was him?"

"I'm positive." He told Escobar about the gold teeth, and the round wound on his torso.

At the mention of teeth, Escobar rubbed his jaw.

"It's that fucking dentist," he said. "We shouldn't have brought him here. He told them how to find us."

"*Patrón*, no!" Aguilar said. "He and Maribel were blindfolded both ways. They couldn't see a thing, I made sure of it."

"Blindfolds aren't always that effective. You can't tell—you're not the one looking through it."

"I'm positive it wasn't them, Don Pablo. Maribel's the one who warned us about the villagers, remember?"

"Of course she did. Because she knew they were planning to attack. But she didn't tell you when they were coming, did she?"

"If she had known, she would have. I know it."

Escobar eyed him with what seemed like contempt. "You've been spending every spare moment with that bitch," he said. "I trusted you, Jaguar, but I don't think I can now."

"I stayed right here and defended the door! If not for me, they would have come inside and found you."

"We were ready for them," Gaviria said. He was still holding the AR-15.

"La Quica, take some of the guys. Leave Jaguar and Sure Shot here, but take the best of the others. I want the heads of that dentist and his assistant in front of me within two hours. We'll put them on posts as a warning not to betray me."

"Don Pablo, you can't—"

"I'll deal with you later, Jaguar. After I've seen those heads. Somebody make sure Jaguar stays in his room."

La Quica nodded his assent. He picked Pancho, Jairo, and Brayan. Sure Shot went into the bathroom to tend to his wound, while Poison and Big Badmouth went out to check on the laborers and to make sure the villagers didn't come back. That left Gordo with Aguilar, Gaviria, and Escobar. And presumably Camilo, who hadn't come out of his room yet.

"Where do you want us, *Patrón*?" Gordo asked.

"Out of my sight," Escobar said. Disgust was plain in his voice. "Take his guns, though. And his claw."

Gordo held out his hands. Aguilar gauged his chances, but the other three men all had guns, and he'd already put down his rifle. He tugged the pistol from his belt and handed it over, then took his knife from his ankle.

"Let's go into the bedroom," Gordo said. He set the gun on the glass-topped table and carried the knife in his left hand.

For a while, they sat in silence. Aguilar heard water running from the bathroom, which was probably Sure Shot trying to clean his wound. Aguilar hoped his didn't become infected, since he hadn't had a chance to do the same, or to bandage it.

Light thumps and creaks came from another room. Escobar pacing, he suspected.

Then Camilo's high voice squeaked, "Is it safe?"

"It's safe, you fucking coward!" Gaviria answered.

Aguilar made himself sit down and be still. His head was spinning. He couldn't contact Maribel; she had no phone in her home, only at Dr. Mesa's office, and it would be hours before anyone was there. But she needed to be warned, or taken to a safe place.

He'd never spent much time with Gordo. For a *sicario*, he was heavy. When he sat across from Aguilar, his gut spilled over his belt and his thighs strained his jeans. He had curly hair with a reddish cast, and a small mustache. He had tucked away his gun and picked at his nails with Aguilar's knife.

"How many people have you killed, Gordo?"

Gordo shrugged. "Thirty? Maybe forty? I stopped counting after fifteen."

"Why?"

"Why keep counting? It's all the same. Men, women, kids, none of them mean anything to me."

"Do you think there's something wrong with us?"

Gordo laughed, and saliva flecked the corners of his mouth. "There's something wrong with the world. We didn't make it what it is, we're just living in it."

"Do you think there's a better way to live?"

"Sure, we could live like Don Pablo. Billions of pesos, the finest grass, a different woman every day if we wanted. Only one problem. He's Don Pablo, and we're not."

Aguilar rose, a little stiff from the night's events and from sitting against the wall.

"Why are you asking all this shit?" Gordo asked. "What's the difference?"

"Just curious."

Aguilar started toward the door.

"Where are you going?"

"I have to piss."

Gordo heaved his bulk off the floor, awkwardly trying to find his feet.

When he did, Aguilar whirled around and slammed into him, pinning him against the wall. He clapped a hand over Gordo's mouth, and with the other, grabbed the hand holding his knife. Gordo struggled, but he was off-balance. Aguilar pressed his knee into the other man's crotch and increased the pressure, and as he did, Gordo's grip on the knife slackened.

Aguilar snatched it from his hand and whipped it across his throat, stepping away quickly. Arterial spray splashed him. Gordo dropped to his knees, blood cascading from his throat and down his front.

Aguilar moved in close enough to tug the pistol from Gordo's pocket. It felt heavy; he'd reloaded since the battle.

"Thanks for that," he said, placing it in his empty holster.

He had to hurry. Poison and Big Badmouth could come back in at any time, and whenever Sure Shot finished in the bathroom, he might look in. If he went out the front door, he might run into Escobar or Gaviria.

But there was always the window. He slid it open and dropped to the ground.

His motorcycle was parked behind the house, in with the big trucks. Poison and Big Badmouth were back there somewhere, at the workers' camp. Aguilar stayed in the shadows, close to the house, until he had to break out into the open. He sprinted to the cover of the trucks, then found his bike.

Now the hard part. He had to wheel it off the premises, not daring to start the engine while anyone else was close enough to give chase. But he had to do it fast, because somebody could find Gordo at any moment.

The thing felt heavier than it ever had. Aguilar was running on adrenaline and urgency, though. He pushed it, as quietly as possible, down the dirt road that led toward the village. When he was a couple of minutes away, he finally dared to start it. He straddled it, keyed it.

The roar sounded like a volcano in the stillness.

But then he was hurtling down the road, wind whipping at him. He had to hurry; there were no shortcuts to the village, so he would have to pass La Quica and the others en route. If he could time it so they had just arrived at the village, that would be best. He knew where Maribel lived, and they only knew Dr. Mesa's office. Mesa and his wife lived behind it, and under torture they might reveal Maribel's location. But if he could get around them while they were busy with him, or even before they reached him, he could collect Maribel and get out of there.

Yes, that would be the plan.

He kept running through it in his head, until he realized that the sky was turning light.

37

MARIBEL AND MESA had both said something about working from dawn to dusk.

It would be dawn before Aguilar reached the village. So she wouldn't be at home, she would be at the office, right on the plaza.

He tried to coax more speed from the motorcycle. Maybe he could cut them off before they reached the village, find a way to kill them all.

He *needed* Maribel.

He had burned his bridges with Escobar somewhat more dramatically than he'd planned, and with definite finality. No sorrowful embrace, no best wishes. He'd killed one of *El Patrón*'s guys and escaped his clutches. There would be no going back—unless it was as one more head on a pole.

But the motorcycle was already giving everything it could. He flattened himself as much as possible, to cut the wind resistance, but that barely helped.

By the time he saw the first structures at the edge of the village, the sun had climbed well above the horizon.

Over the bike's scream, he thought he heard something. Distant bangs. Gunshots?

It couldn't be. He wasn't that far behind. The motorcycle could make much better time on that dirt road than the truck.

He'd had to delay, though, to give Gordo time to relax, to get comfortable. Too much time?

He tore into the village, leaned into corners, almost colliding with a mule-drawn cart.

Then the plaza opened before him. He cut straight across it, heedless of the other traffic, willing people to see him coming and get out of the way.

Directly ahead was Mesa's office.

A smoking ruin.

The glass door was shattered. Bullet holes pocked the walls. The sign was on the ground, broken off its mount.

Inside, he saw the flicker of flames. He smelled smoke and kerosene.

He stopped the bike, put down the kickstand, and went through the door, brushing off glass with his shoulders.

"Don't be here," he said, over and over. "Don't be here. Don't be here."

The lobby was empty. The telephone and the appointment book had been knocked onto the floor and doused with kerosene; they were burning, and flames were licking up the wall, reaching for the beams at the ceiling.

Aguilar took a deep breath, held it, and waded through thicker smoke into the back.

The walls and ceiling and half of the floor were on fire.

Dr. Mesa lay on his own dental chair, as if for an

examination. But his chest and white lab coat were covered in blood, and his head was gone, his neck a ragged, glistening stump. His clothes were smoldering, and flames were toying around the bottom of the chair, seeking a foothold.

But no Maribel! Aguilar forgot to hold his breath. He blew out a sigh of relief, sucked in air and dense smoke, and started coughing. Eyes closed and tearing up, head down, his foot bumped into something.

He opened his eyes.

Maribel lay on the floor, on her stomach.

Even without her head, he was certain that it was her. He recognized the blue scrubs, the shape of her.

"*No-o-o!*" he cried. He dropped to his knees, wincing from the pain in his leg but scarcely noticing the flames. He touched her. Still so warm, pliable. So... so Maribel.

He had a gun at his hip. He thought about staying here with her, forever. Let the fire take them both.

He reached down, touched the grip... and released it.

He couldn't take that step.

If he had anything to live for, he didn't know what it was.

But he couldn't end his life without trying to find it.

The flames danced closer. He kissed her shoulder, then made his way through the smoke and back outside. People were streaming toward the office, now. Probably the initial attack had frightened everyone away, but enough time had passed to restore their courage.

He ignored them, got on the motorcycle. Started the engine.

Only then did he see the truck, parked in front of

the little restaurant that always smelled of coffee. If the guys were inside, he could take his revenge.

He started toward it, drawing his gun and holding it beside his leg.

He'd only made it a few steps when Maribel's face loomed in his mind.

She wouldn't want this. She wouldn't have wanted to be slaughtered, beheaded. But knowing that she had been, she wouldn't want more killing to follow from it. The only thing that would bring her peace would be for the killing to stop.

So he would honor what he knew to be her wish. He wouldn't seek revenge. He wouldn't go into that restaurant and blow those guys away.

But there was one thing he had to do. Since the truck was directly in front of the restaurant, it was likely that Maribel's and Mesa's heads were inside it, rather than in the restaurant with the *sicarios*.

He could, at least, make sure those were never delivered to Escobar, for him to gloat over.

Instead of storming right up to the restaurant, he holstered the weapon and took a more circuitous route, into the plaza and across and up to the truck from behind. The back was empty, so he went to the driver's side door, climbed up and looked in the window.

On the floor, on the passenger side, was a zippered gym bag. That had to be it.

He opened the driver's door—the *sicarios* never locked these trucks; anybody foolish enough to take anything from them would pay with his life—and crawled onto the bench seat. Remaining below the window line, he reached for the bag and grasped a handle. It was heavier than it looked. As he raised it, he felt the contents shift.

Definitely the heads.

He had originally thought he would take them back to the burning office and toss them in the fire, but by now villagers had crowded around it, trying to extinguish the flames. Instead, he would take them along, bury them in the jungle somewhere.

Maribel had loved the jungle. She would be happy there.

He was almost to the motorcycle when he heard someone shout, "Jaguar!"

He spun around, shifting the bag to his left hand and snaking the gun from its holster.

Pancho was closest to him. He was reaching for his gun, but he was too slow. Aguilar fired two shots into his chest. The first stopped him in his tracks, the second knocked him to his knees.

Jairo was close behind; when Pancho went down, he reached for his friend and instead tripped over him.

Behind them were La Quica and Brayan. Brayan had pulled his pistol and fired three rounds. The first went low, and by the time he fired again, Aguilar was moving, heading for the bike in a zigzag pattern, and firing back. The closest Brayan's rounds came was one that hit the bag, and something in the bag, but didn't pass through.

Behind him, people around Mesa's office started screaming. Aguilar thought maybe one of Brayan's rounds had hit somebody, but he couldn't tear his gaze away from the *sicarios* to be sure.

One of Aguilar's shots got lucky, scraping across Brayan's outstretched arm and into his cheek.

Just Jairo and La Quica left. Aguilar made it to the motorcycle, got on. He'd left it running, anticipating a hurried escape.

Jairo disentangled himself from the fallen Pancho and drew his gun.

But La Quica put a hand on his shoulder, spoke a single word.

His gaze met Aguilar's. He said something else. Aguilar couldn't hear him over the screams, but he could read his lips.

"Go."

EPILOGUE

Cheyenne, Wyoming, United States, 1993

LUIS ROBERTS—SOMETIMES known as Lou, other times as Jaguar, but born Jose Aguilar Gonzales—sat at the bar stool, gripping the bar so tightly that his knuckles had gone white. A bottle of Dos Equis sat sweating in front of him, but he had barely touched it.

At the corner of the bar, mounted high on the wall, the TV was tuned to CNN. The sound was off, but the screen showed a man's body on a tiled rooftop. The man was overweight, with long hair and a black beard streaked with silver. He wore a dark blue shirt, tugged up to show a fleshy belly, and light blue jeans. He was barefoot. The shirt was bloody, and blood had spattered his arms. Three men crouched around him, holding guns, with men in uniform behind them.

The banner at the bottom of the screen said DRUG KINGPIN PABLO ESCOBAR DEAD.

A few of the others at the bar had glanced at the TV. Some commented, most went back to their own conversations or their private, internal discussions.

Luis couldn't look away.

He had packed everything he cared about keeping into a used Isuzu Trooper that he'd bought for cash, and hit the road the day after the incident in Scottsdale. Flagstaff that first night, then Gallup, Albuquerque, Trinidad, Denver. Tonight it would be Cheyenne, tomorrow night somewhere in Nebraska.

He liked big cities, because it was easier to feel lost in them. Cheyenne wasn't big, but it would do. There was always a cheap motel on the outskirts of town, the kind of place where nobody asked too many questions. There was always an anonymous restaurant or bar where a man could eat alone without raising suspicions.

He felt like a fugitive from the law, a man on the run.

But he wasn't. He had broken a few laws—who hadn't?—since he had entered the country illegally, so many years ago. But mostly he had lived an honest life. He worked hard, he paid his taxes, he followed the rules.

It had been a lonely life, to be sure. Always afraid of entering into any kind of long-term relationship, especially a romantic one, because the possibility of seeing yet another lover killed—or leaving her behind at a moment's notice—was too awful to bear. Instead, he had befriended neighbors and their families, and certain coworkers. He could enjoy the warmth of their family lives and pretend, at least for a little while, that he was part of those.

Now, once again, he was alone and moving. The journey had been a long one, from Colombia through Panama, Costa Rica, Nicaragua—where, once again, he had almost been killed in a gun battle, although not one he was personally involved in. Then Honduras, Guatemala, Mexico, and across the border into Texas.

Once in the United States, he had allowed himself to slow down. A few years in Texas, then some in California. When he settled in Arizona, he told himself that it was the end. He wasn't moving again.

Last week, that had changed.

But now?

With Escobar dead, did he really have to run?

The better question was this: Was Escobar really dead?

The body on TV hardly looked like the man he remembered. It had been more than a decade, though. For Escobar, too, the intervening years had been hard ones. The last couple of years, Escobar had been the one on the run, chased by the Search Bloc and Los Pepes and the American DEA. Luis had followed the news, always hoping for the day that Pablo Escobar found himself in a prison from which he couldn't escape.

Instead, they'd killed him. Or killed someone who looked sort of like him.

He watched the silent news channel, and he should have felt at ease.

But he didn't. Because even if it was Escobar, even if he was dead, he was in Colombia.

And strange things happened in Colombia. Things that Americans, who prided themselves on rationality, would never believe.

In Colombia, jaguars could talk. A poor man could become a billionaire and build himself an estate stocked with dinosaurs and hippos and rare African birds.

In Colombia, a man could be killed, yet live again.

In Colombia, the truth of magic could not be dismissed. Literary types talked about "magical realism," but magic *was* realism. It was as real as bullets.

Luis Roberts sat on his barstool, surrounded by Americans who would never believe such things.

But he could never be an American. Colombia didn't let go that easily. Colombia didn't let go at all. You could leave Colombia, but it never left you.

Luis drank some beer and he stared at the screen, and he wondered.